P9-DFJ-229

THE ADVENTURE OF THE THIMBLEWITCH

by
ERIC ORCHARD

TOP SHELF PRODUCTIONS
Atlanta • Portland • New York

For Julie, Henry, and Thomas,
with whom I also have adventures.

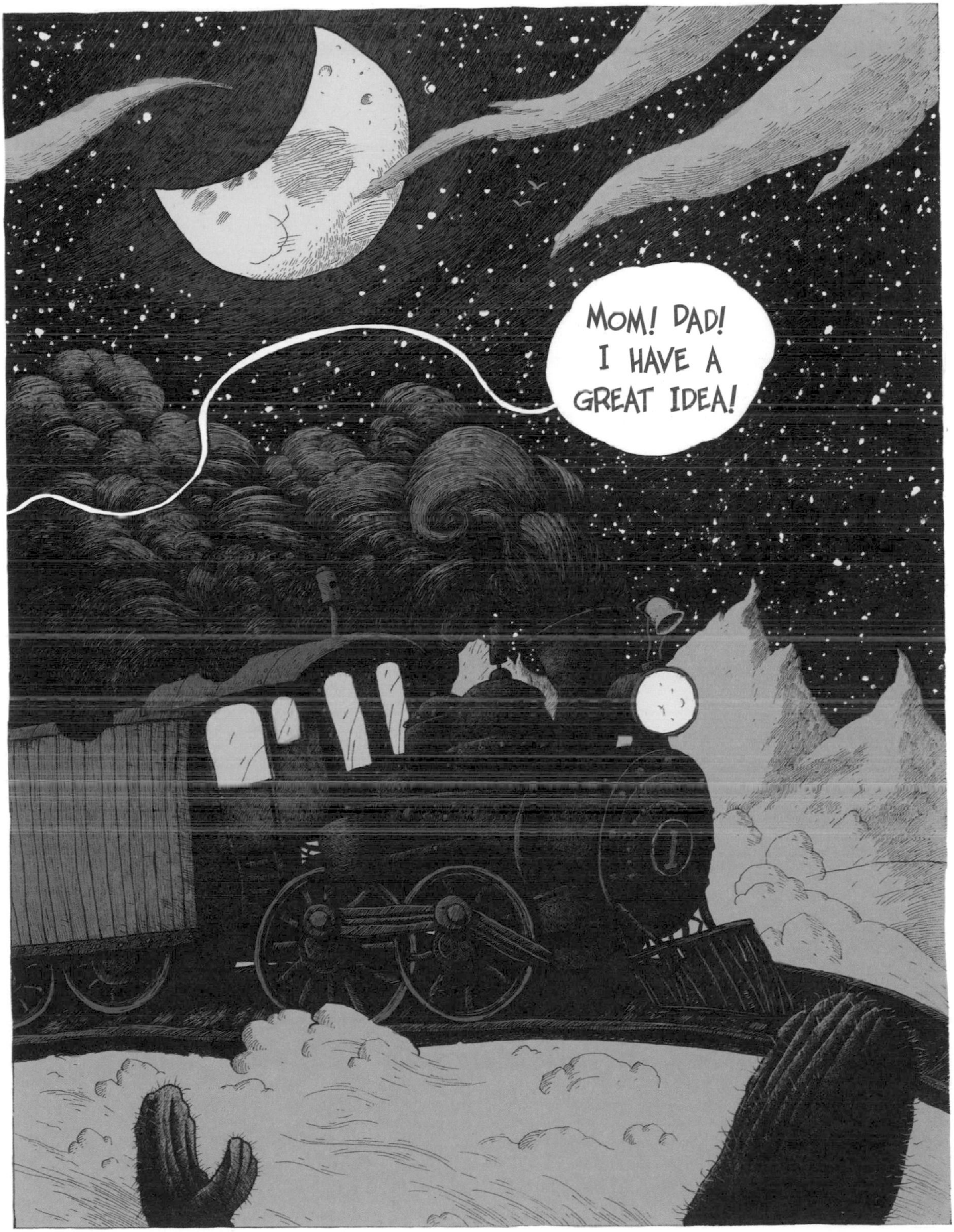
MOM! DAD! I HAVE A GREAT IDEA!

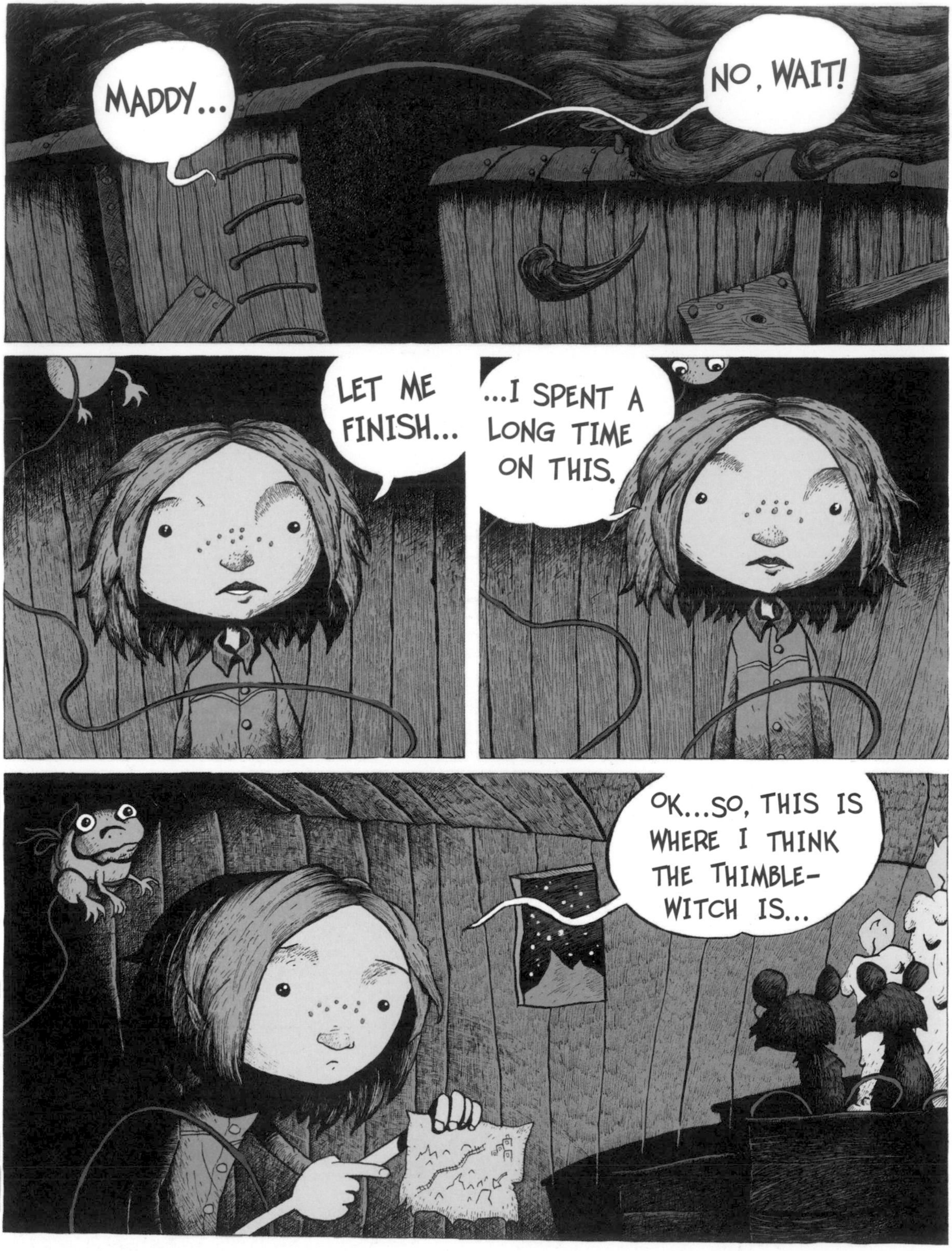
MADDY...
NO, WAIT!
LET ME FINISH...
...I SPENT A LONG TIME ON THIS.
OK...SO, THIS IS WHERE I THINK THE THIMBLE-WITCH IS...

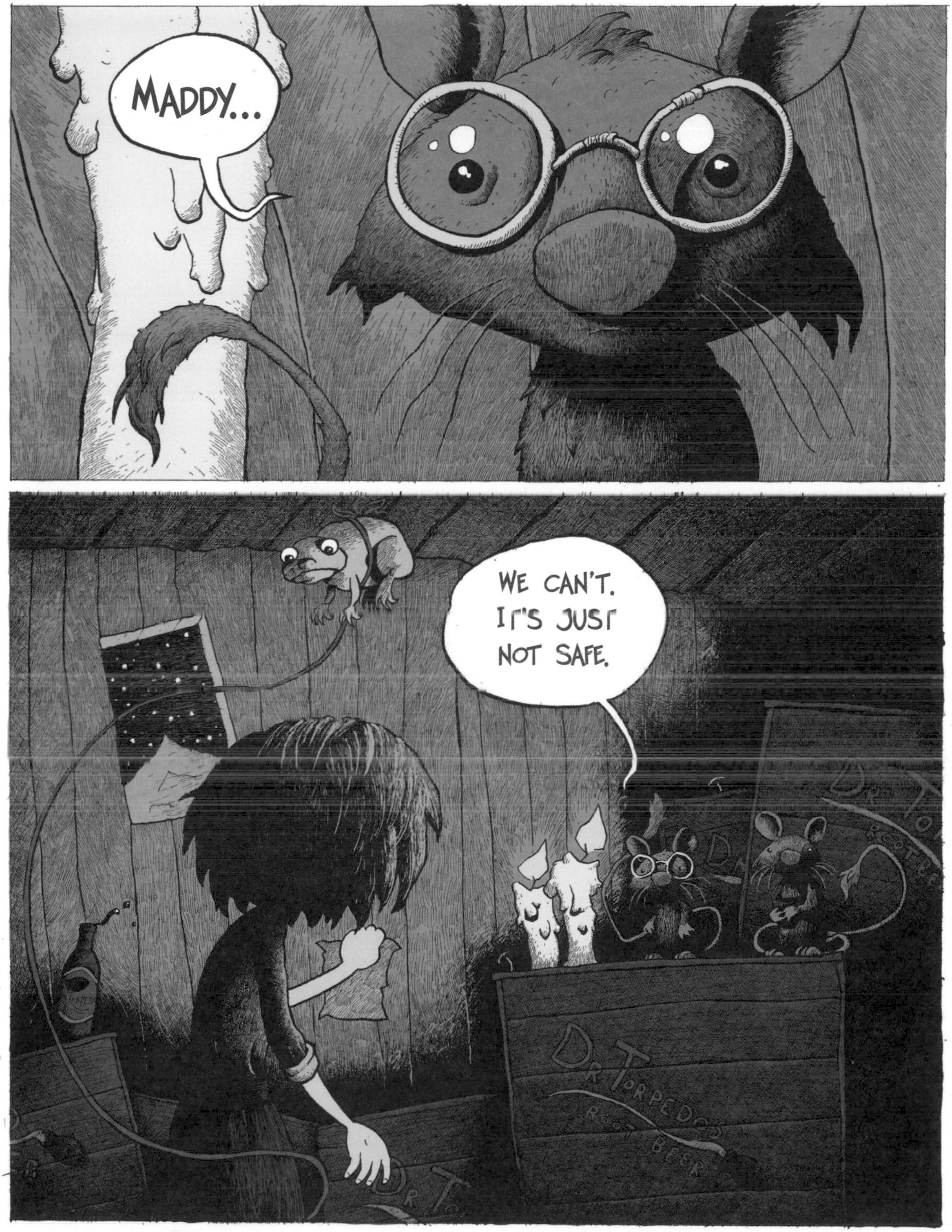
MADDY...
WE CAN'T. IT'S JUST NOT SAFE.
DR TORPEDO'S ROOT BEER

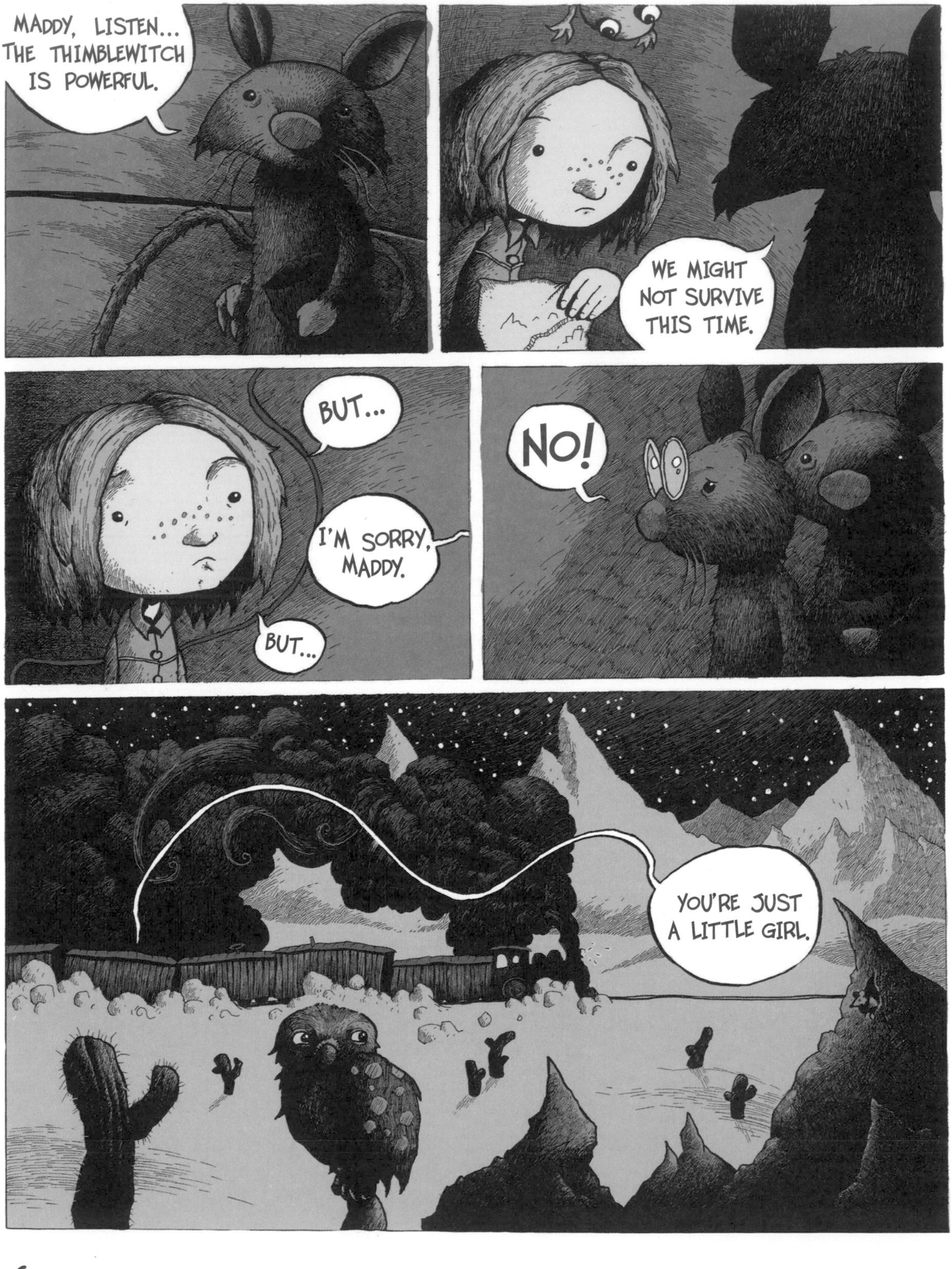
MADDY, LISTEN... THE THIMBLEWITCH IS POWERFUL.
WE MIGHT NOT SURVIVE THIS TIME.
BUT...
I'M SORRY, MADDY.
BUT...
NO!
YOU'RE JUST A LITTLE GIRL.

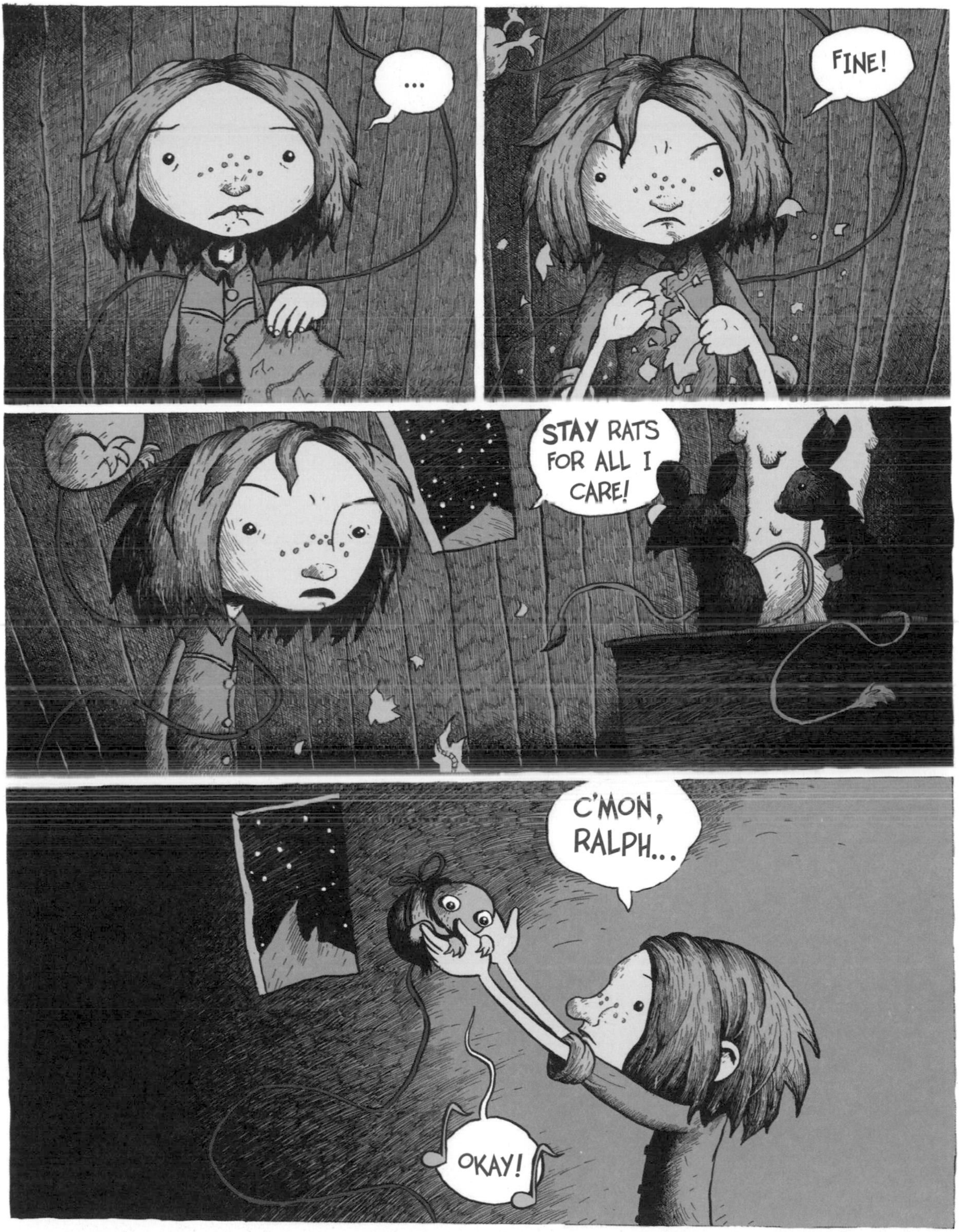
...
FINE!
STAY RATS FOR ALL I CARE!
C'MON, RALPH...
OKAY!

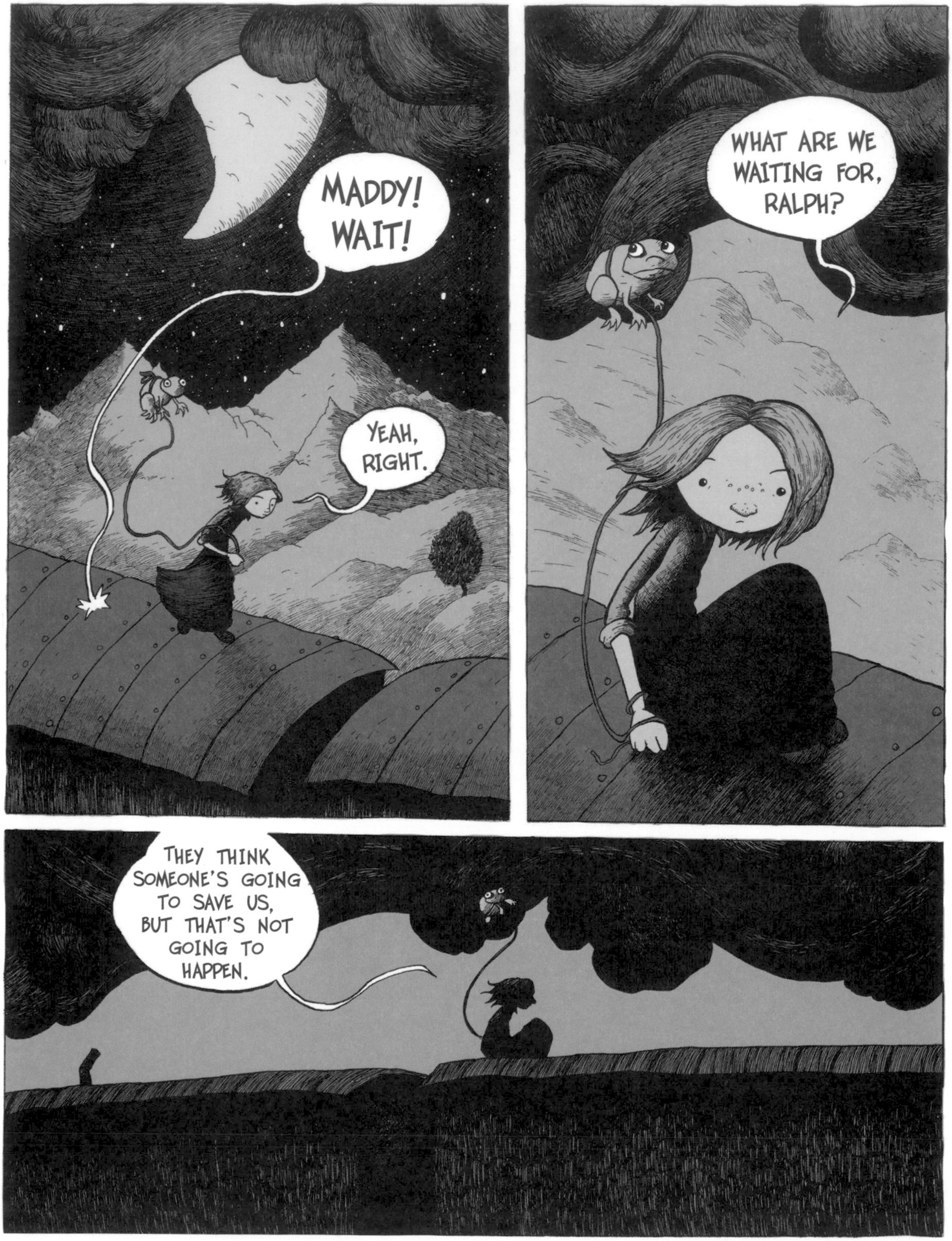
MADDY! WAIT!
YEAH, RIGHT.
WHAT ARE WE WAITING FOR, RALPH?
THEY THINK SOMEONE'S GOING TO SAVE US, BUT THAT'S NOT GOING TO HAPPEN.

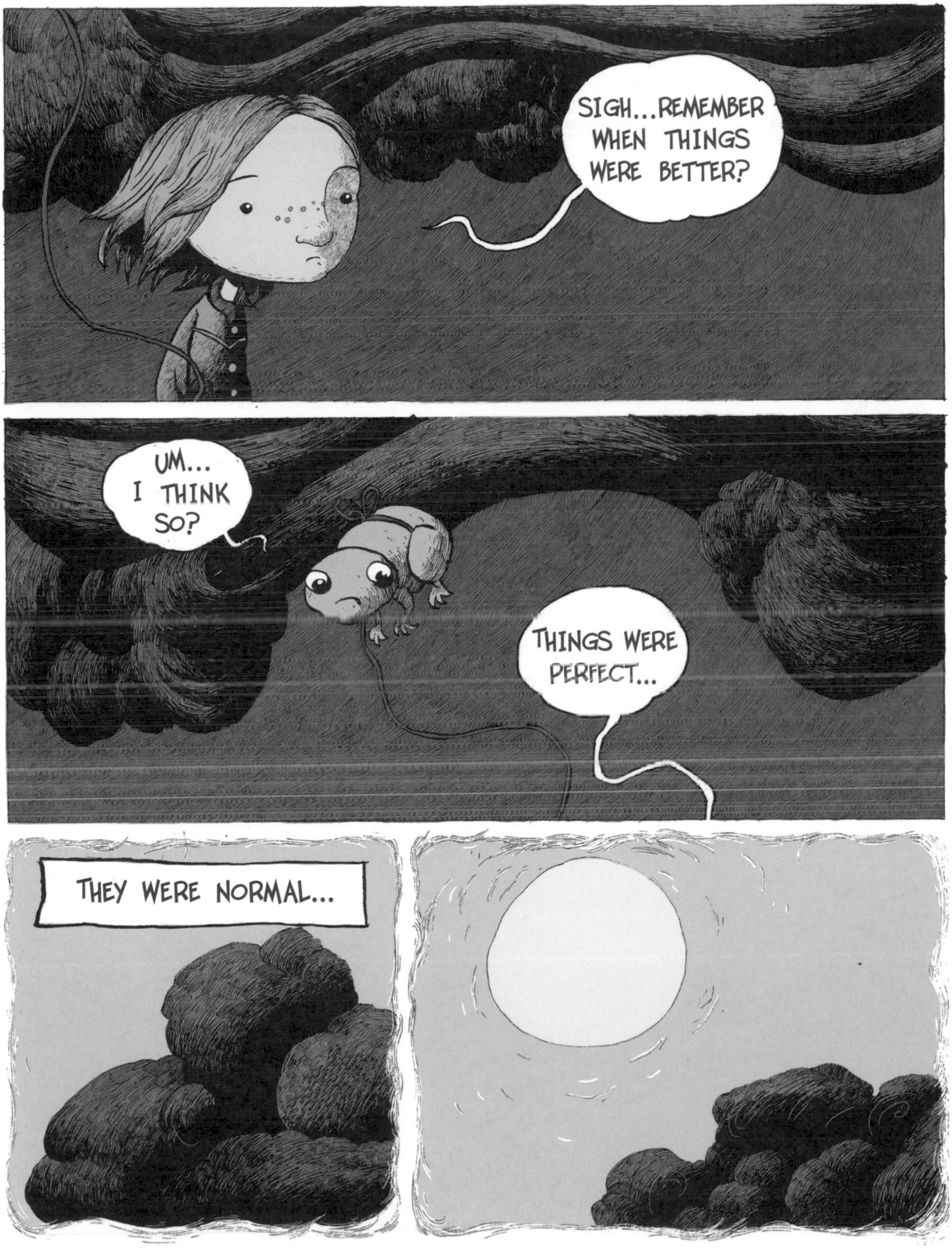
SIGH...REMEMBER WHEN THINGS WERE BETTER?
UM... I THINK SO?
THINGS WERE PERFECT...
THEY WERE NORMAL...

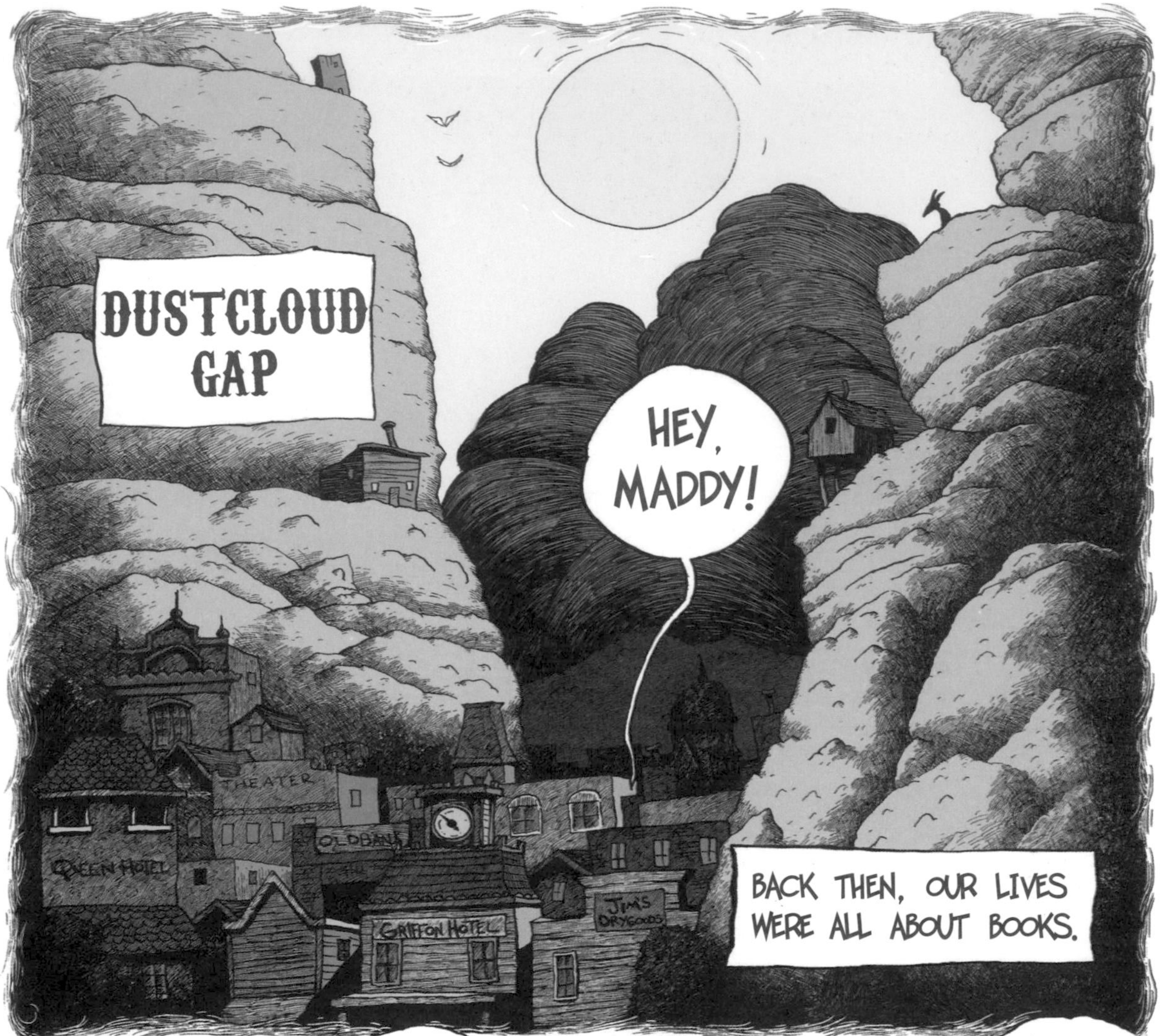
DUSTCLOUD GAP
HEY, MADDY!
THEATER
QUEEN HOTEL
OLD BANK
GRIFFON HOTEL
JIM'S DRYGOODS
BACK THEN, OUR LIVES WERE ALL ABOUT BOOKS.

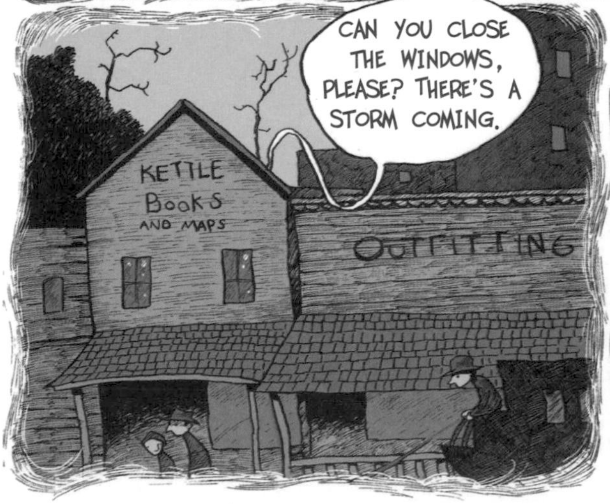
CAN YOU CLOSE THE WINDOWS, PLEASE? THERE'S A STORM COMING.
KETTLE BOOKS AND MAPS
OUTFITTING

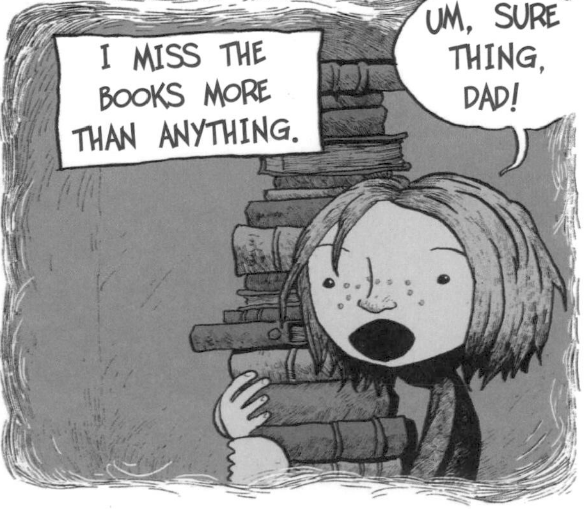
I MISS THE BOOKS MORE THAN ANYTHING.
UM, SURE THING, DAD!

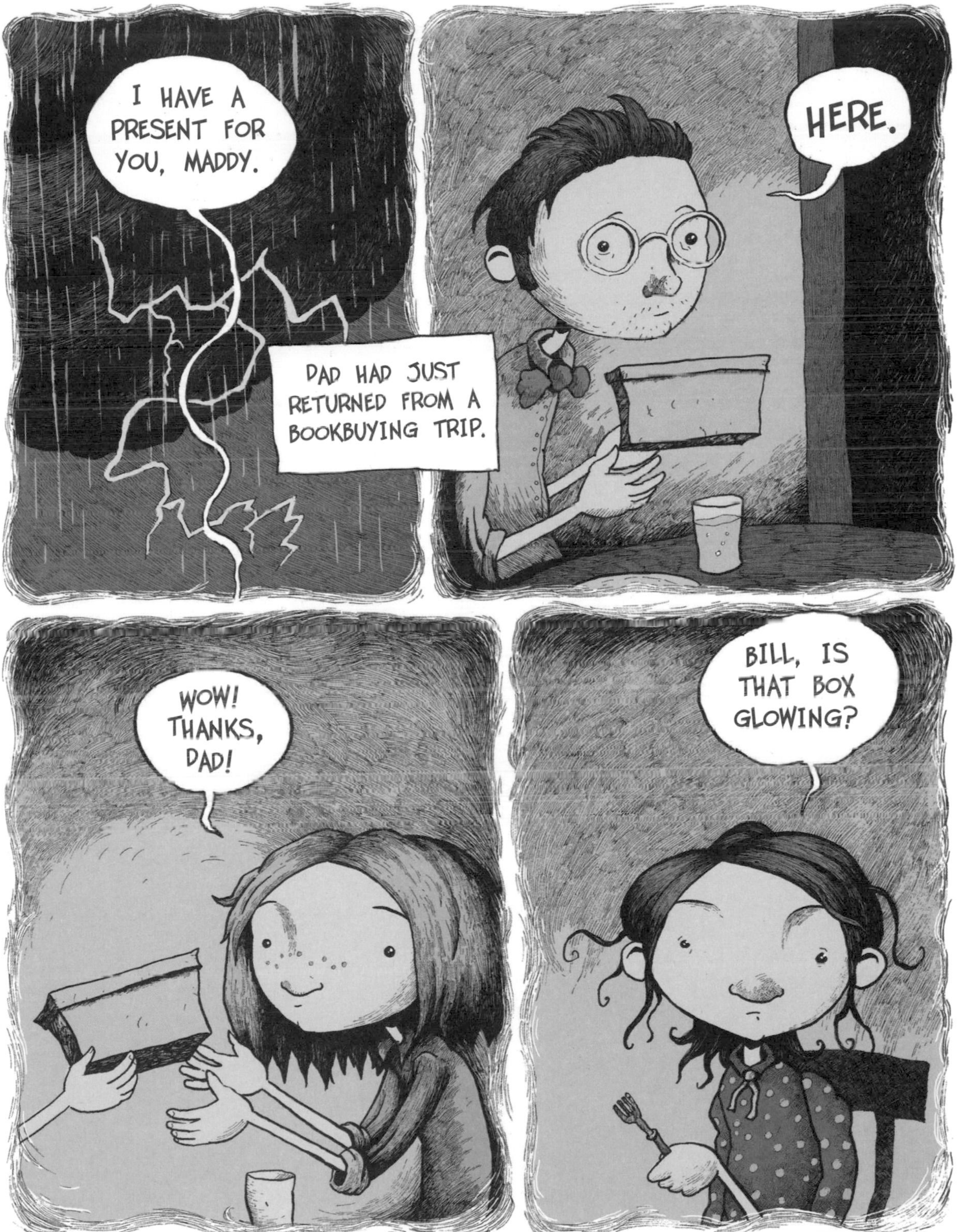
I HAVE A PRESENT FOR YOU, MADDY.
DAD HAD JUST RETURNED FROM A BOOKBUYING TRIP.
HERE.
WOW! THANKS, DAD!
BILL, IS THAT BOX GLOWING?

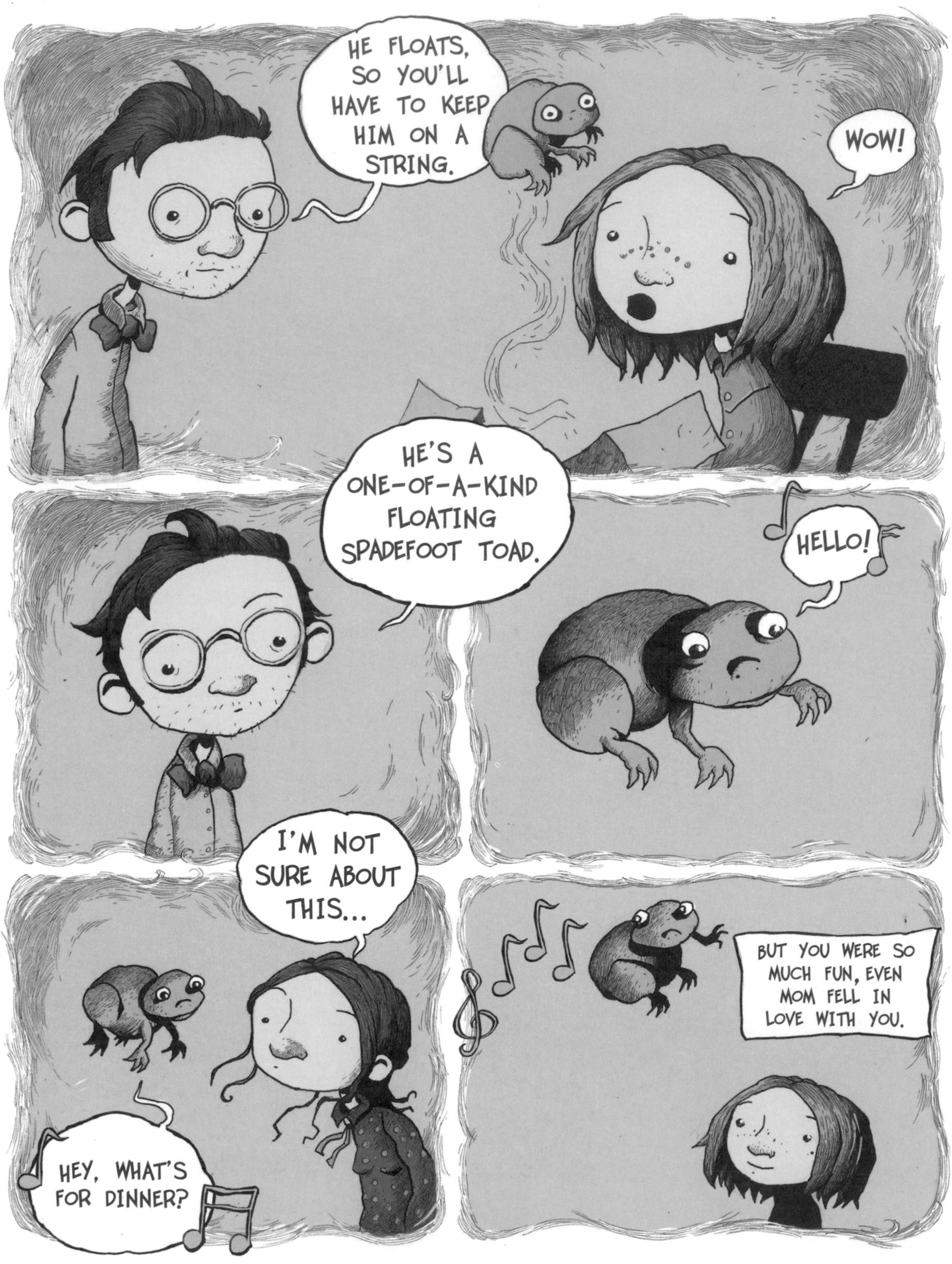
HE FLOATS, SO YOU'LL HAVE TO KEEP HIM ON A STRING.
WOW!
HE'S A ONE-OF-A-KIND FLOATING SPADEFOOT TOAD.
HELLO!
I'M NOT SURE ABOUT THIS...
HEY, WHAT'S FOR DINNER?
BUT YOU WERE SO MUCH FUN, EVEN MOM FELL IN LOVE WITH YOU.

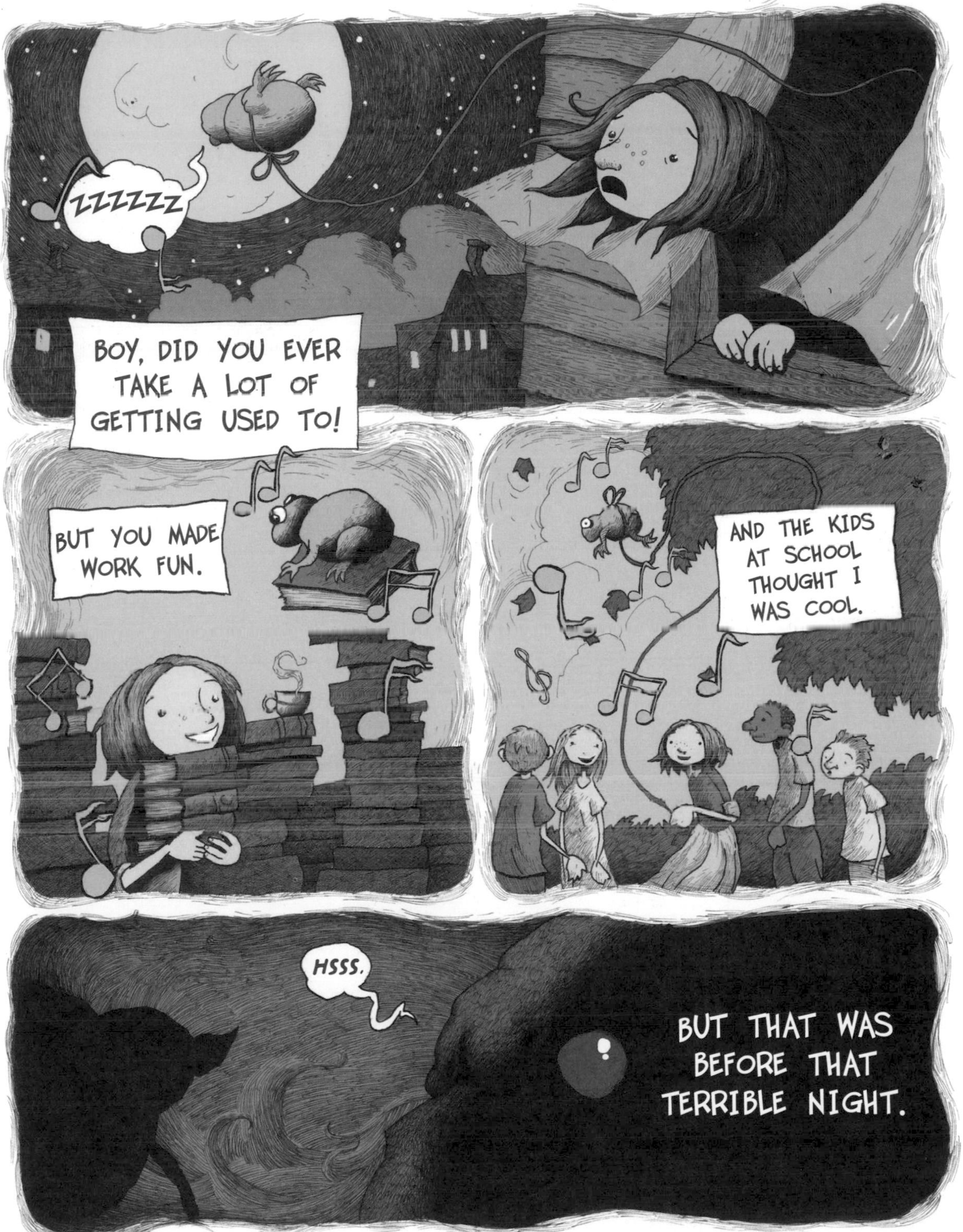
ZZZZZZ
BOY, DID YOU EVER TAKE A LOT OF GETTING USED TO!
BUT YOU MADE WORK FUN.
AND THE KIDS AT SCHOOL THOUGHT I WAS COOL.
HSSS.
BUT THAT WAS BEFORE THAT TERRIBLE NIGHT.

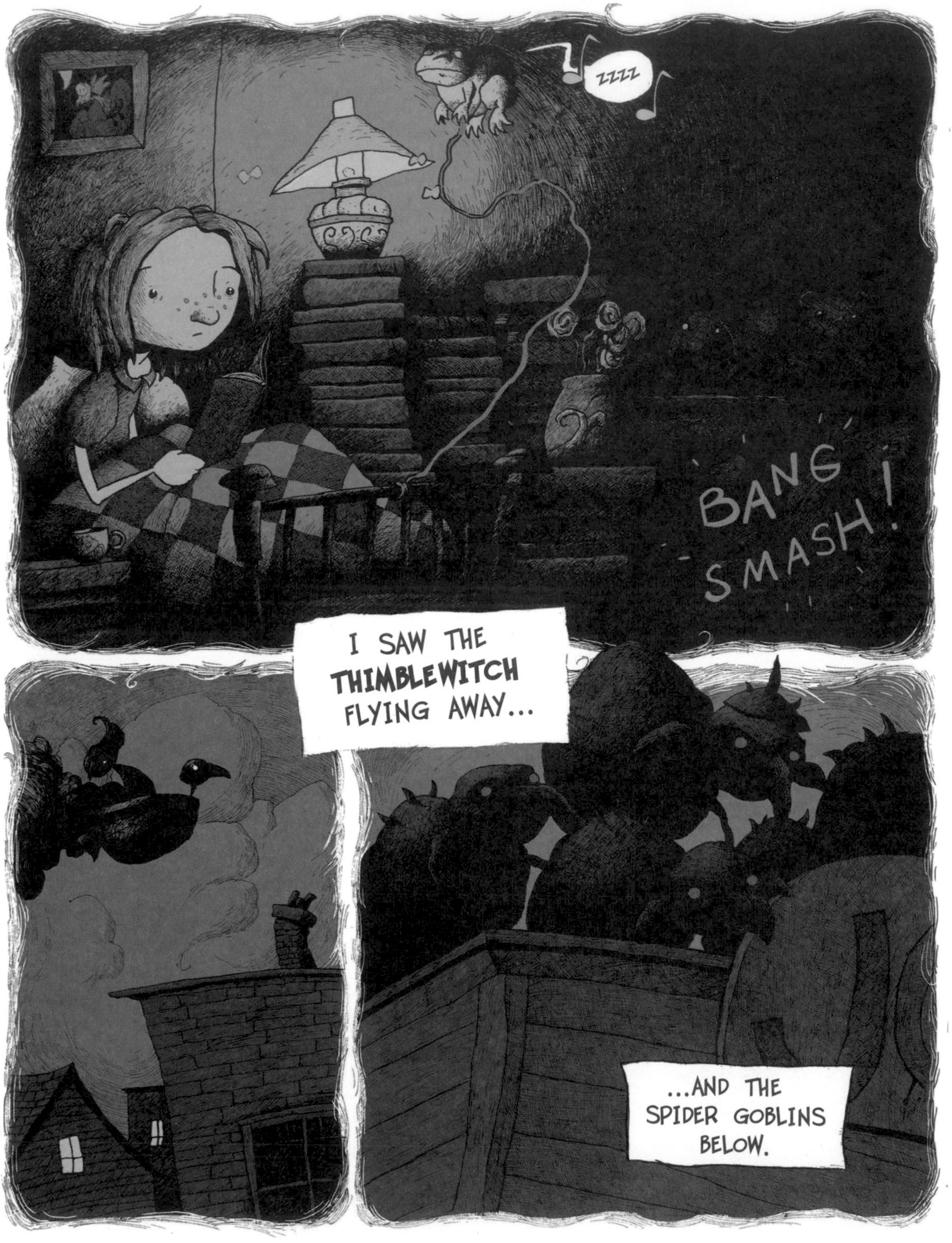
ZZZZ
BANG
SMASH!
I SAW THE THIMBLEWITCH FLYING AWAY...
...AND THE SPIDER GOBLINS BELOW.

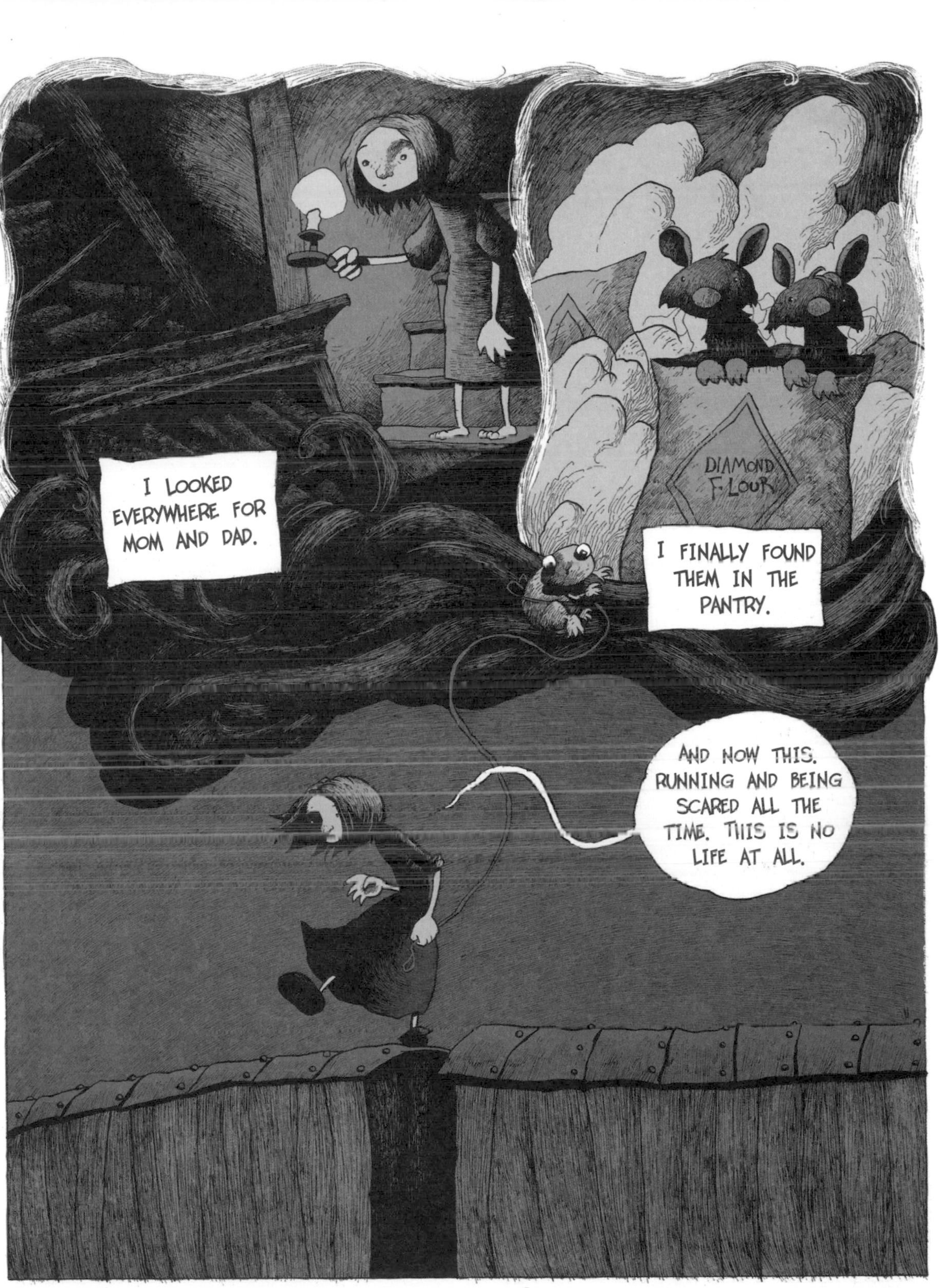
I LOOKED EVERYWHERE FOR MOM AND DAD.
DIAMOND F·LOUR
I FINALLY FOUND THEM IN THE PANTRY.
AND NOW THIS. RUNNING AND BEING SCARED ALL THE TIME. THIS IS NO LIFE AT ALL.

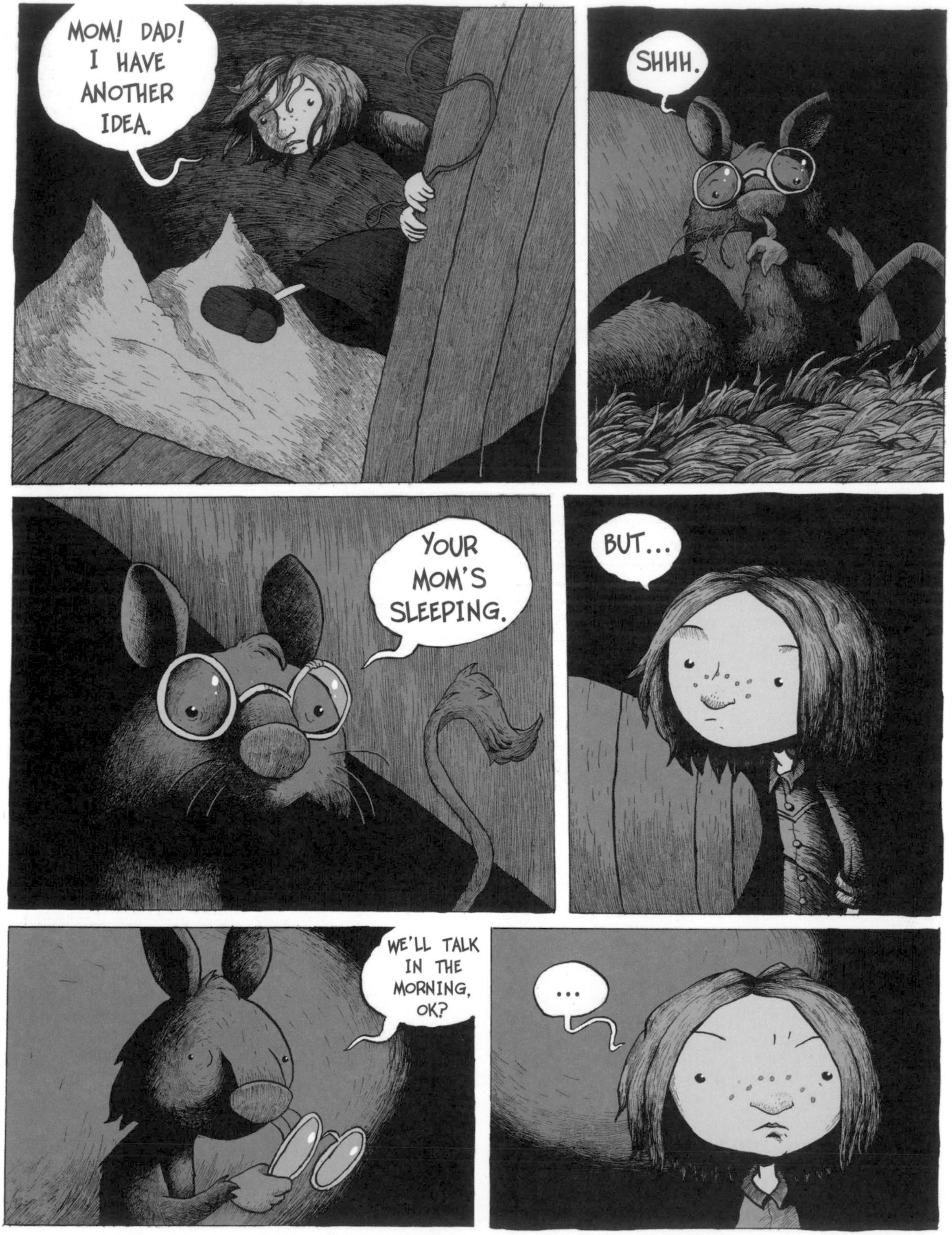
MOM! DAD! I HAVE ANOTHER IDEA.
SHHH.
YOUR MOM'S SLEEPING.
BUT...
WE'LL TALK IN THE MORNING, OK?
...

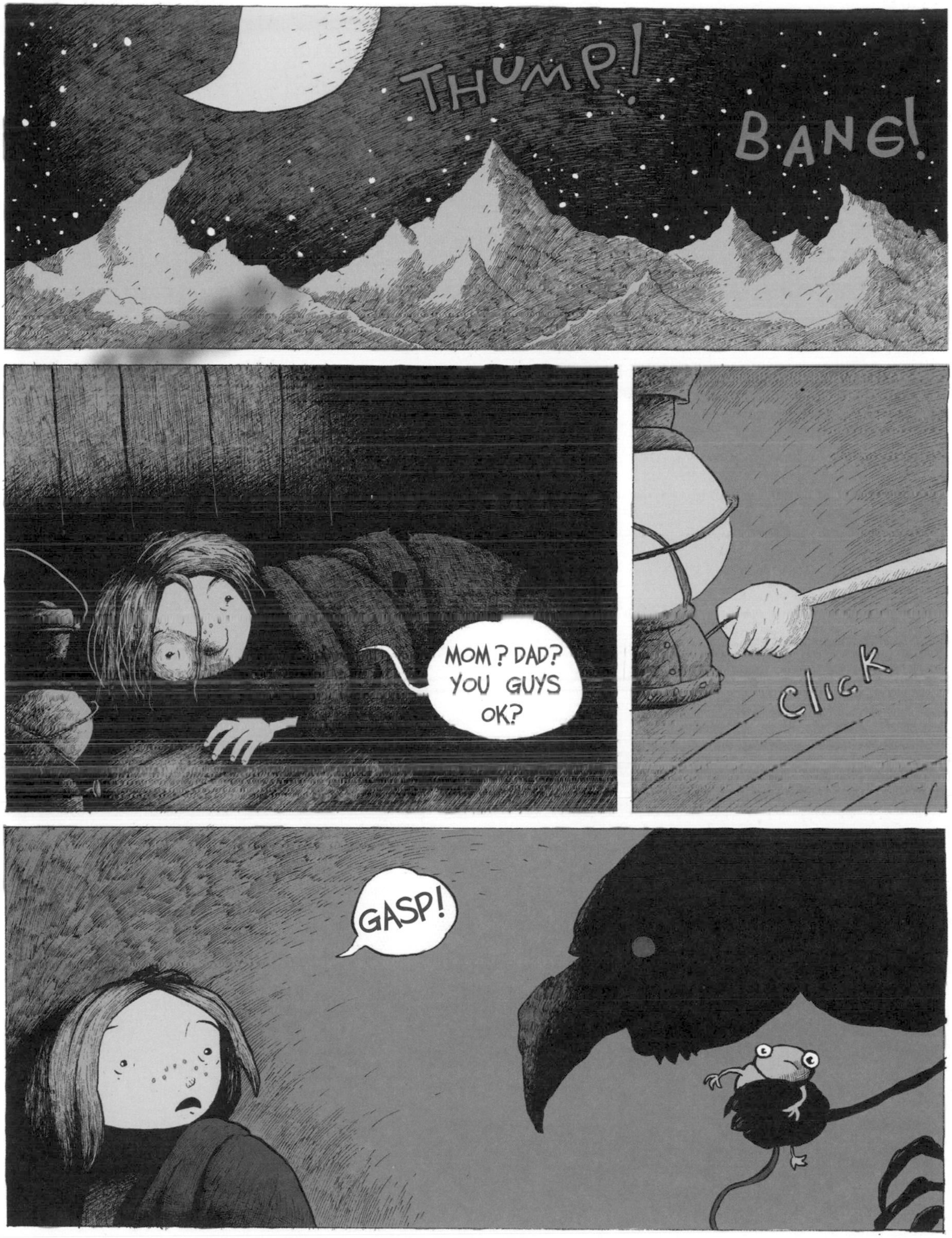
THUMP!
BANG!
MOM? DAD? YOU GUYS OK?
CLICK
GASP!

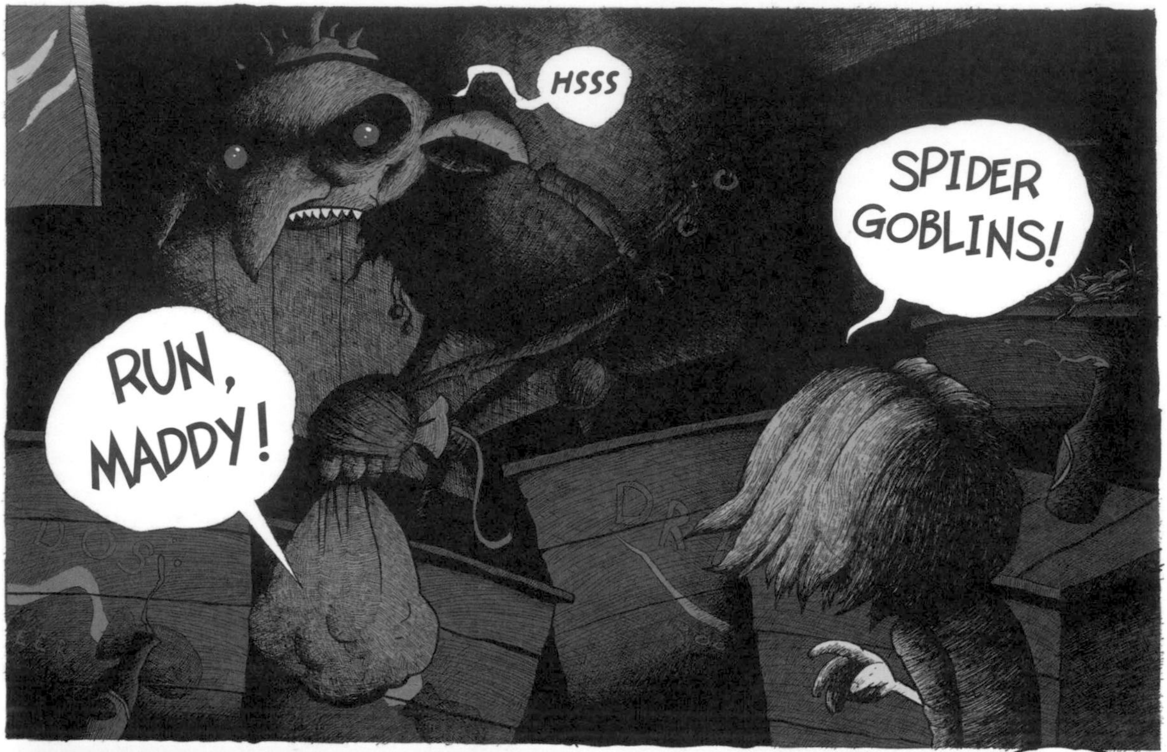
HSSS
SPIDER GOBLINS!
RUN, MADDY!
OOF
HSSS
NOOO!
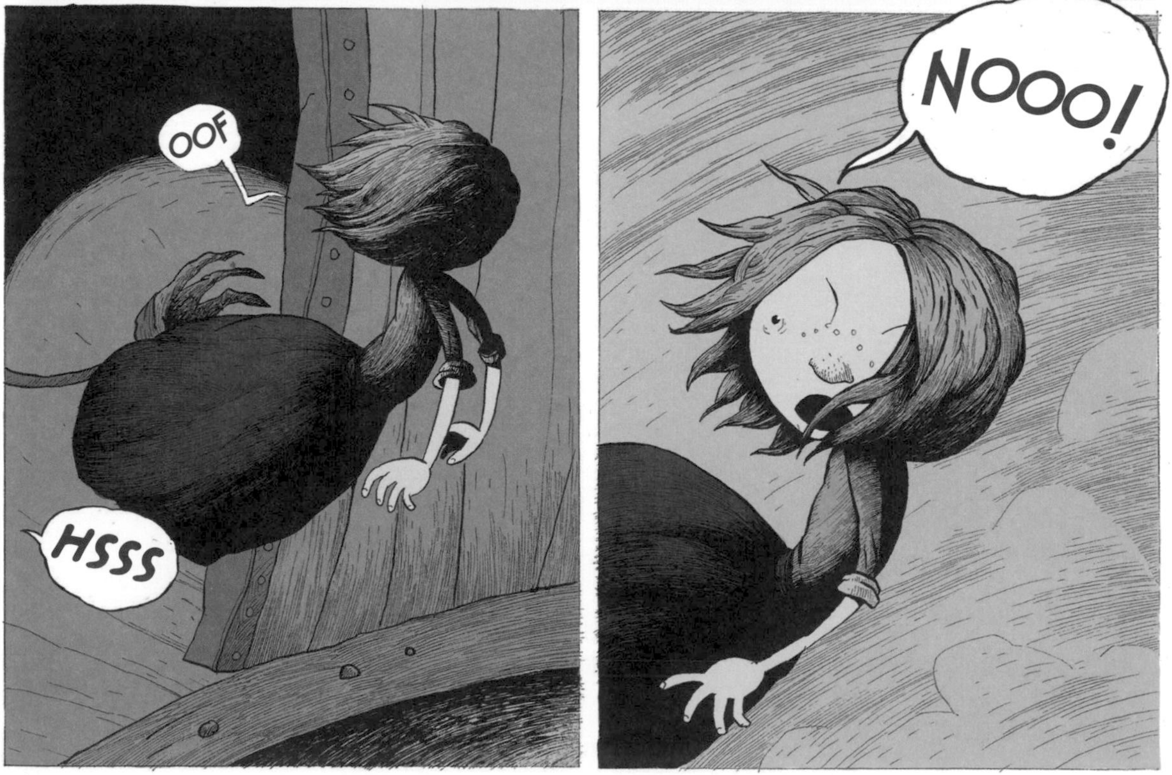

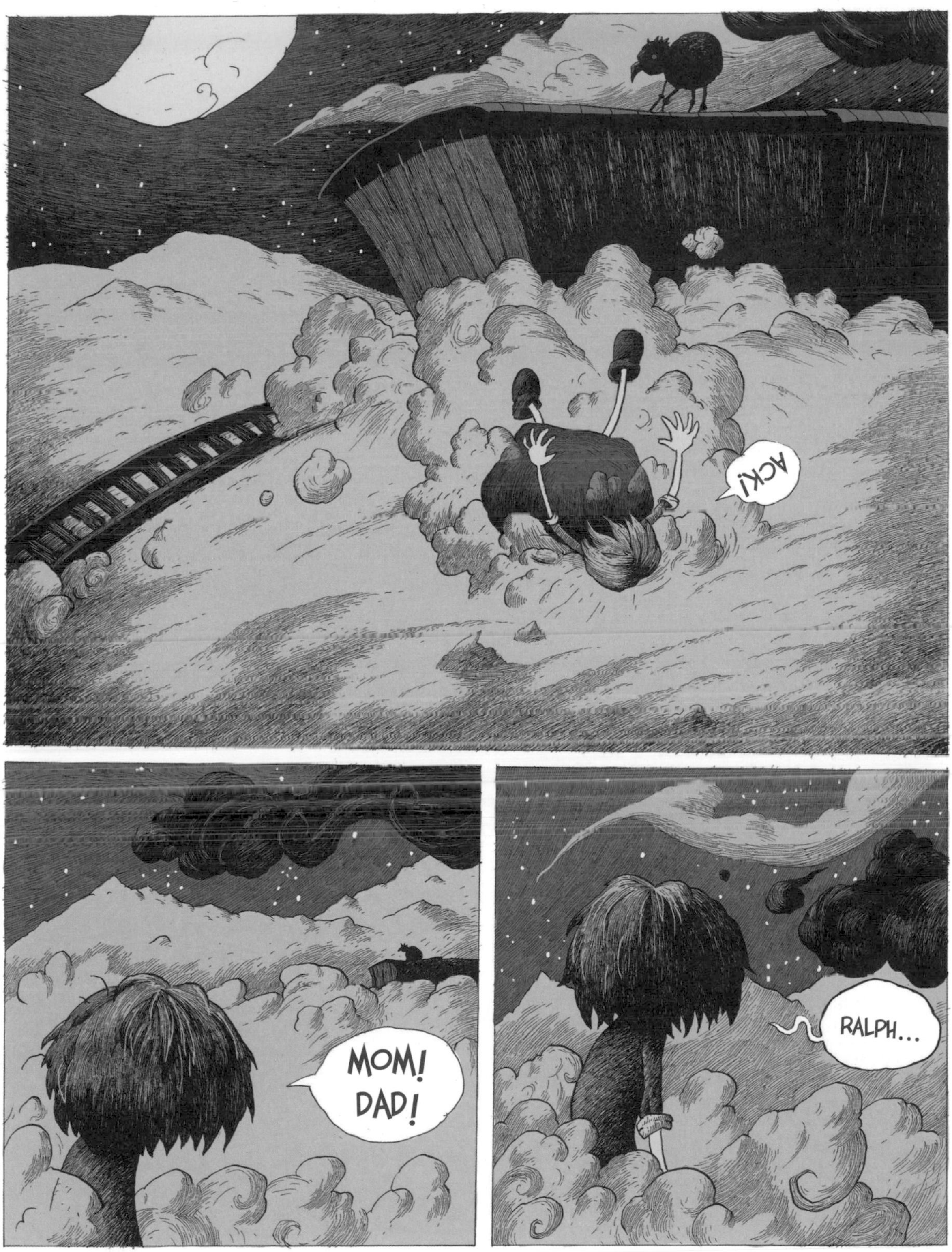
ACK!
MOM! DAD!
RALPH...

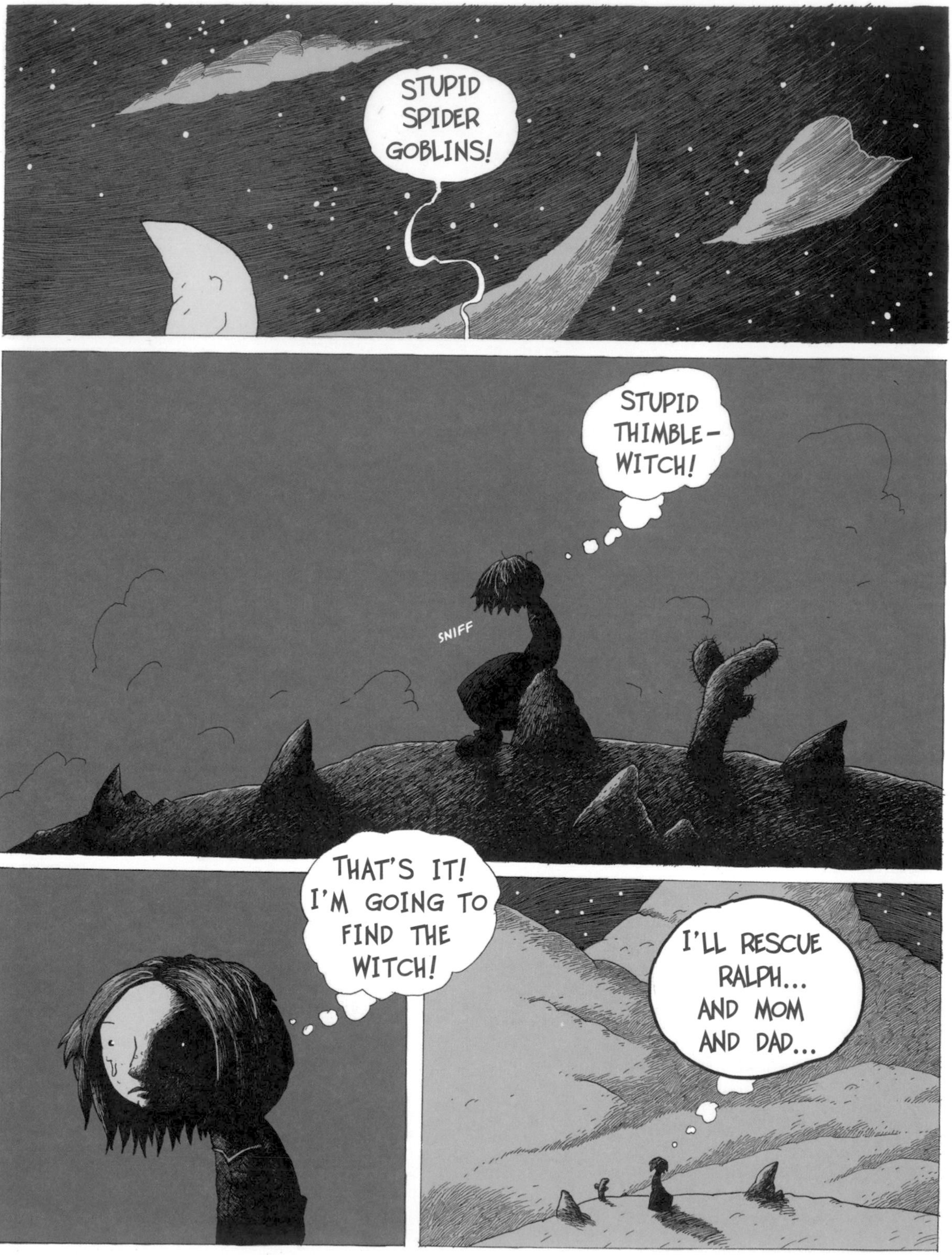
STUPID SPIDER GOBLINS!
STUPID THIMBLE-WITCH!
SNIFF
THAT'S IT! I'M GOING TO FIND THE WITCH!
I'LL RESCUE RALPH... AND MOM AND DAD...

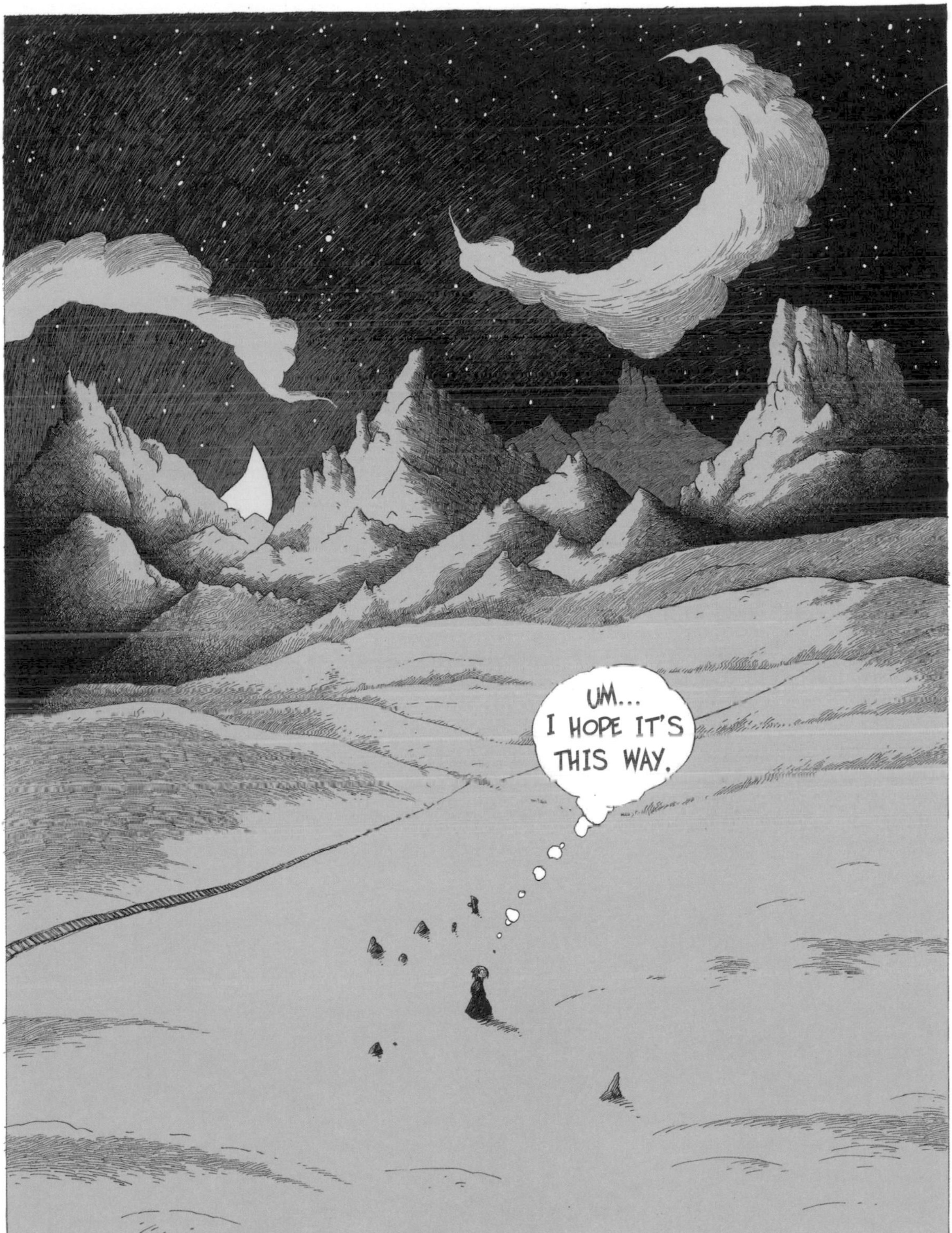
UM... I HOPE IT'S THIS WAY.

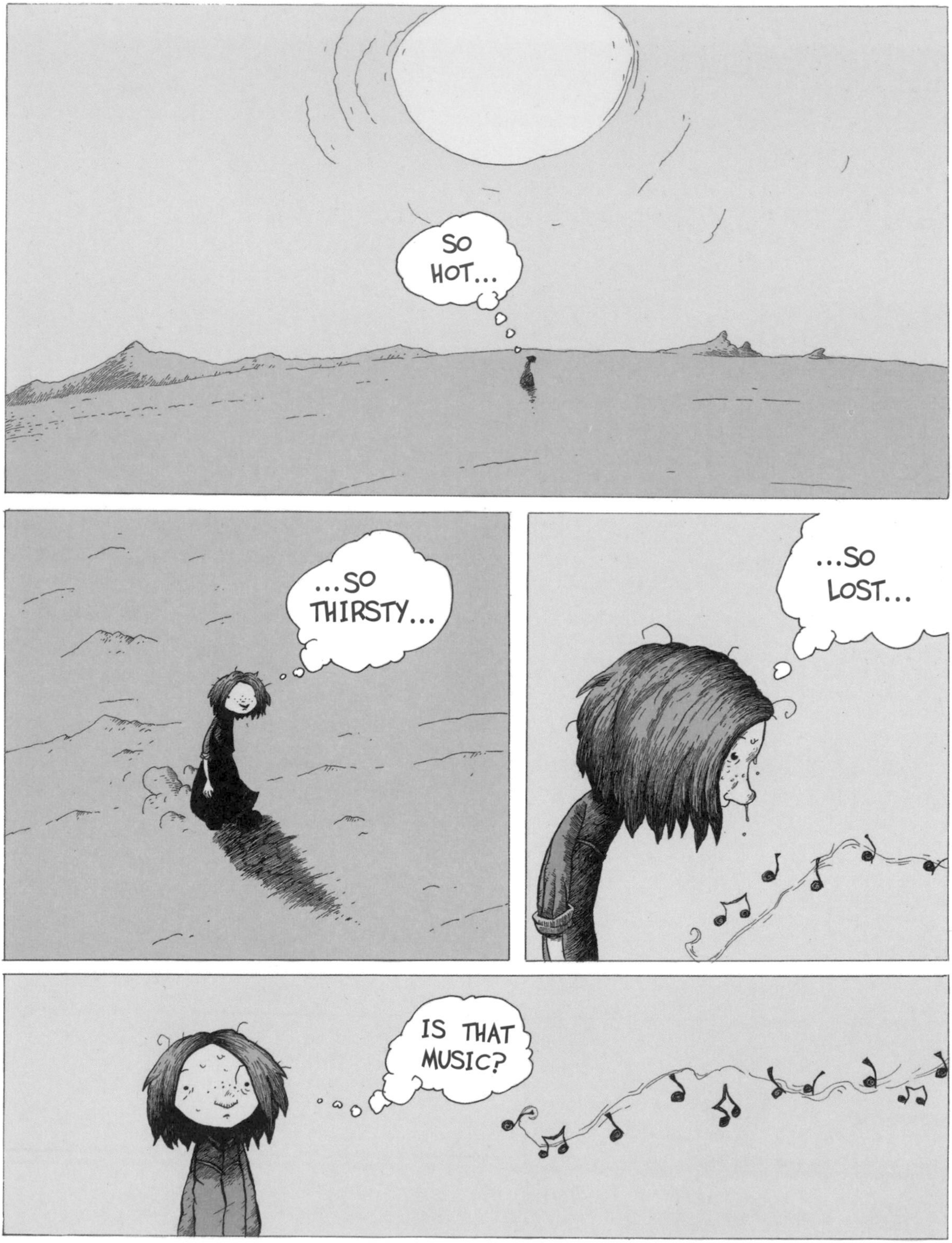
SO HOT...
...SO THIRSTY...
...SO LOST...
IS THAT MUSIC?

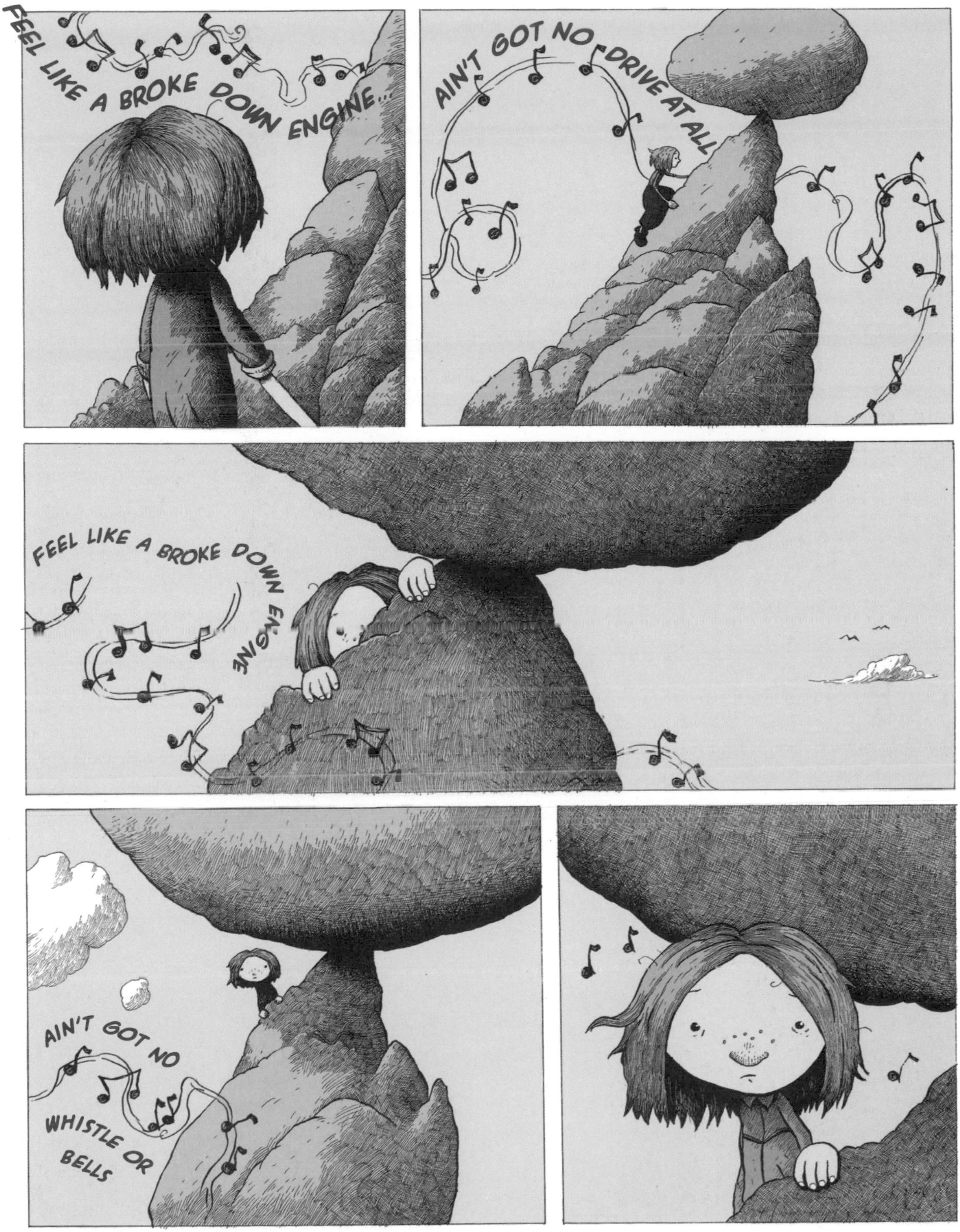
FEEL LIKE A BROKE DOWN ENGINE...
AIN'T GOT NO DRIVE AT ALL
FEEL LIKE A BROKE DOWN ENGINE
AIN'T GOT NO
WHISTLE OR BELLS

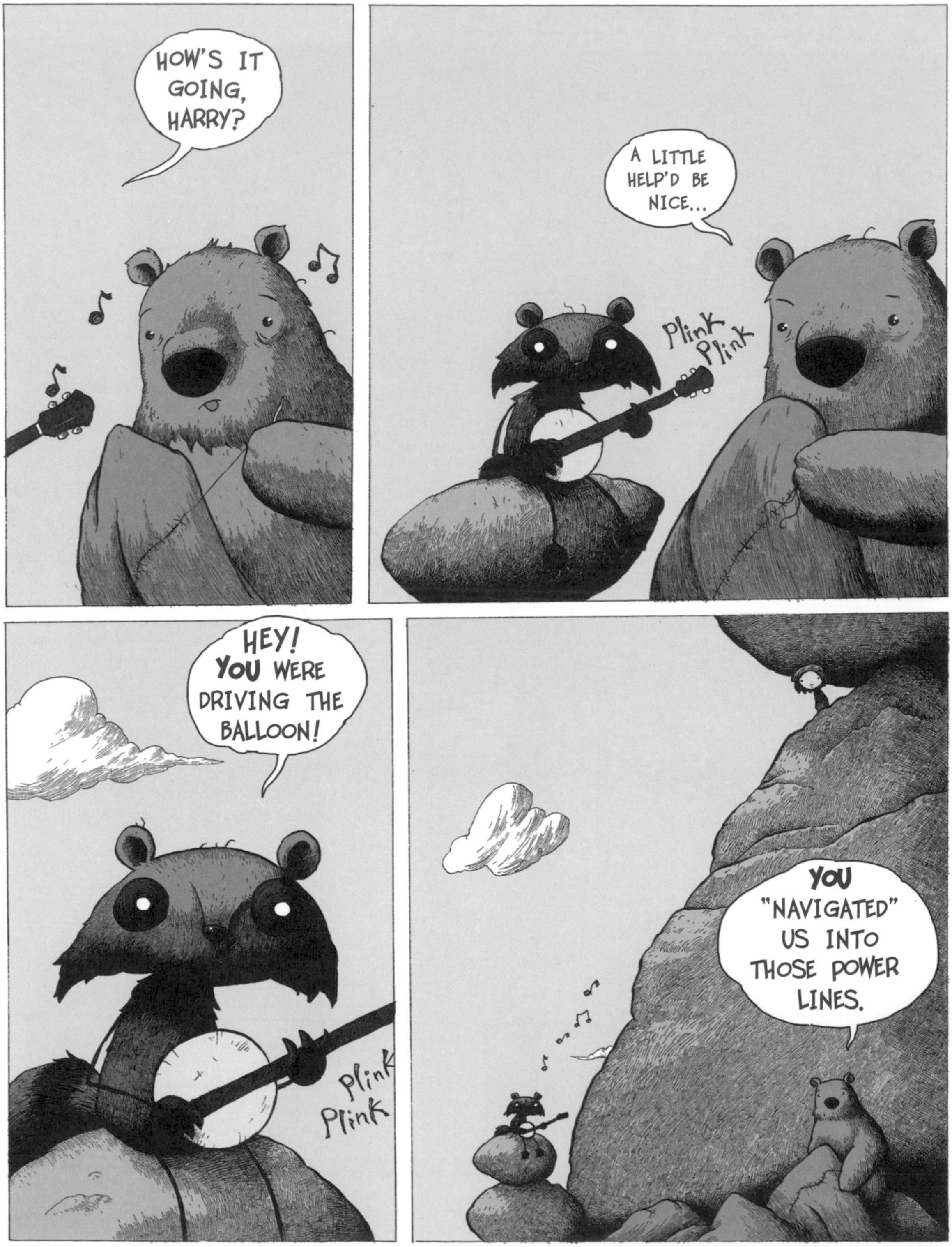
HOW'S IT GOING, HARRY?
A LITTLE HELP'D BE NICE...
Plink Plink
HEY! YOU WERE DRIVING THE BALLOON!
Plink Plink
YOU "NAVIGATED" US INTO THOSE POWER LINES.

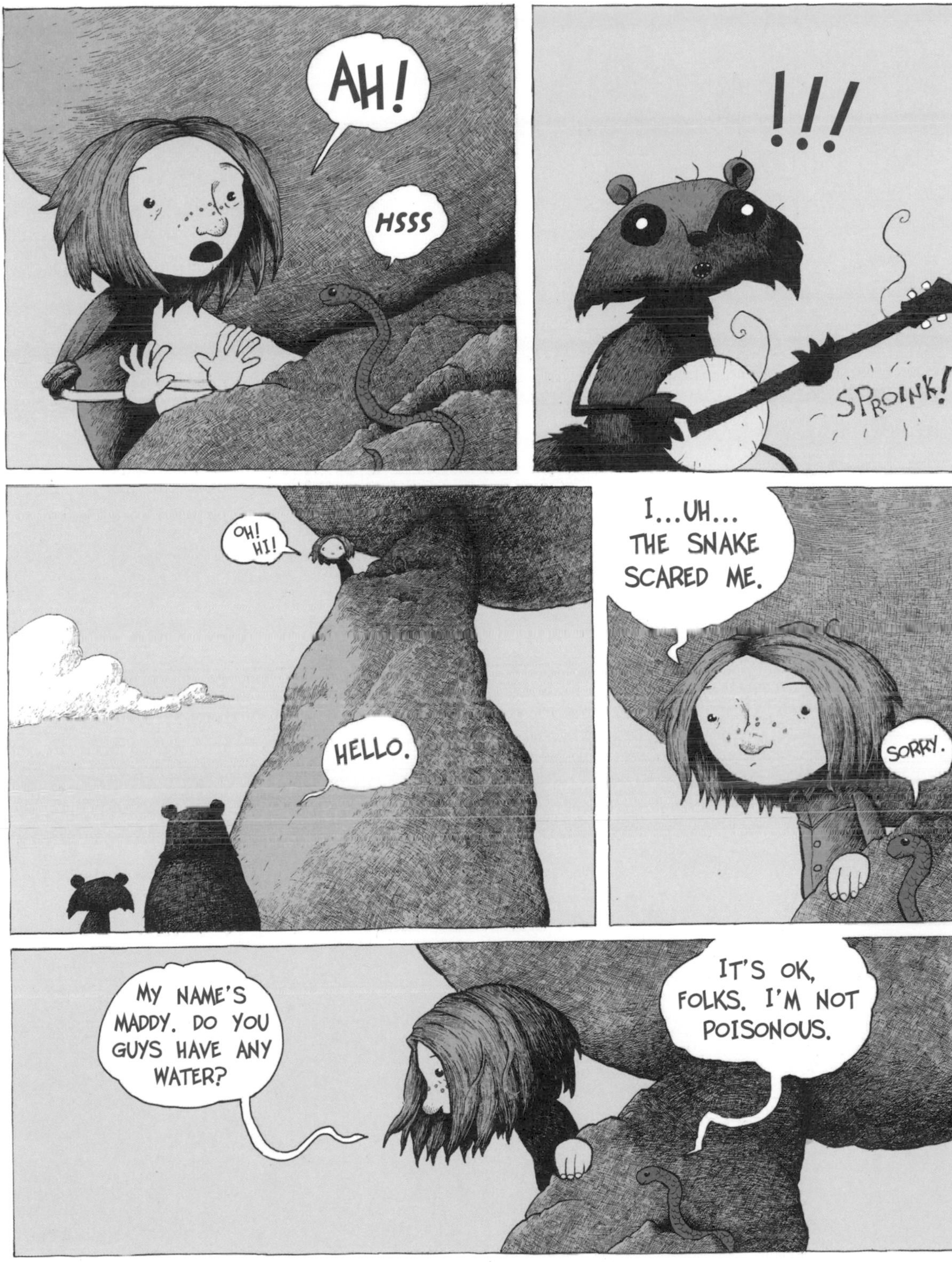
AH!
HSSS
!!!
SPROINK!
OH! HI!
HELLO.
I...UH... THE SNAKE SCARED ME.
SORRY.
MY NAME'S MADDY. DO YOU GUYS HAVE ANY WATER?
IT'S OK, FOLKS. I'M NOT POISONOUS.

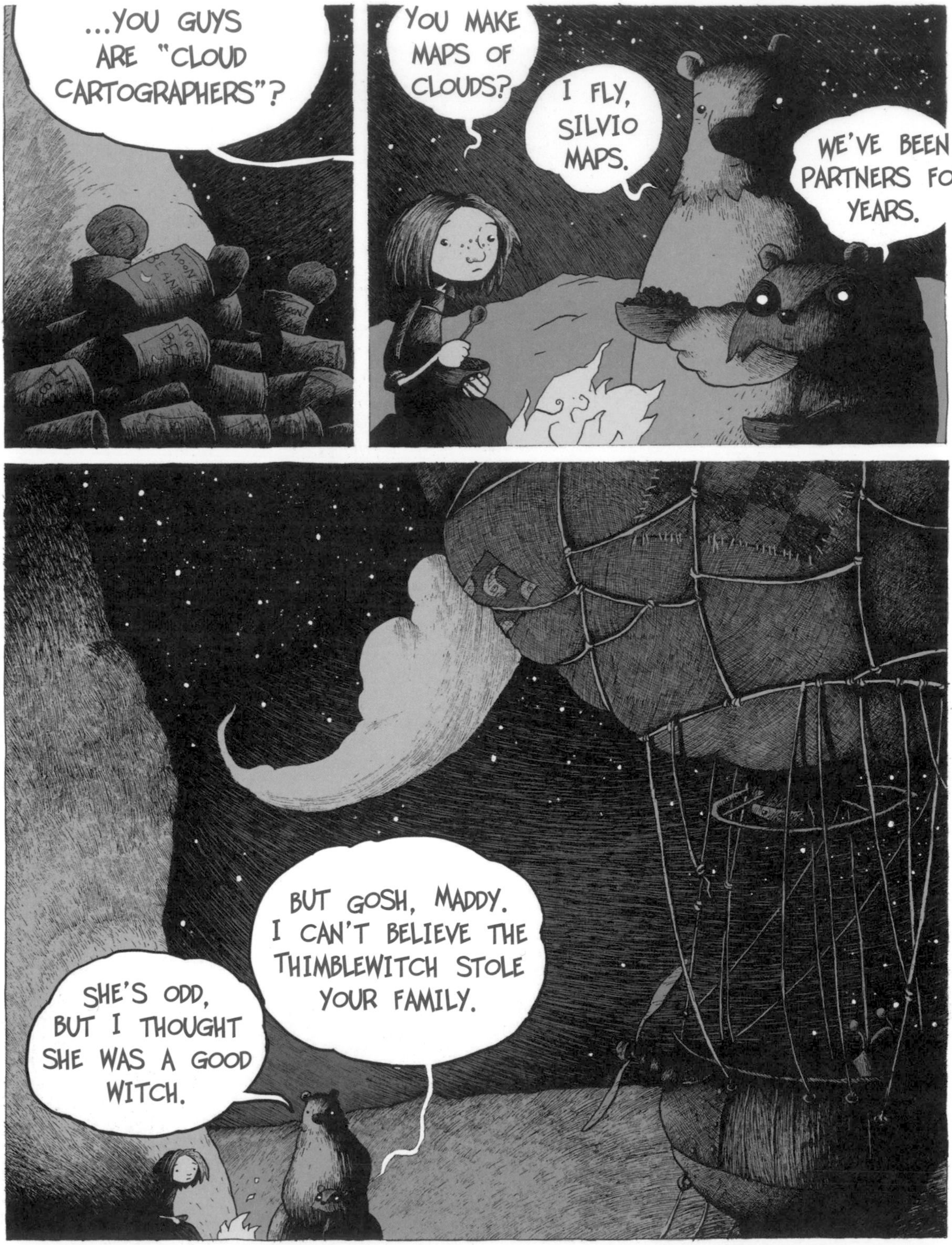
...YOU GUYS ARE "CLOUD CARTOGRAPHERS"?
YOU MAKE MAPS OF CLOUDS?
I FLY, SILVIO MAPS.
WE'VE BEEN PARTNERS FOR YEARS.
BUT GOSH, MADDY. I CAN'T BELIEVE THE THIMBLEWITCH STOLE YOUR FAMILY.
SHE'S ODD, BUT I THOUGHT SHE WAS A GOOD WITCH.

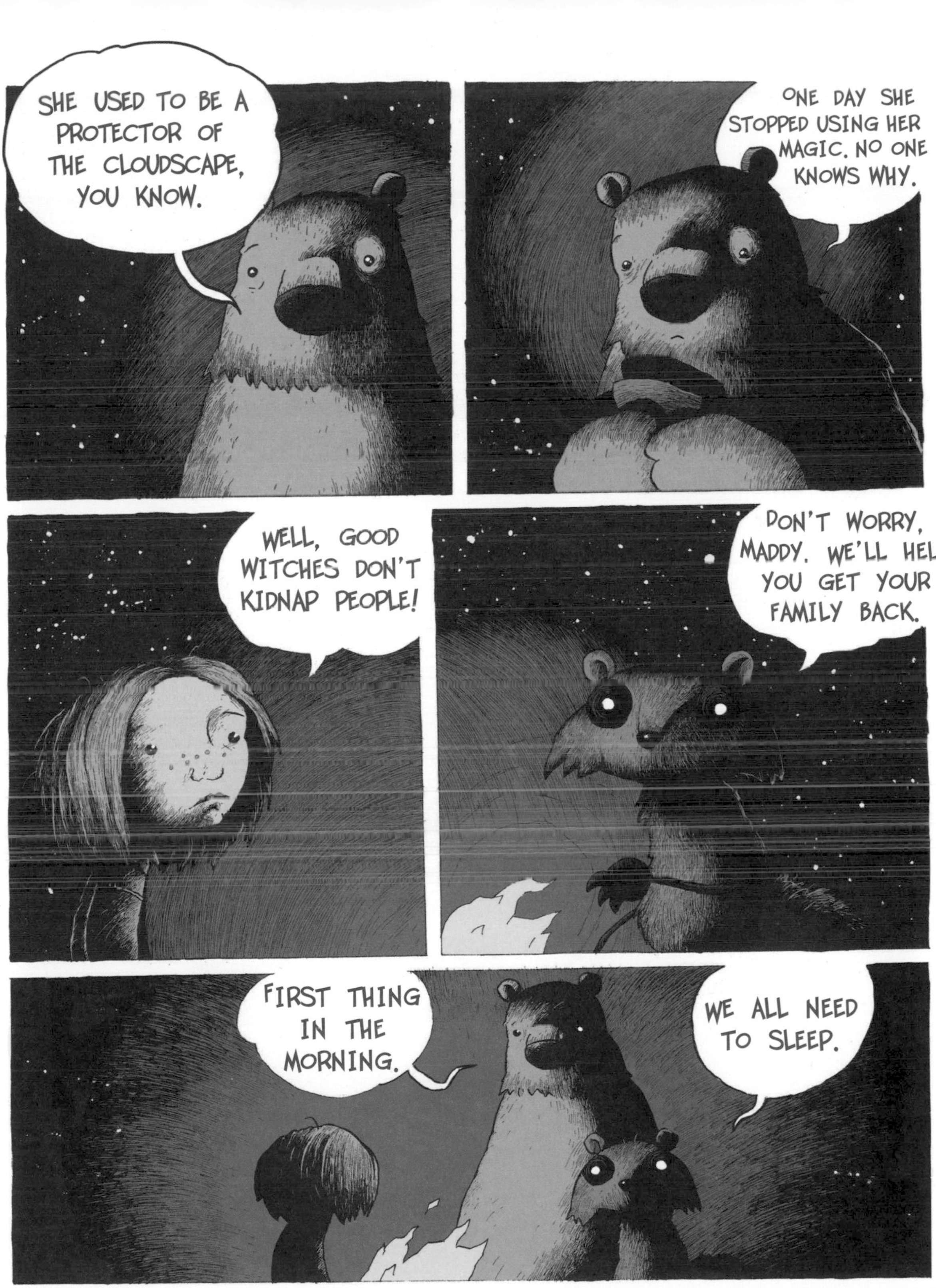
SHE USED TO BE A PROTECTOR OF THE CLOUDSCAPE, YOU KNOW.
ONE DAY SHE STOPPED USING HER MAGIC. NO ONE KNOWS WHY.
WELL, GOOD WITCHES DON'T KIDNAP PEOPLE!
DON'T WORRY, MADDY. WE'LL HELP YOU GET YOUR FAMILY BACK.
FIRST THING IN THE MORNING.
WE ALL NEED TO SLEEP.

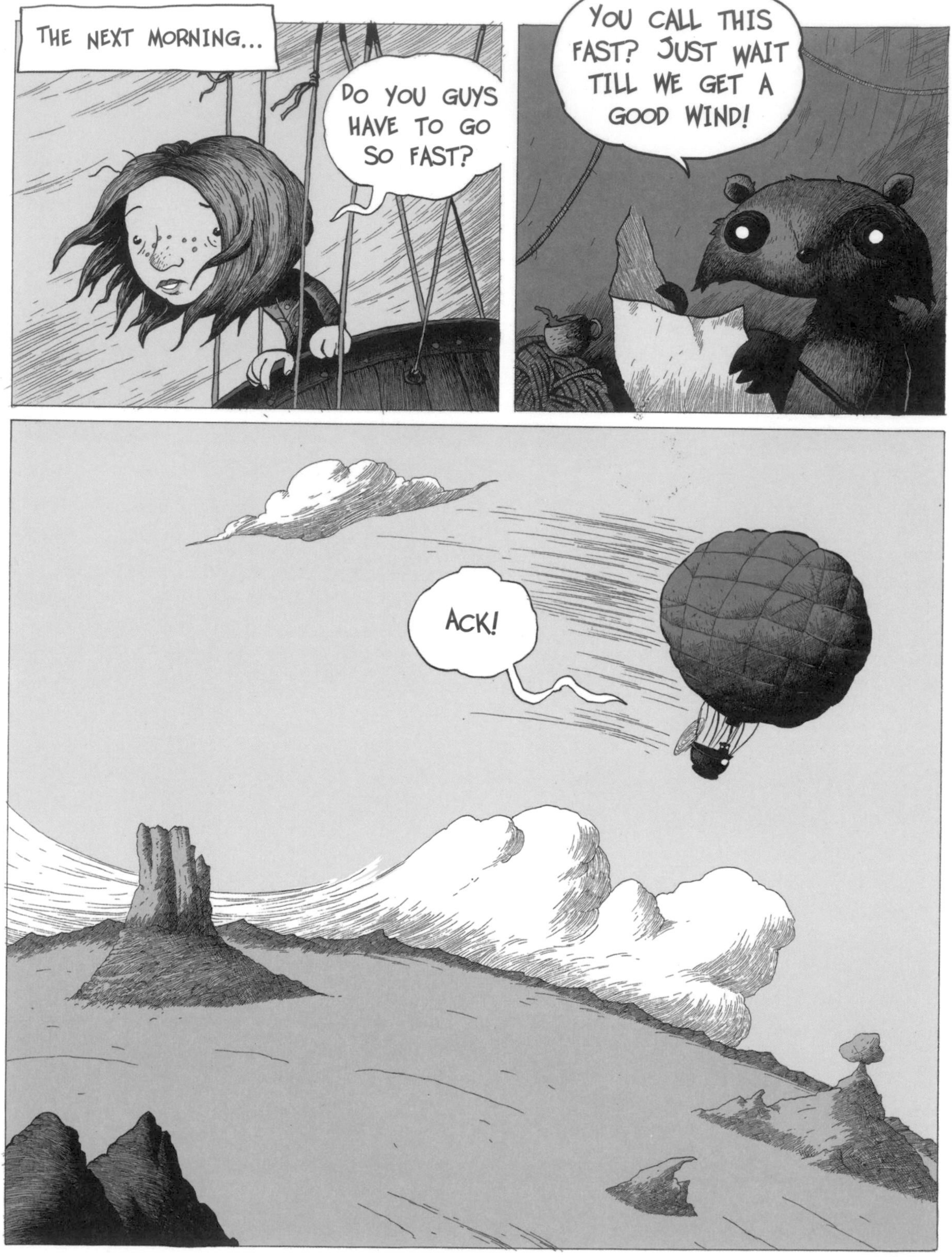
THE NEXT MORNING...
DO YOU GUYS HAVE TO GO SO FAST?
YOU CALL THIS FAST? JUST WAIT TILL WE GET A GOOD WIND!
ACK!

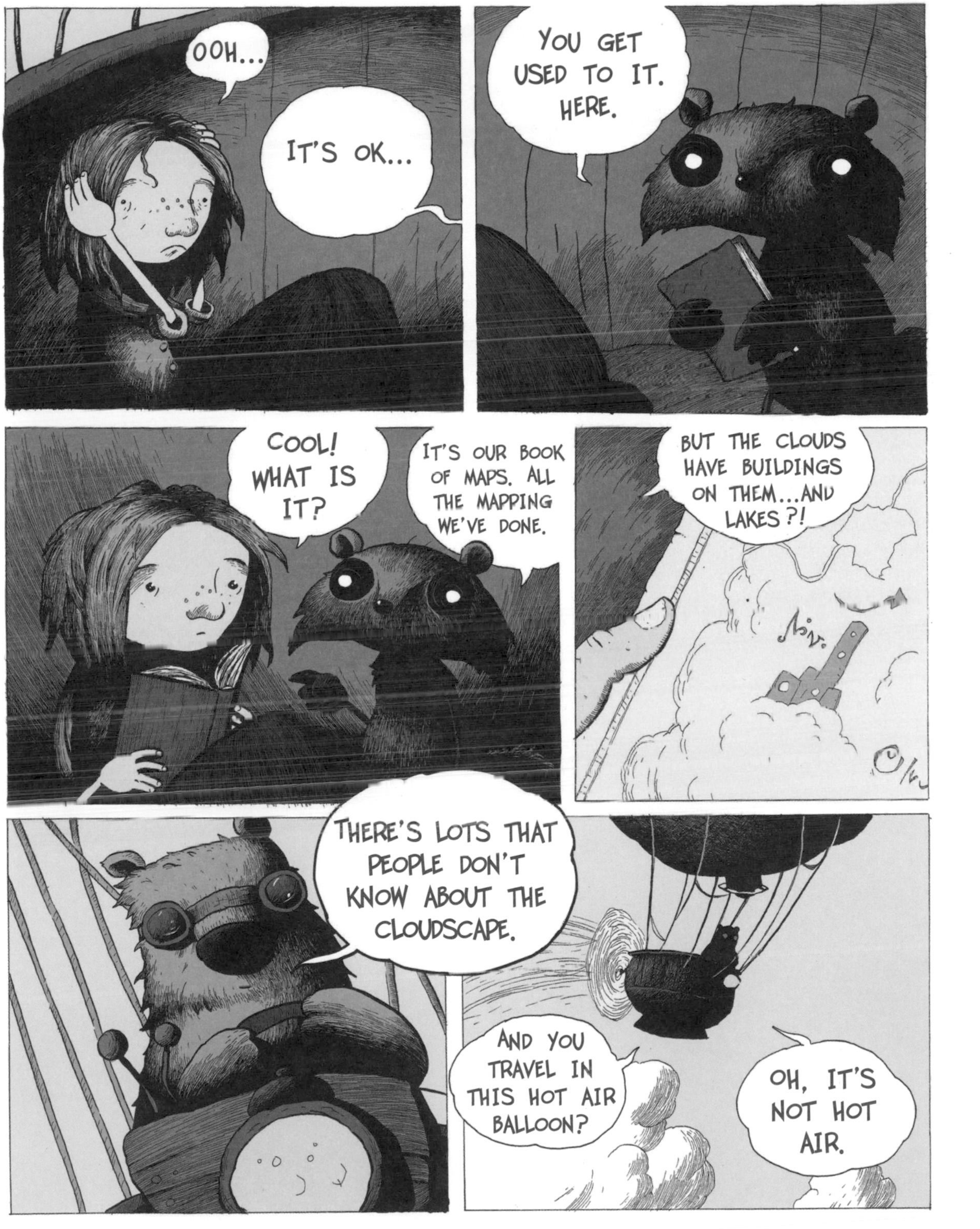
OOH...
IT'S OK...
YOU GET USED TO IT. HERE.
COOL! WHAT IS IT?
IT'S OUR BOOK OF MAPS. ALL THE MAPPING WE'VE DONE.
BUT THE CLOUDS HAVE BUILDINGS ON THEM...AND LAKES?!
THERE'S LOTS THAT PEOPLE DON'T KNOW ABOUT THE CLOUDSCAPE.
AND YOU TRAVEL IN THIS HOT AIR BALLOON?
OH, IT'S NOT HOT AIR.

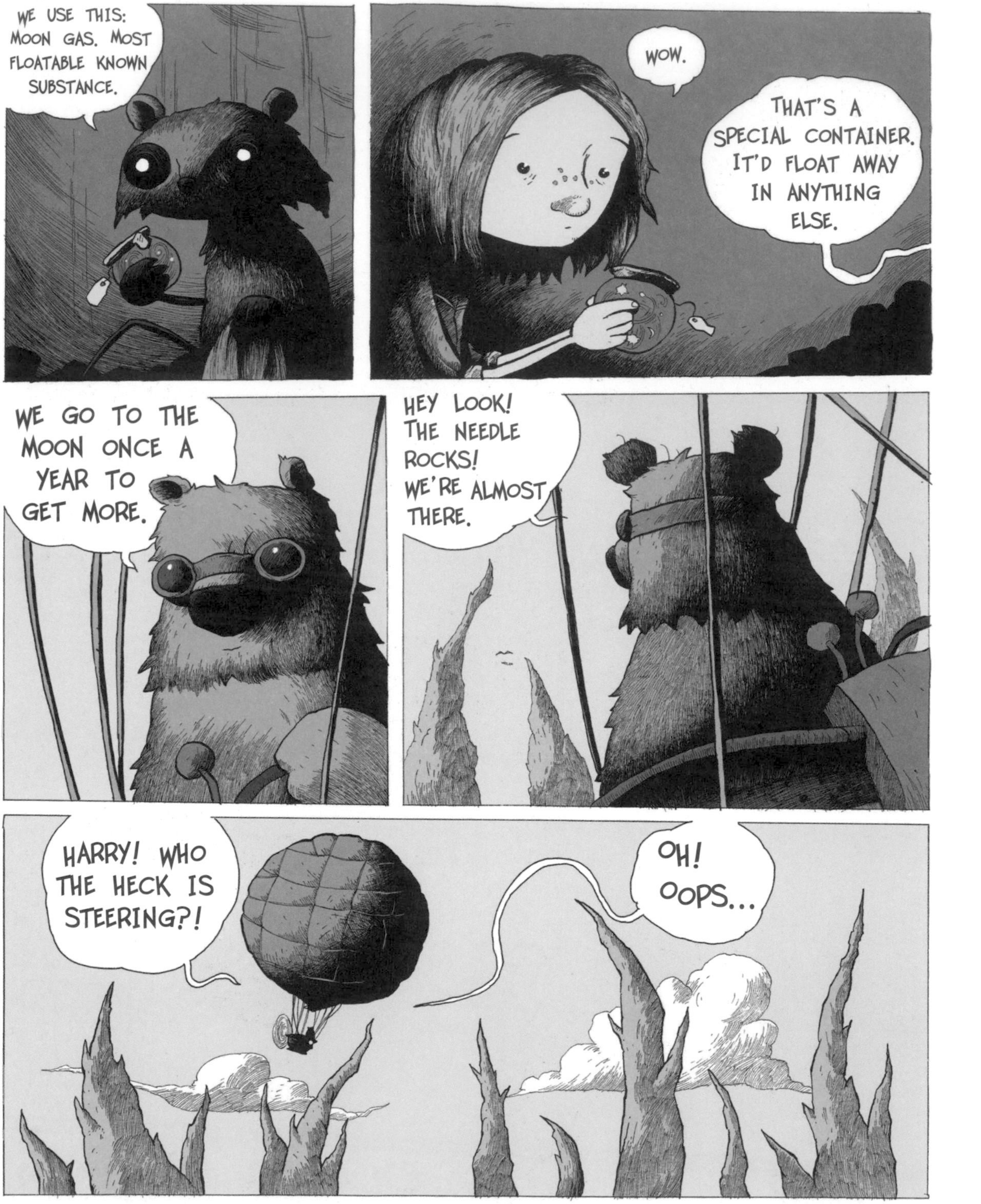
WE USE THIS: MOON GAS. MOST FLOATABLE KNOWN SUBSTANCE.
WOW.
THAT'S A SPECIAL CONTAINER. IT'D FLOAT AWAY IN ANYTHING ELSE.
WE GO TO THE MOON ONCE A YEAR TO GET MORE.
HEY LOOK! THE NEEDLE ROCKS! WE'RE ALMOST THERE.
HARRY! WHO THE HECK IS STEERING?!
OH! OOPS...

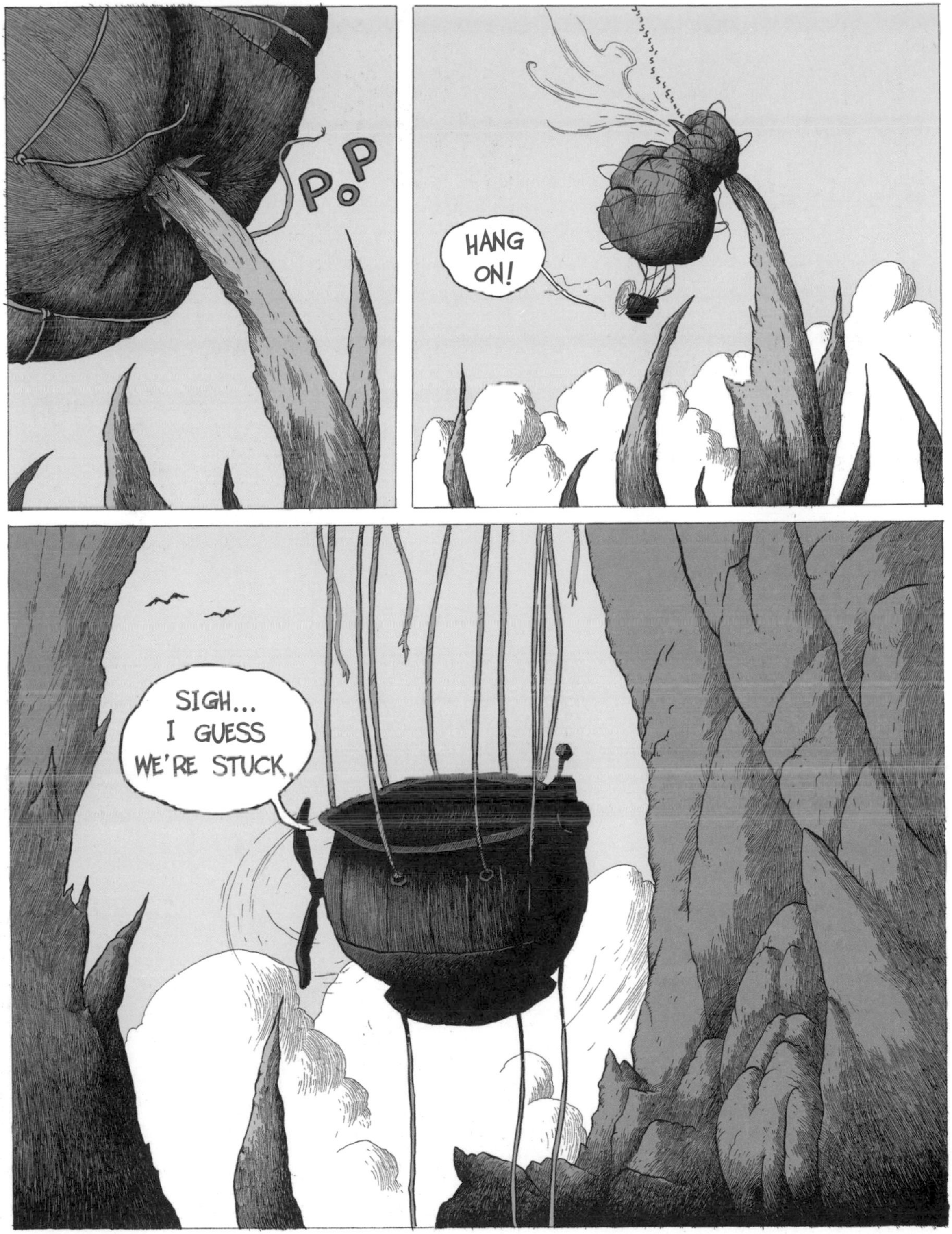
POP
HANG ON!
SIGH... I GUESS WE'RE STUCK.

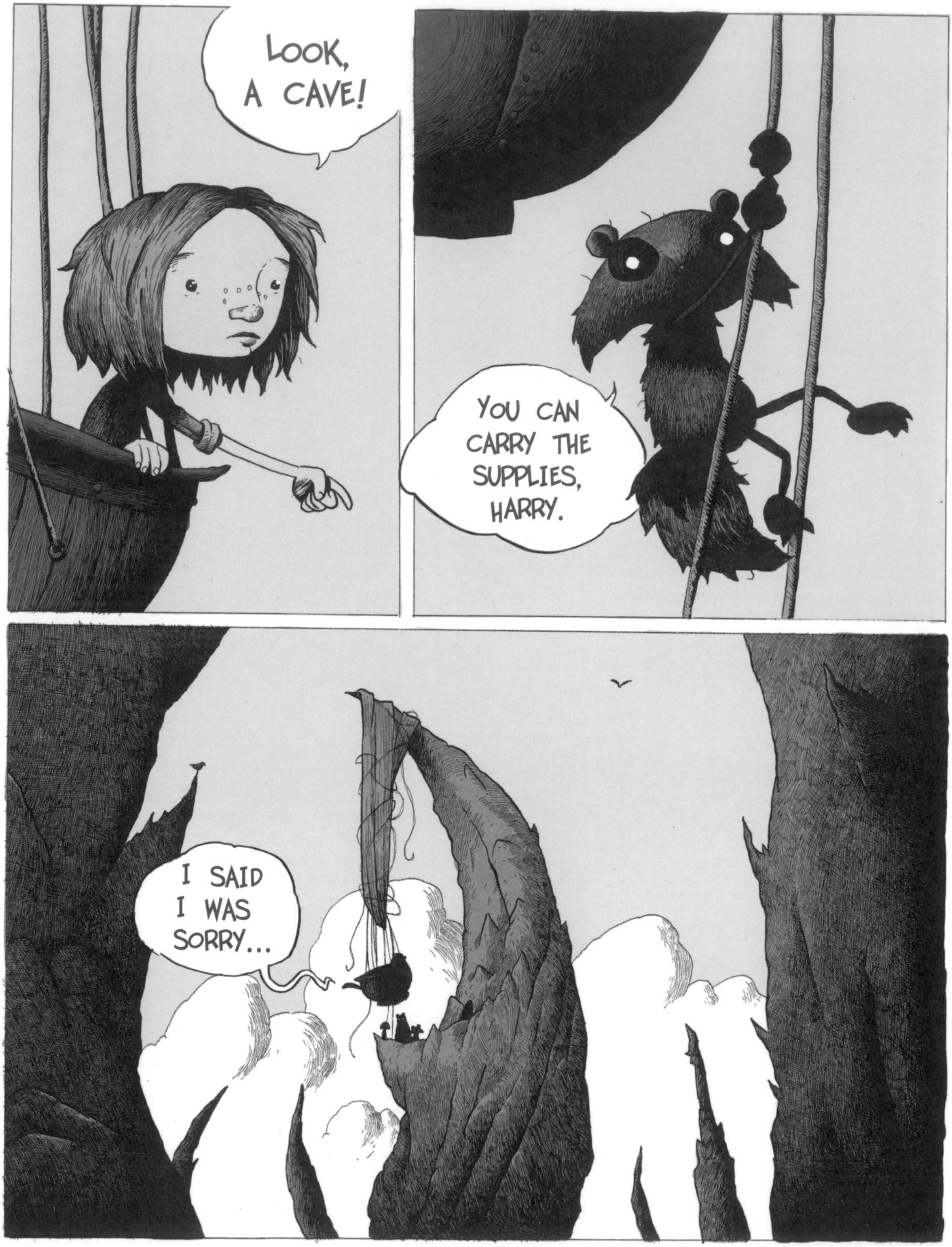
LOOK, A CAVE!
YOU CAN CARRY THE SUPPLIES, HARRY.
I SAID I WAS SORRY...

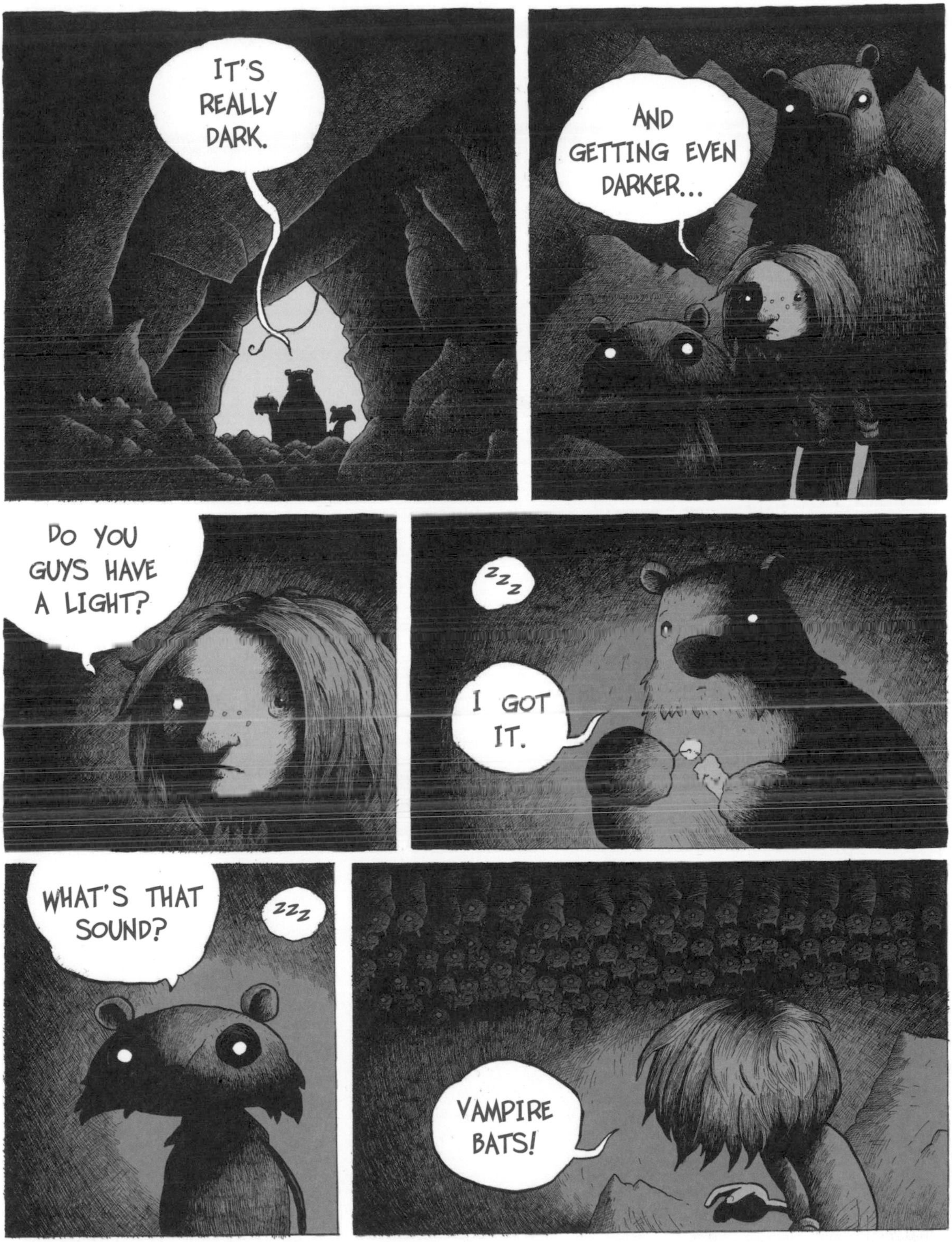
IT'S REALLY DARK.
AND GETTING EVEN DARKER...
DO YOU GUYS HAVE A LIGHT?
ZZZ
I GOT IT.
WHAT'S THAT SOUND?
ZZZ
VAMPIRE BATS!

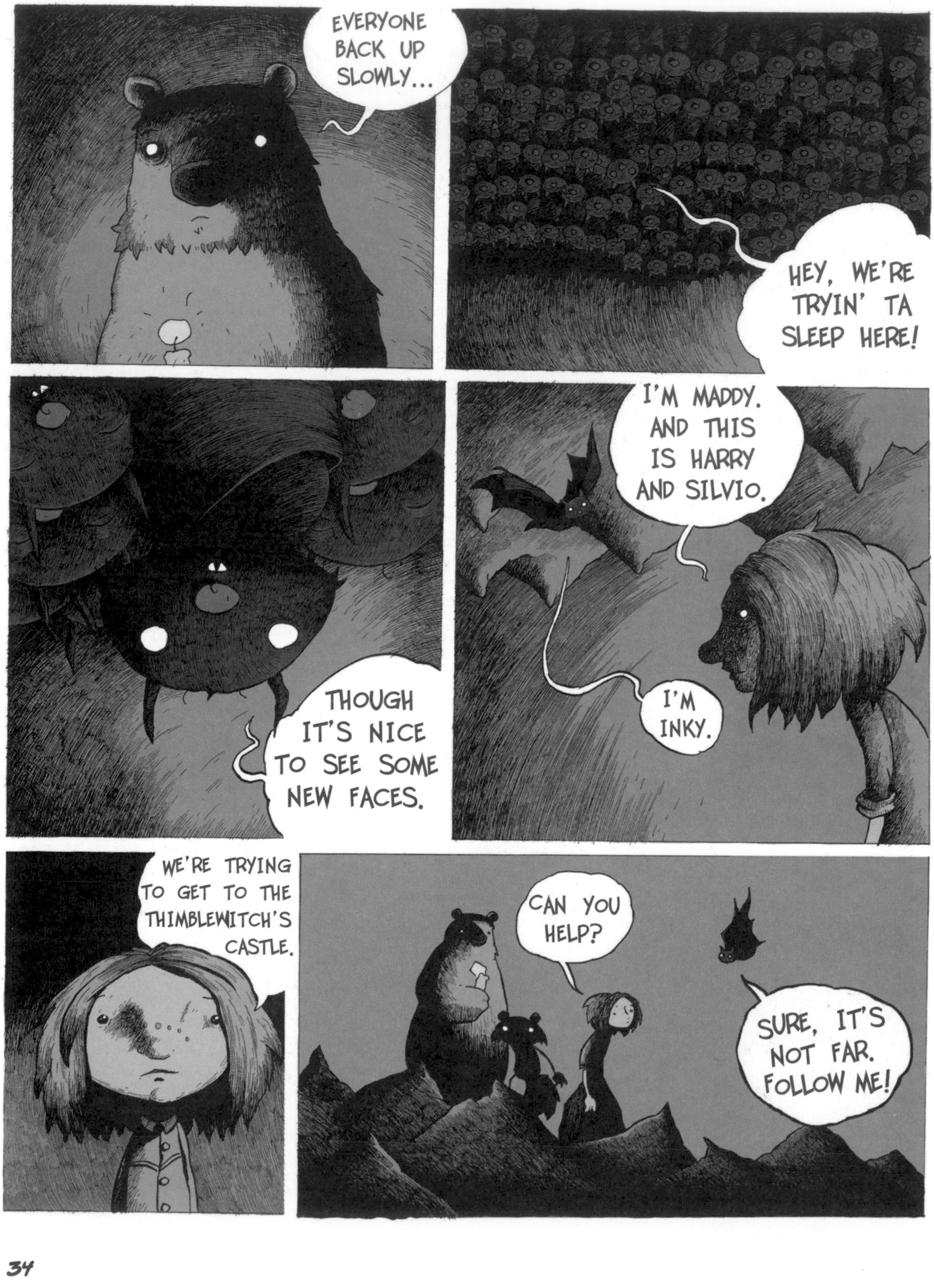

EVERYONE BACK UP SLOWLY...
HEY, WE'RE TRYIN' TA SLEEP HERE!
THOUGH IT'S NICE TO SEE SOME NEW FACES.
I'M MADDY. AND THIS IS HARRY AND SILVIO.
I'M INKY.
WE'RE TRYING TO GET TO THE THIMBLEWITCH'S CASTLE.
CAN YOU HELP?
SURE, IT'S NOT FAR. FOLLOW ME!

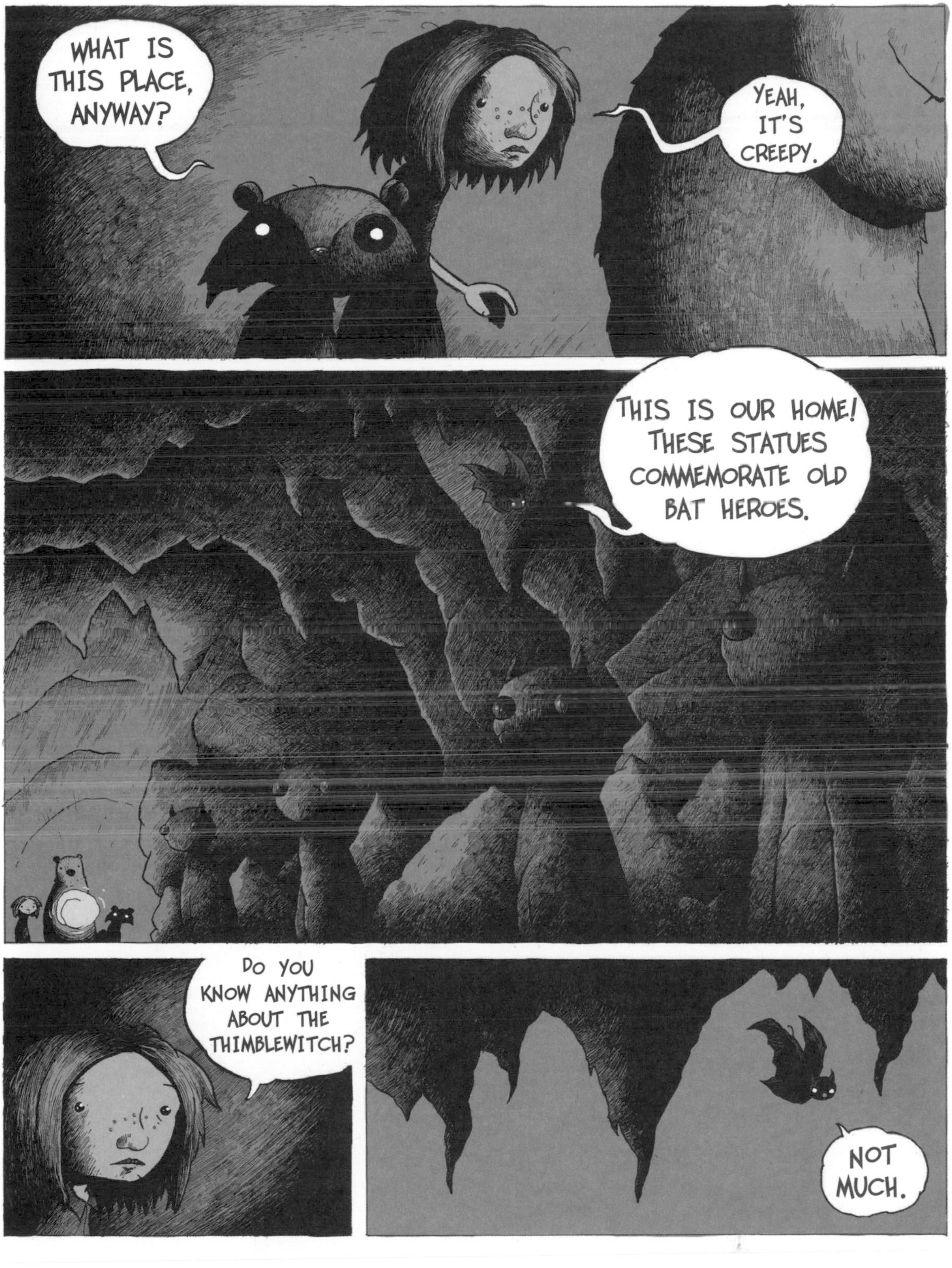
WHAT IS THIS PLACE, ANYWAY?
YEAH, IT'S CREEPY.
THIS IS OUR HOME! THESE STATUES COMMEMORATE OLD BAT HEROES.
DO YOU KNOW ANYTHING ABOUT THE THIMBLEWITCH?
NOT MUCH.

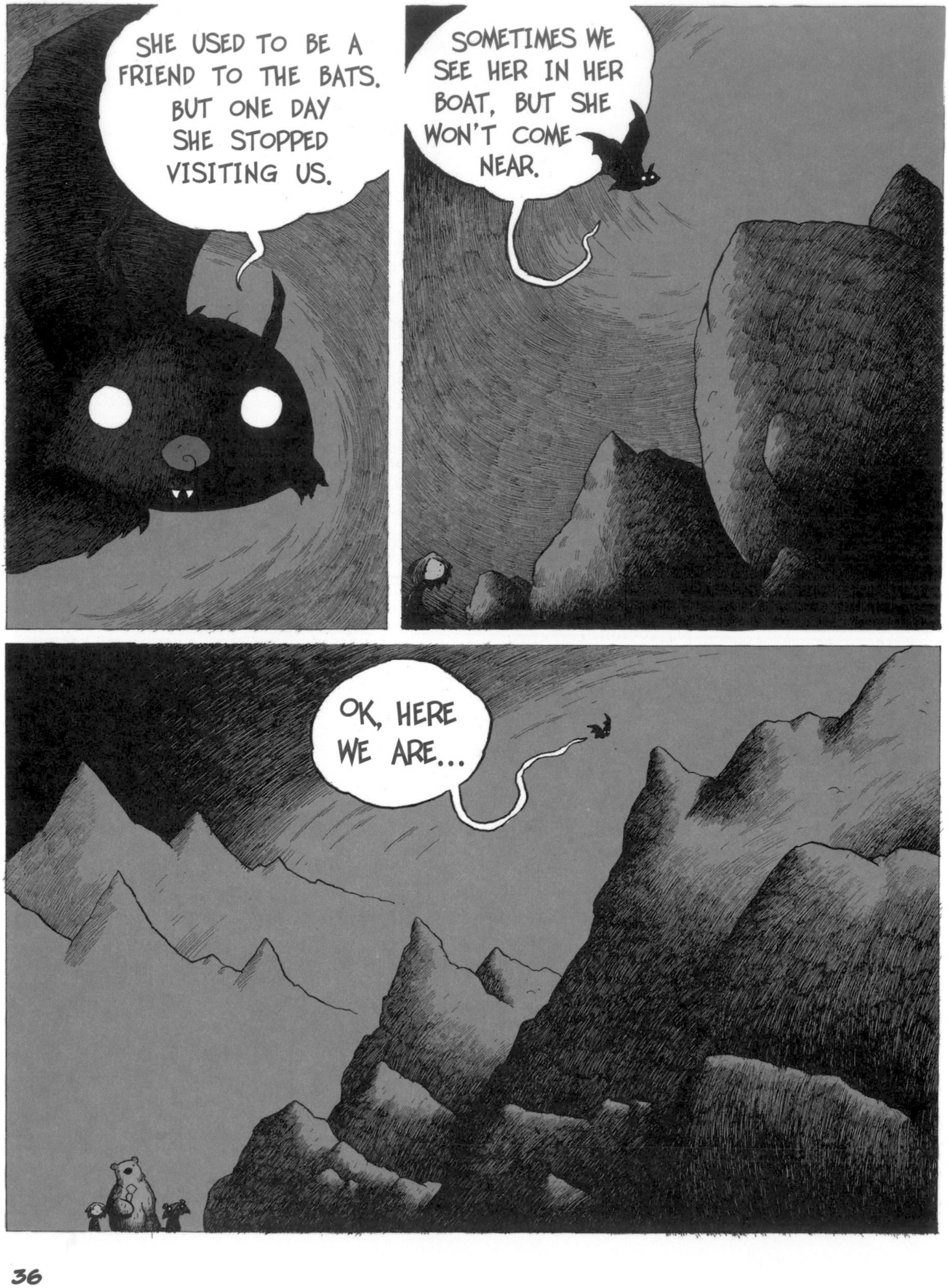
SHE USED TO BE A FRIEND TO THE BATS. BUT ONE DAY SHE STOPPED VISITING US.
SOMETIMES WE SEE HER IN HER BOAT, BUT SHE WON'T COME NEAR.
OK, HERE WE ARE...

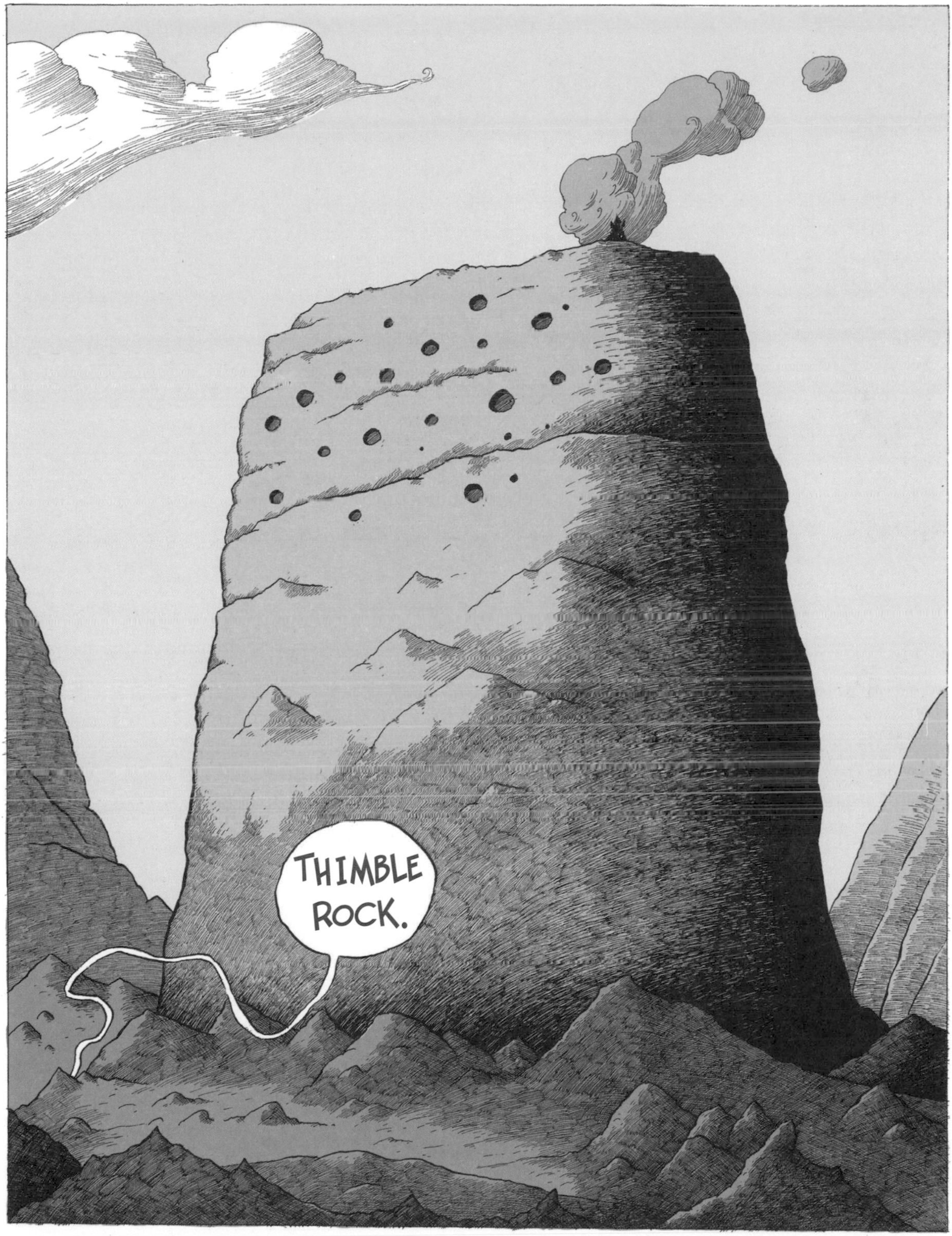
THIMBLE ROCK.

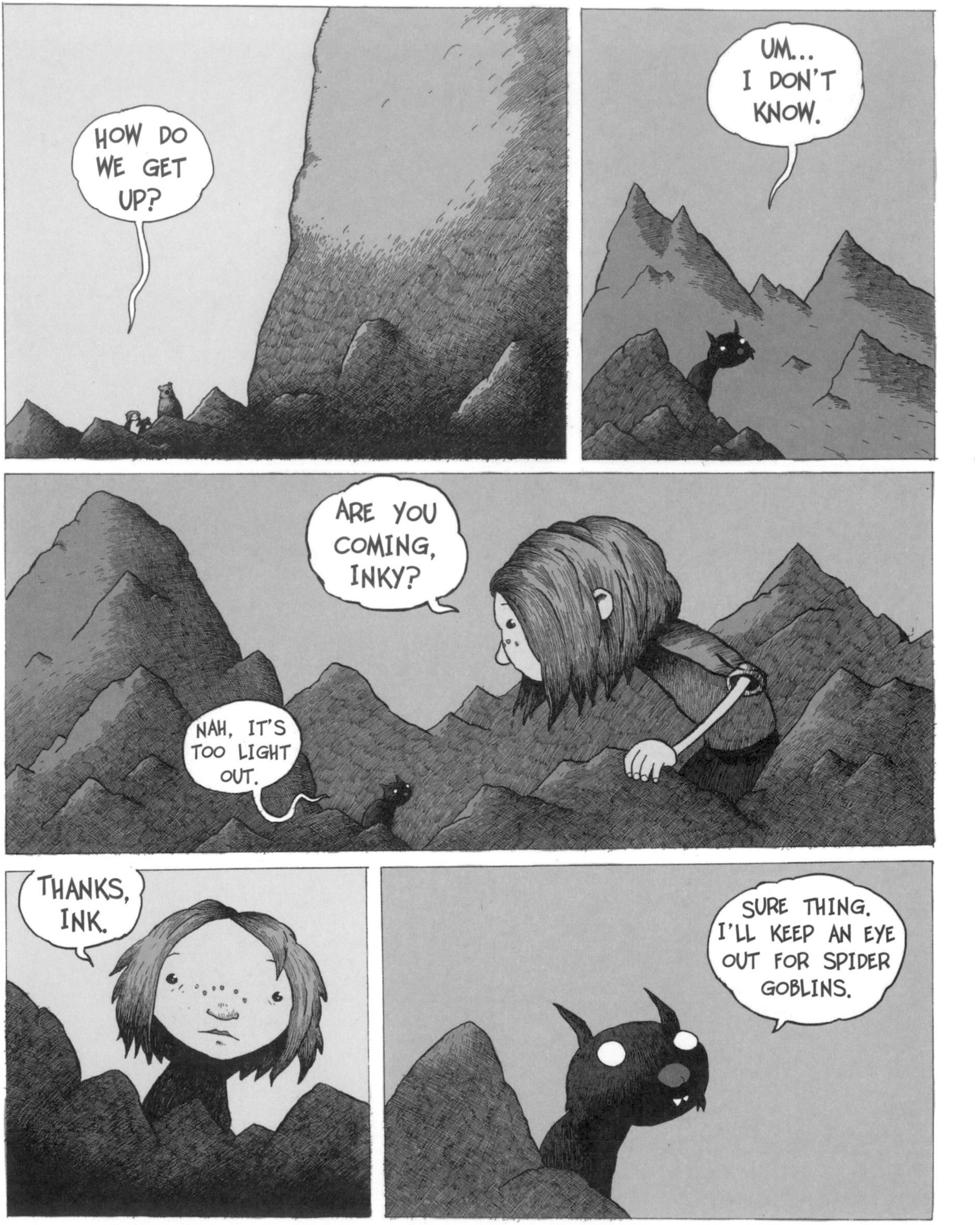
HOW DO WE GET UP?
UM... I DON'T KNOW.
ARE YOU COMING, INKY?
NAH, IT'S TOO LIGHT OUT.
THANKS, INK.
SURE THING. I'LL KEEP AN EYE OUT FOR SPIDER GOBLINS.

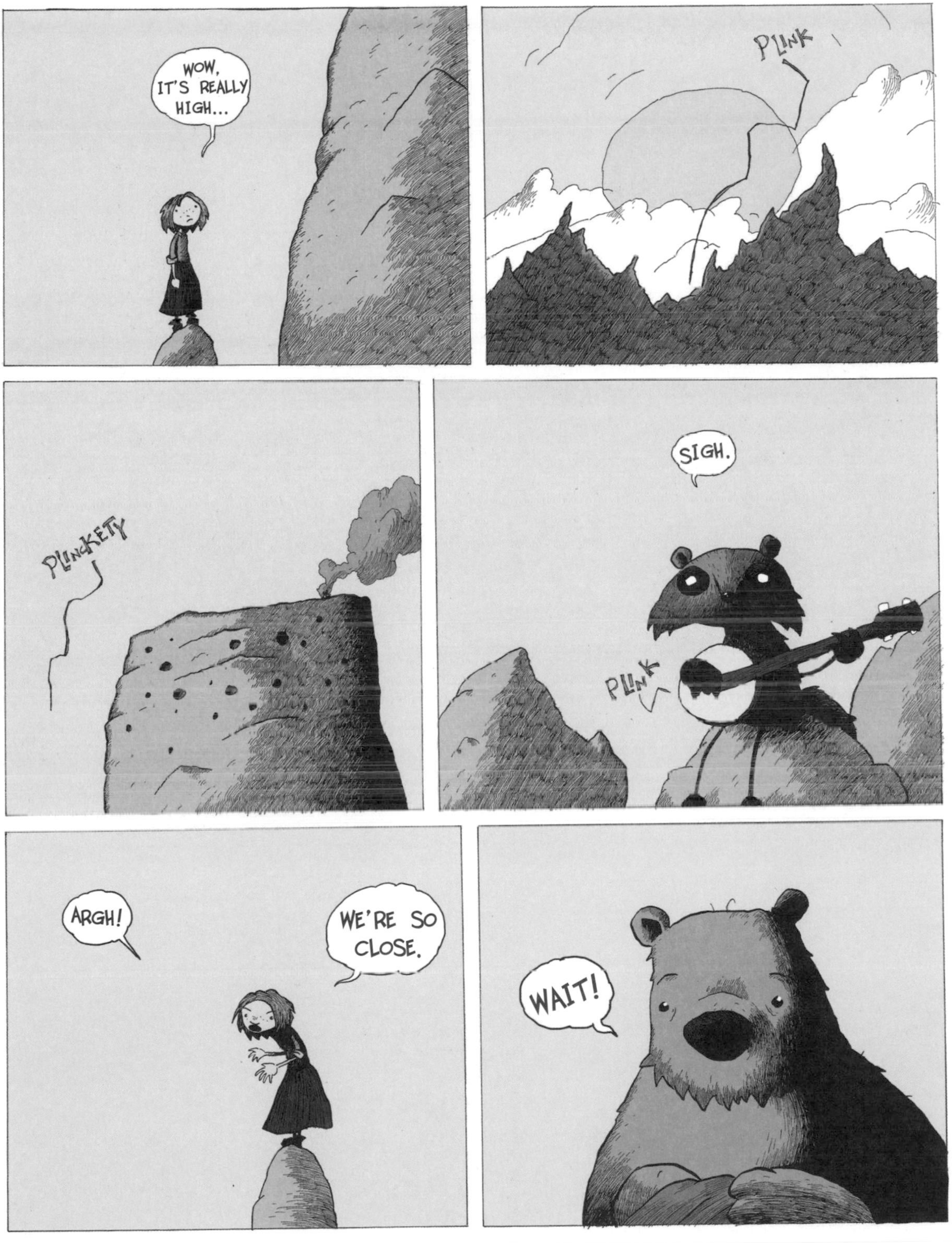
WOW, IT'S REALLY HIGH...
PLINK
PLINCKETY
SIGH.
PLINK
ARGH!
WE'RE SO CLOSE.
WAIT!

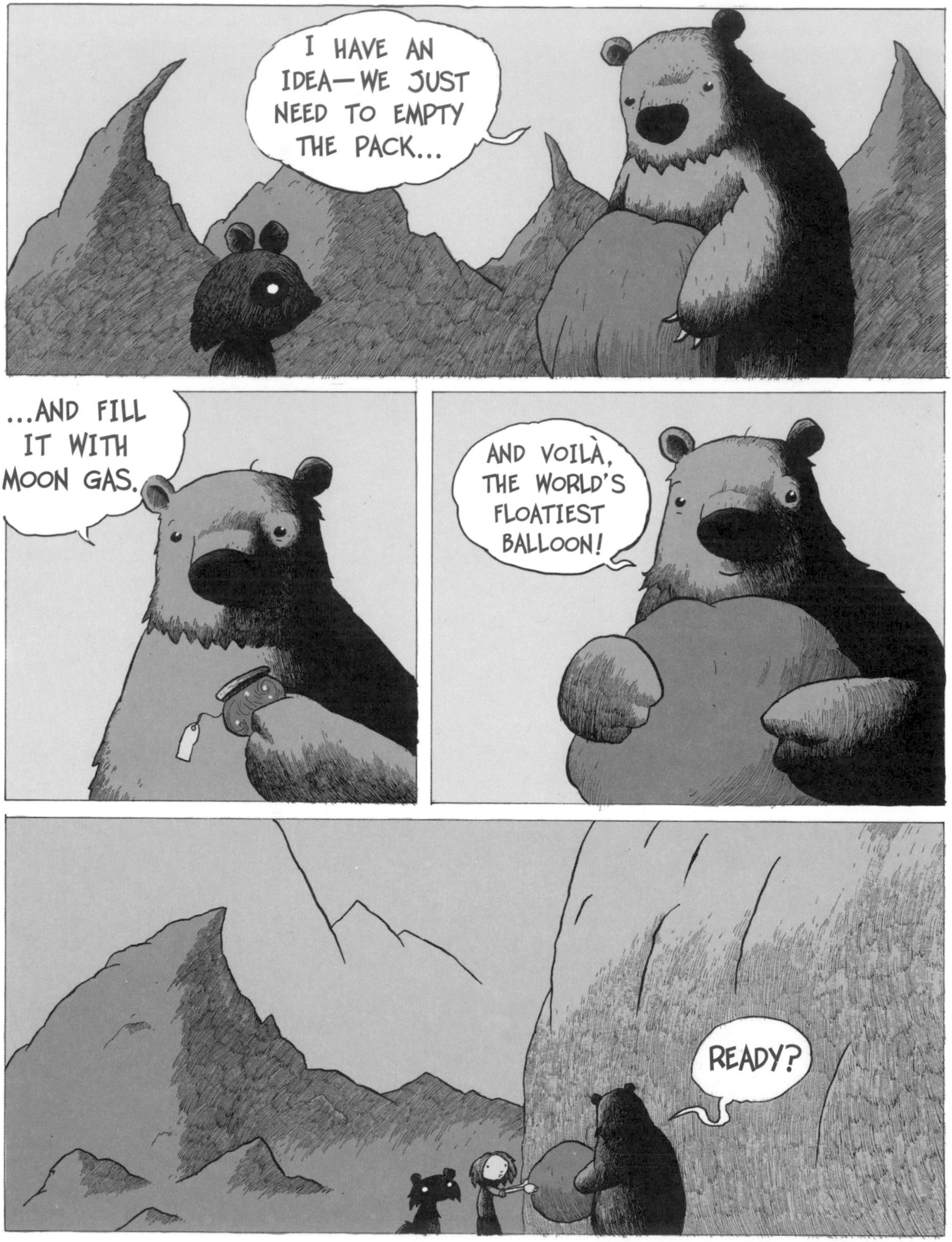
I HAVE AN IDEA—WE JUST NEED TO EMPTY THE PACK...
...AND FILL IT WITH MOON GAS.
AND VOILÀ, THE WORLD'S FLOATIEST BALLOON!
READY?

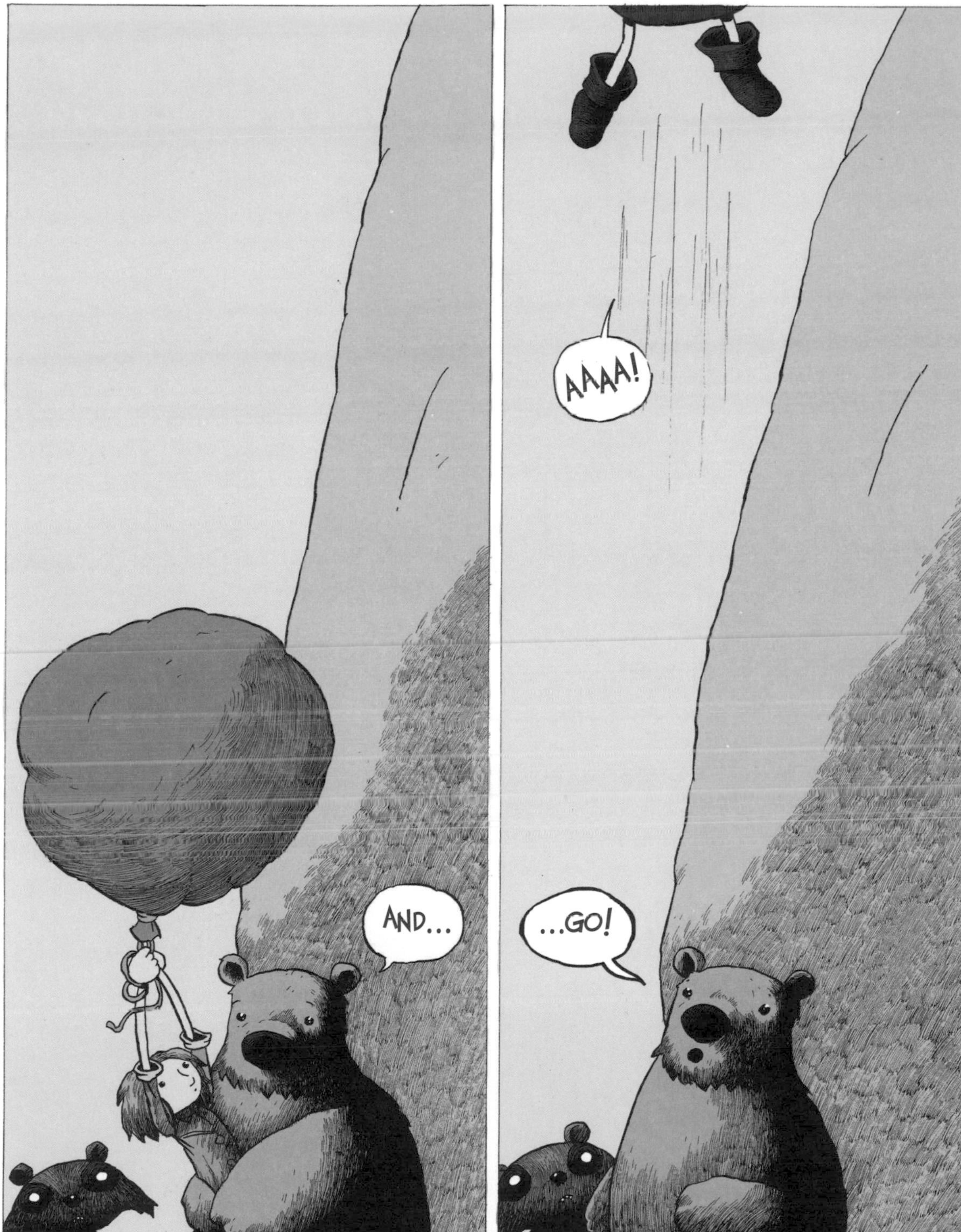
AND...
...GO!
AAAA!

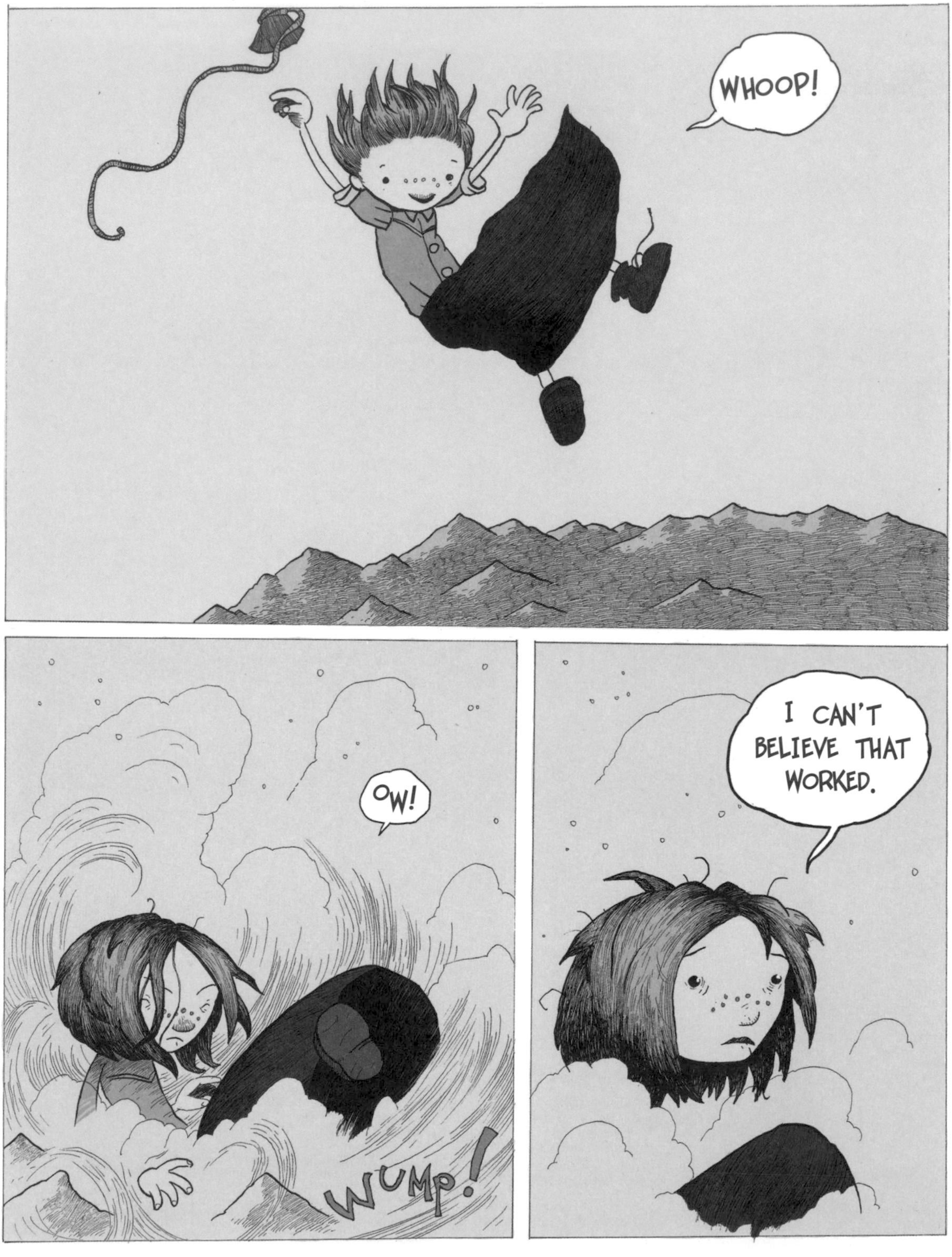
WHOOP!
OW!
WUMP!
I CAN'T BELIEVE THAT WORKED.

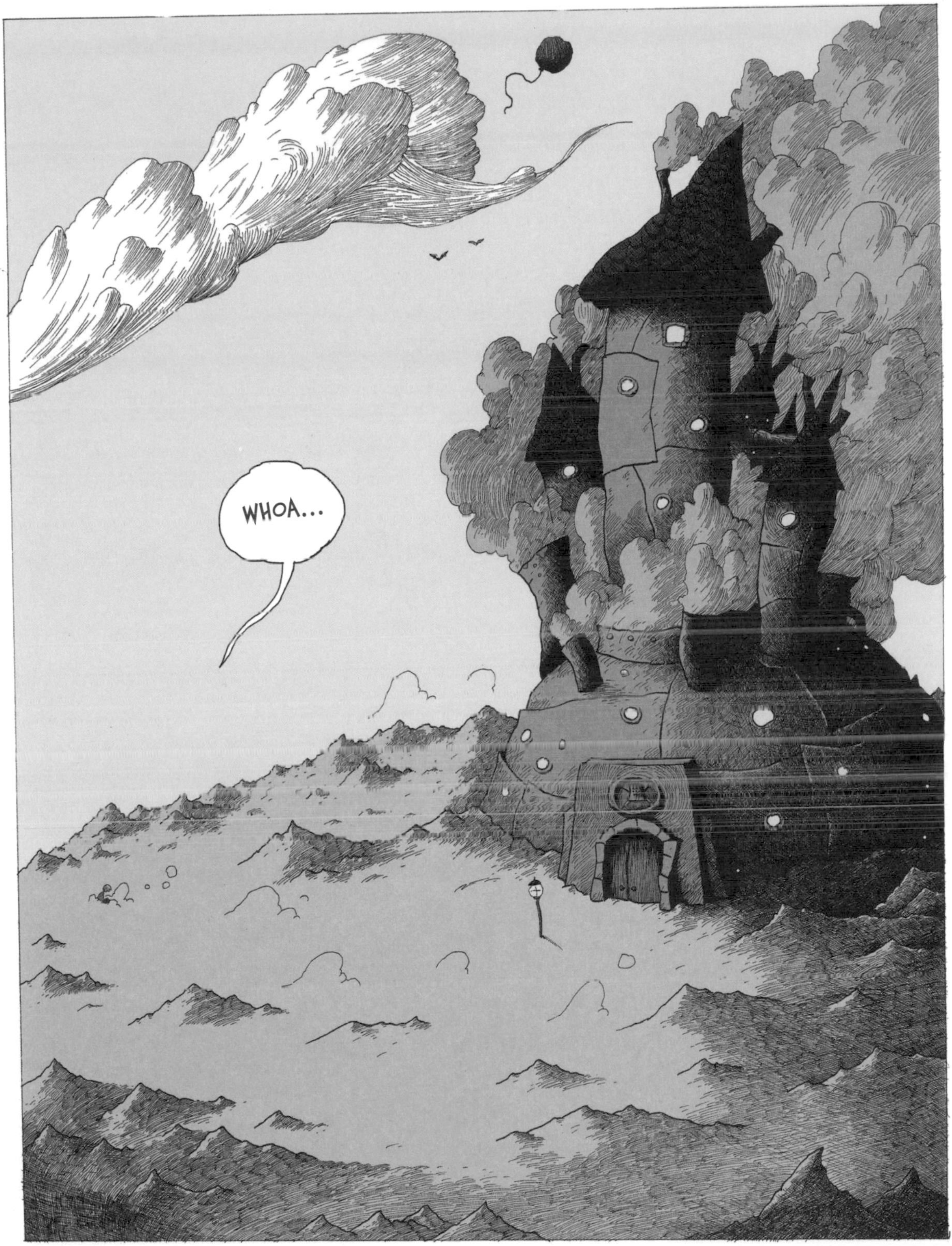
WHOA...

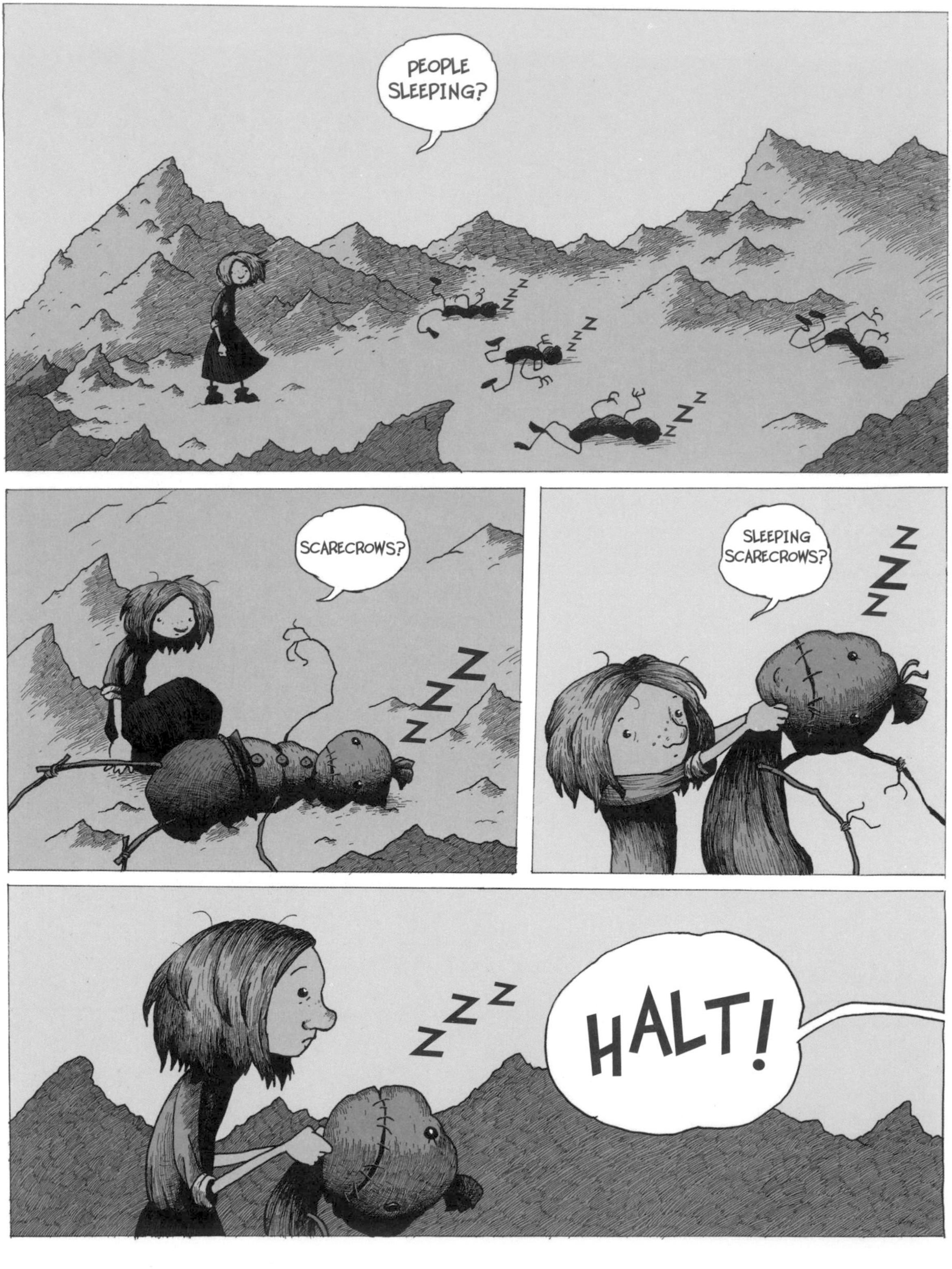
PEOPLE SLEEPING?
Z Z Z
Z Z Z
Z Z Z
Z Z Z
SCARECROWS?
Z Z Z
SLEEPING SCARECROWS?
Z Z Z
Z Z Z
HALT!

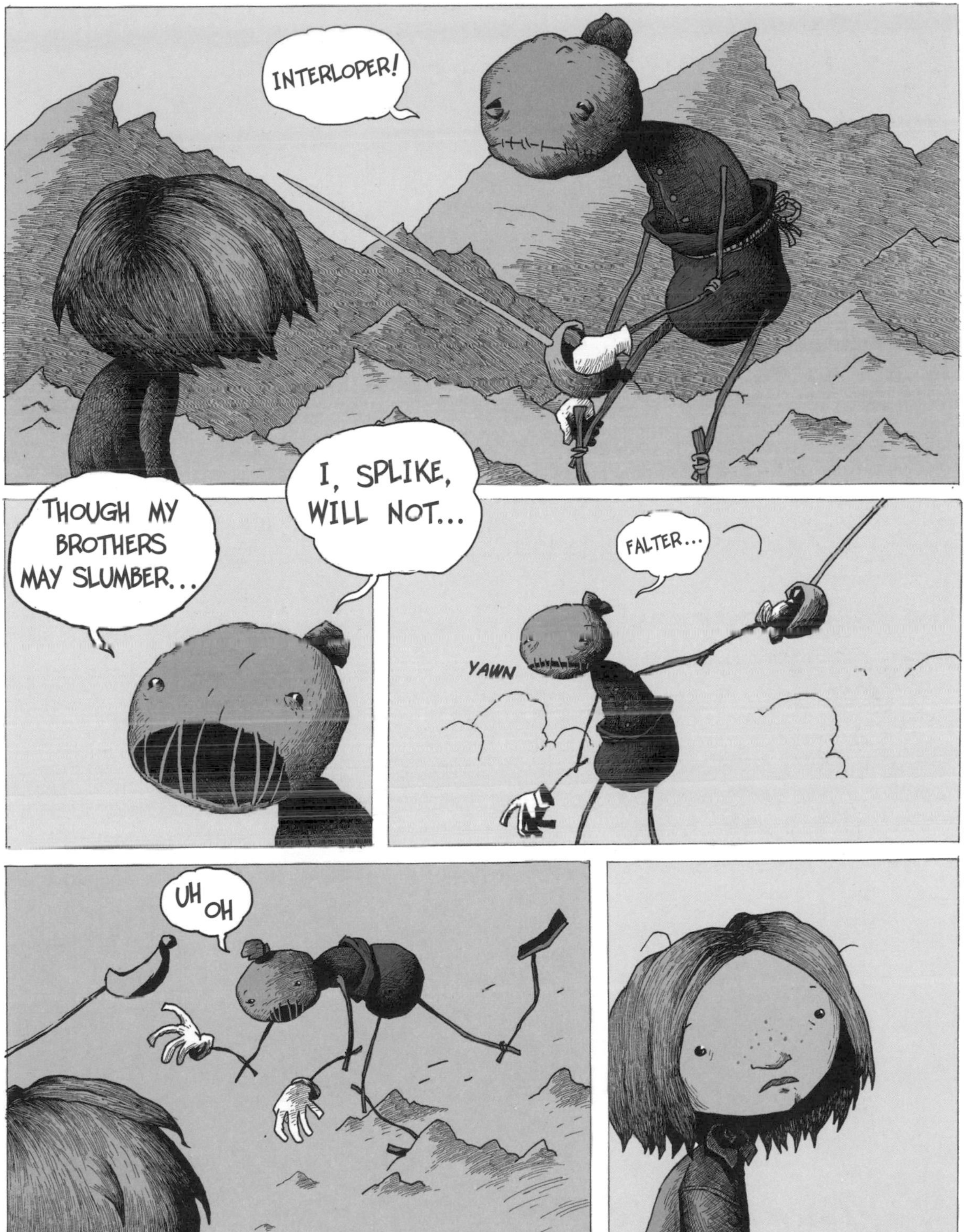
INTERLOPER!
THOUGH MY BROTHERS MAY SLUMBER...
I, SPLIKE, WILL NOT...
FALTER...
YAWN
UH OH

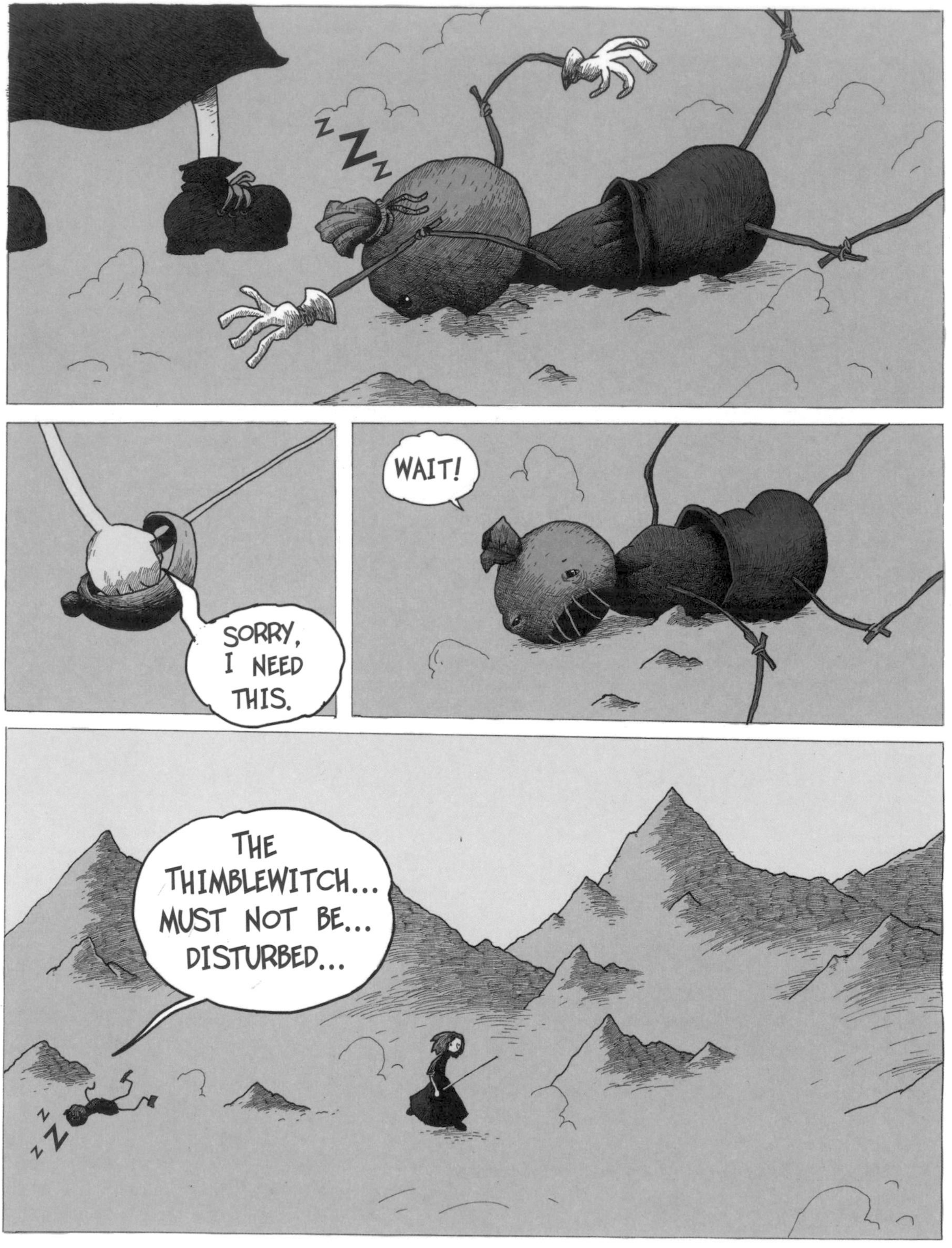
ZZZ
SORRY, I NEED THIS.
WAIT!
THE THIMBLEWITCH... MUST NOT BE... DISTURBED...
ZZZ

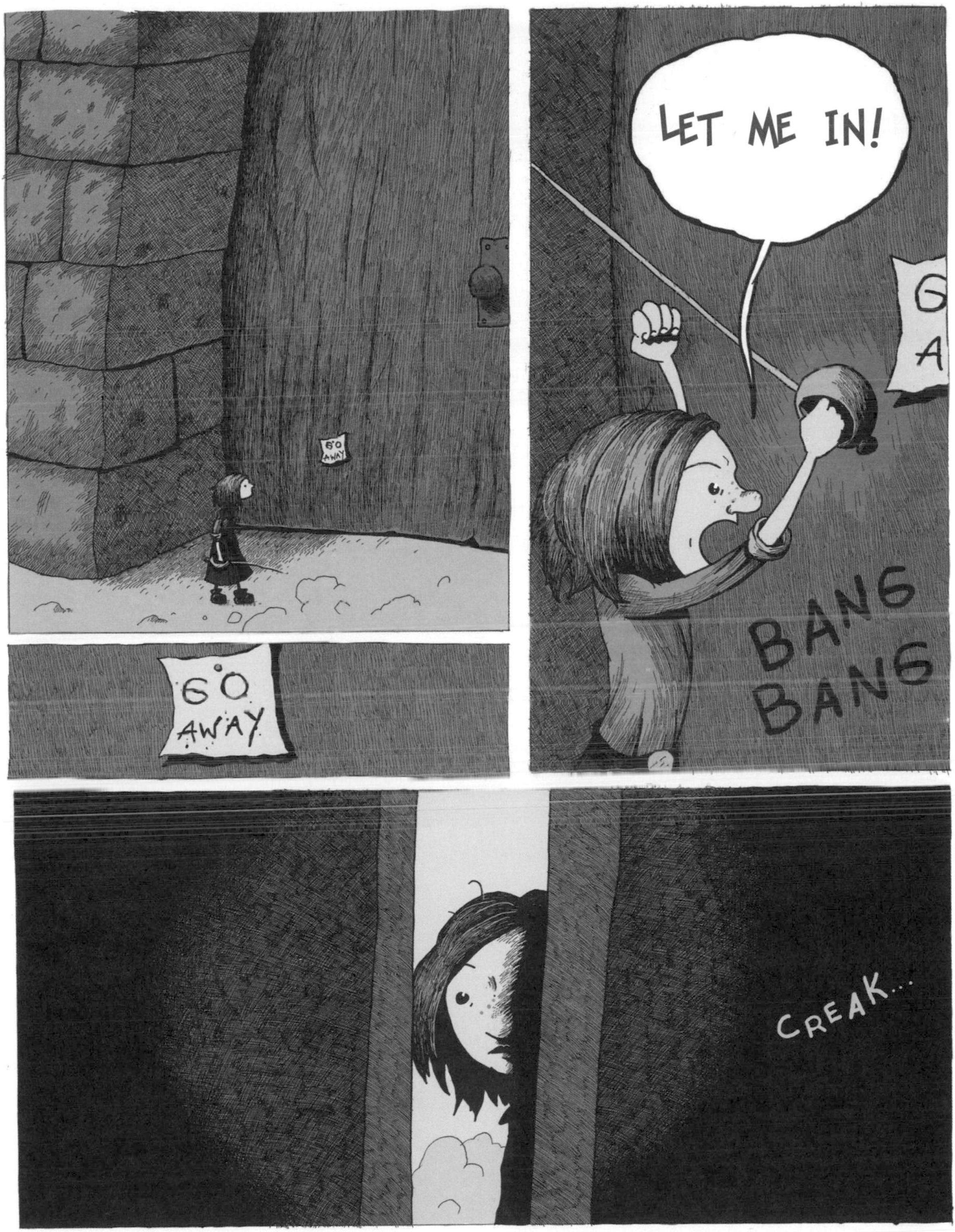
GO AWAY
GO AWAY
LET ME IN!
BANG BANG
CREAK...

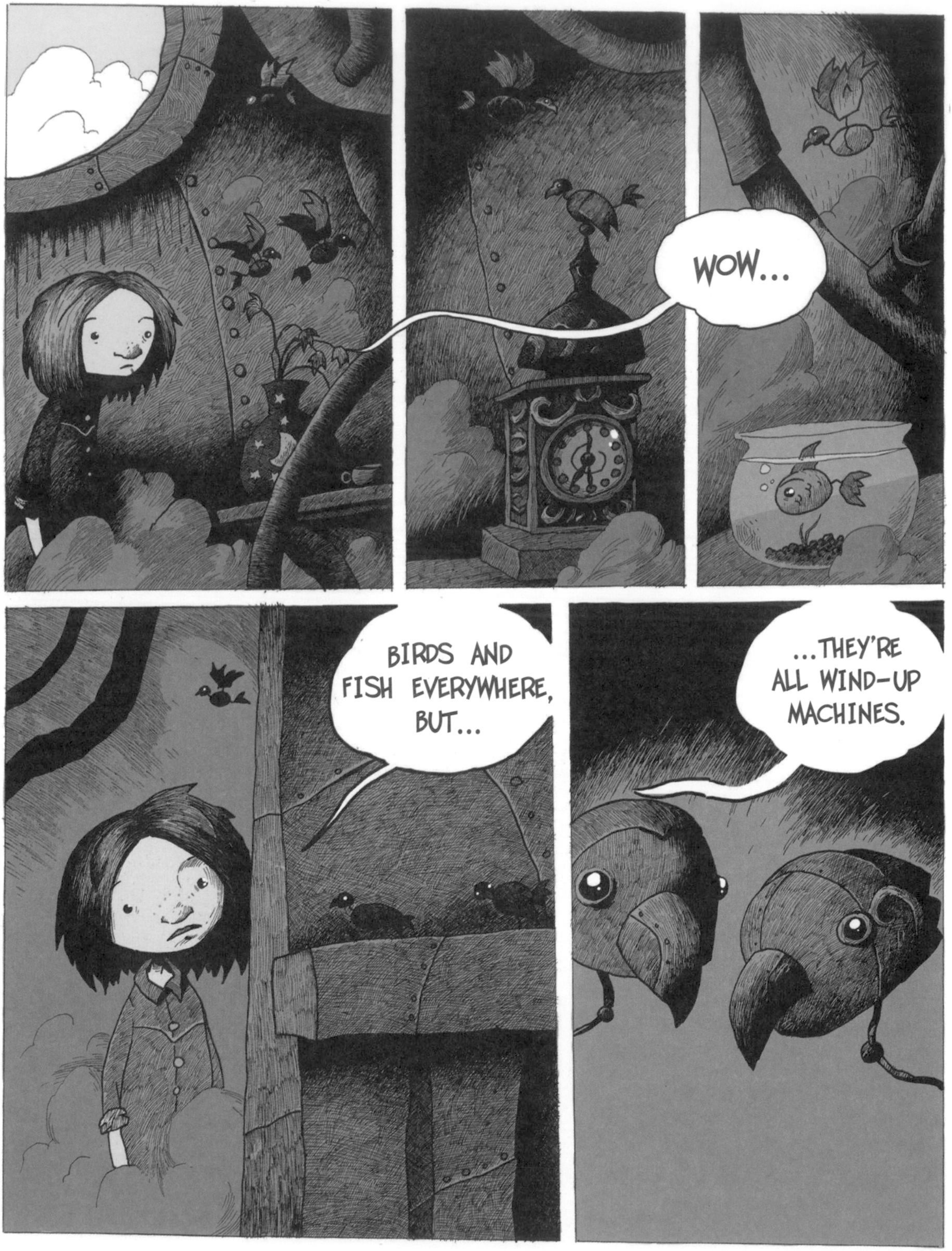
WOW...
BIRDS AND FISH EVERYWHERE, BUT...
...THEY'RE ALL WIND-UP MACHINES.

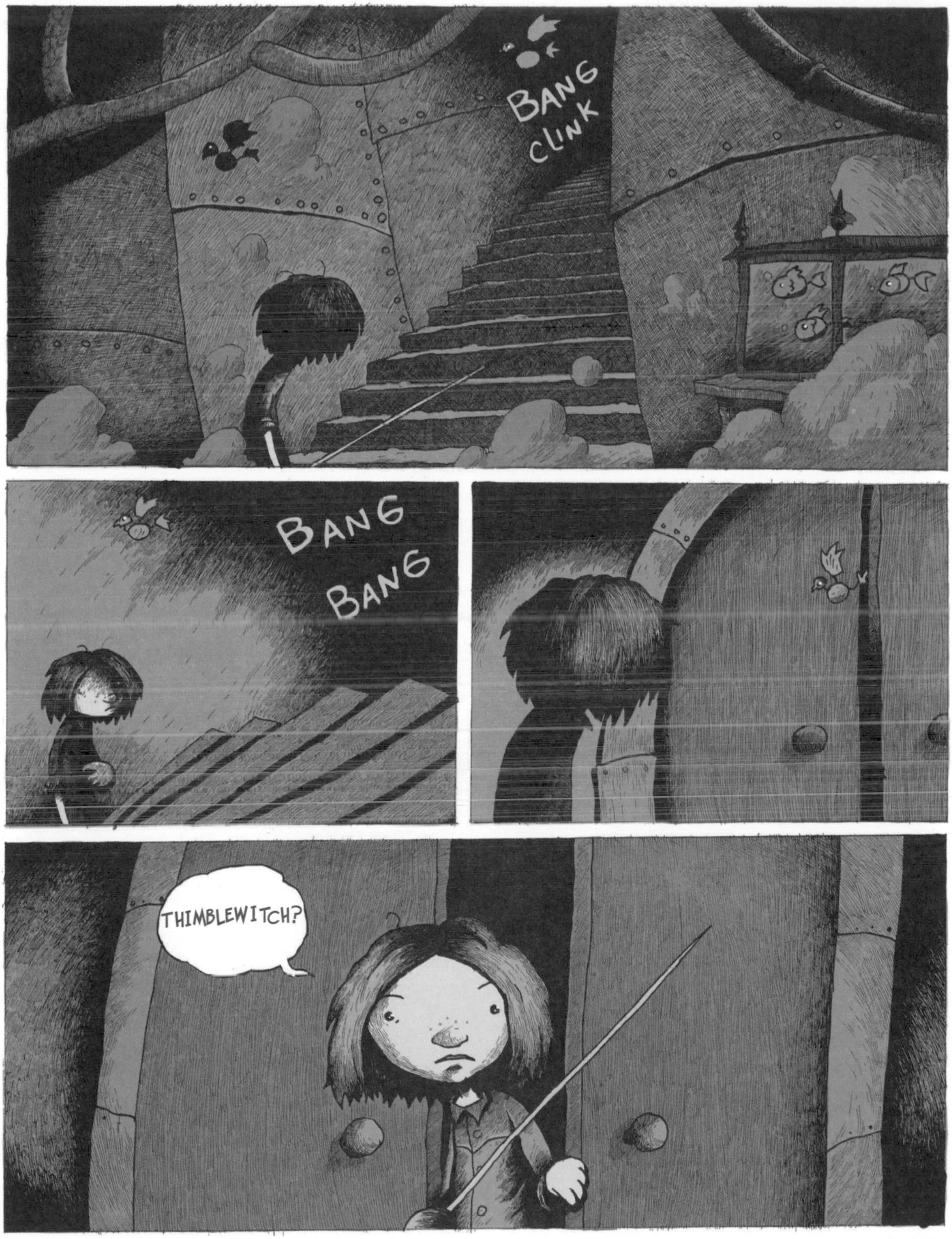
BANG
CLINK
BANG
BANG
THIMBLEWITCH?

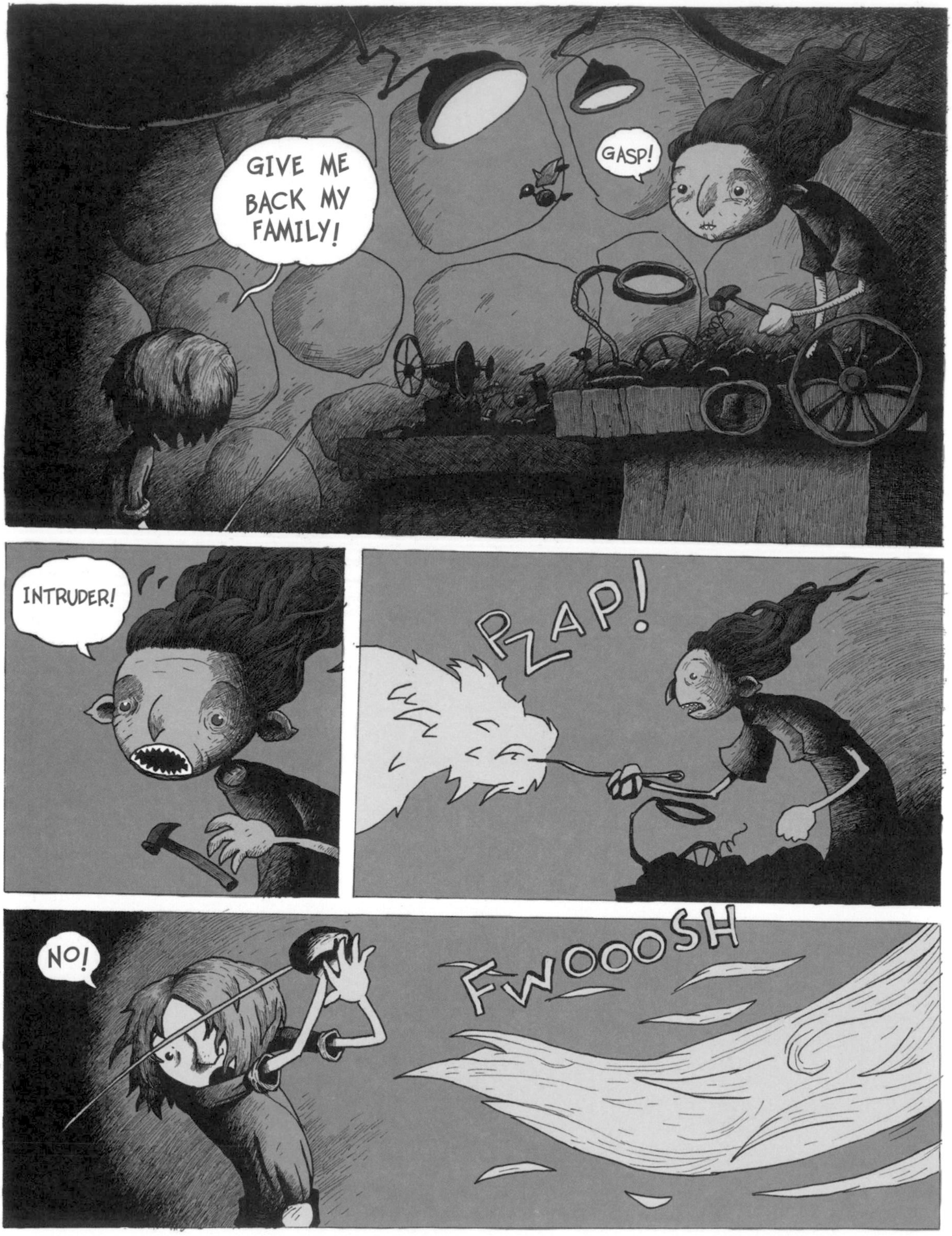
GIVE ME BACK MY FAMILY!
GASP!
INTRUDER!
PZAP!
NO!
FWOOOOSH

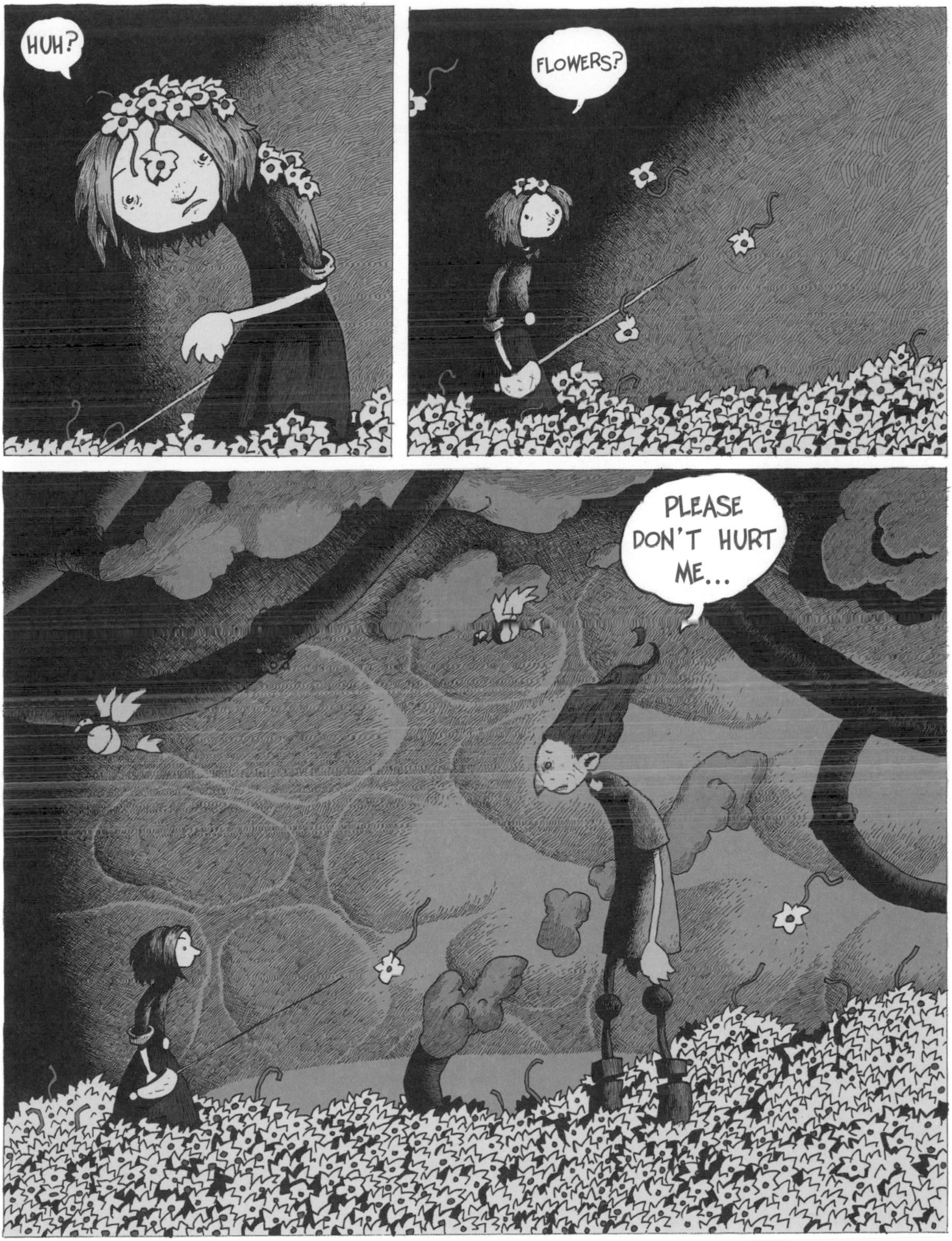
HUH?
FLOWERS?
PLEASE DON'T HURT ME...

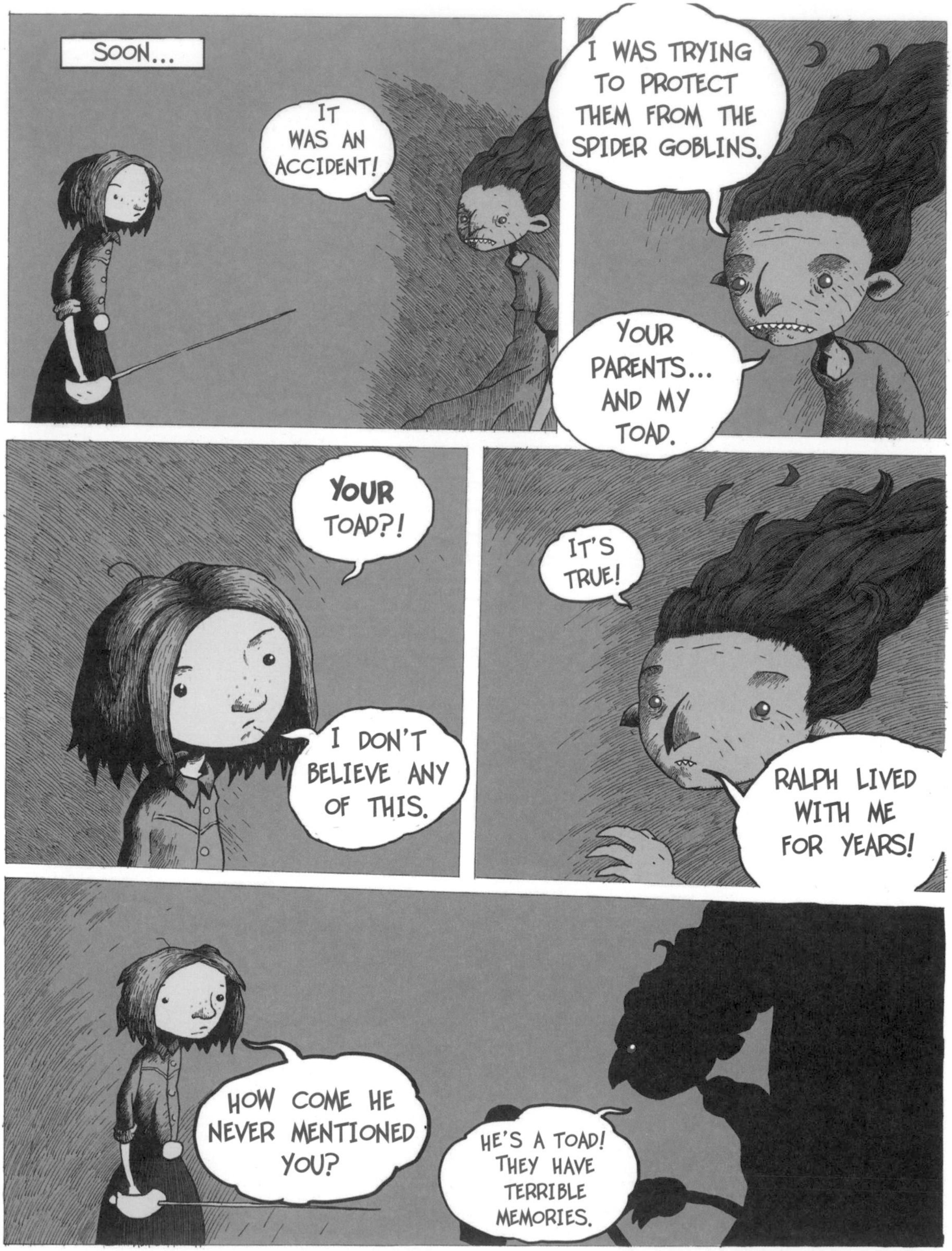
SOON...
IT WAS AN ACCIDENT!
I WAS TRYING TO PROTECT THEM FROM THE SPIDER GOBLINS.
YOUR PARENTS... AND MY TOAD.
YOUR TOAD?!
I DON'T BELIEVE ANY OF THIS.
IT'S TRUE!
RALPH LIVED WITH ME FOR YEARS!
HOW COME HE NEVER MENTIONED YOU?
HE'S A TOAD! THEY HAVE TERRIBLE MEMORIES.

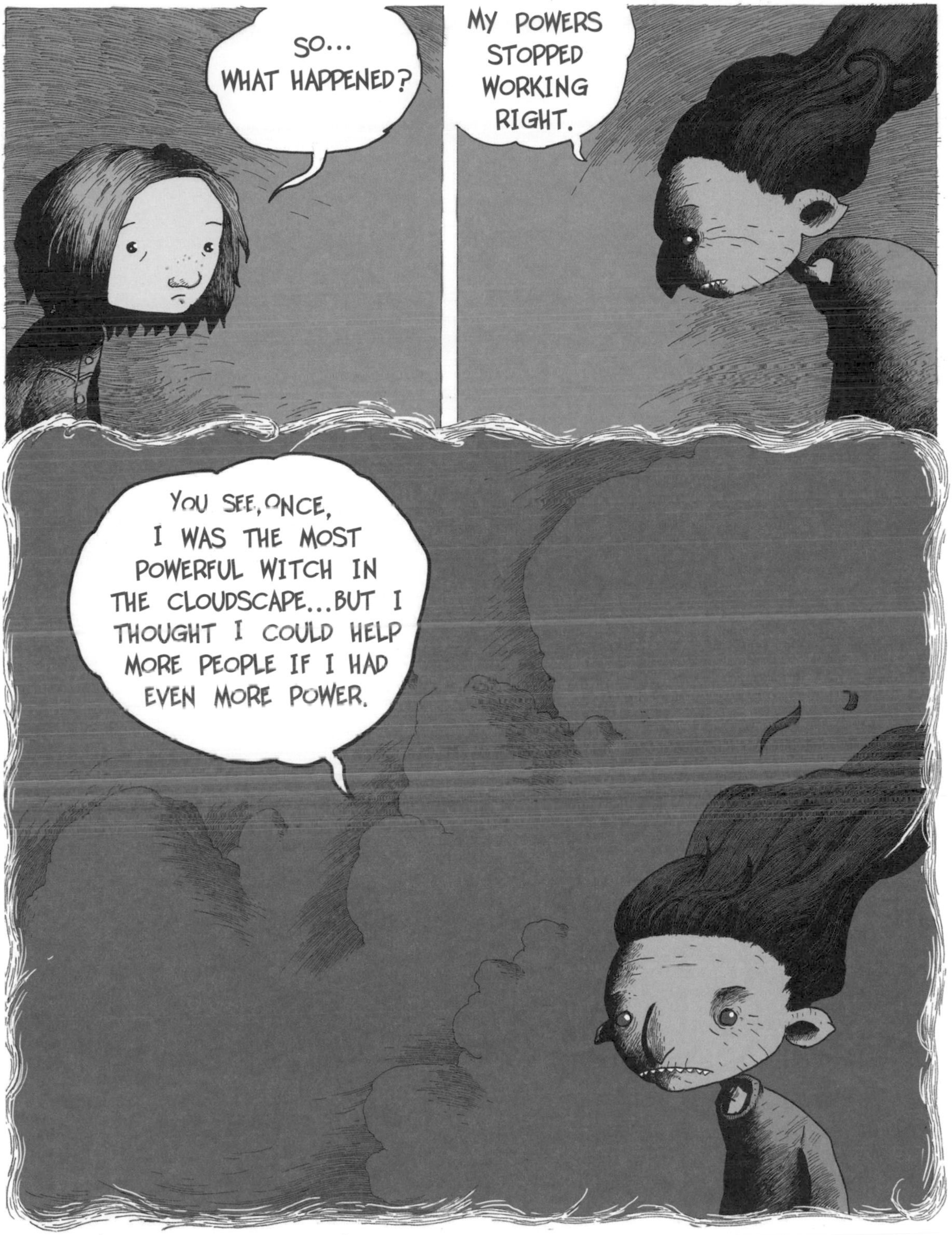
SO... WHAT HAPPENED?
MY POWERS STOPPED WORKING RIGHT.
YOU SEE, ONCE, I WAS THE MOST POWERFUL WITCH IN THE CLOUDSCAPE...BUT I THOUGHT I COULD HELP MORE PEOPLE IF I HAD EVEN MORE POWER.

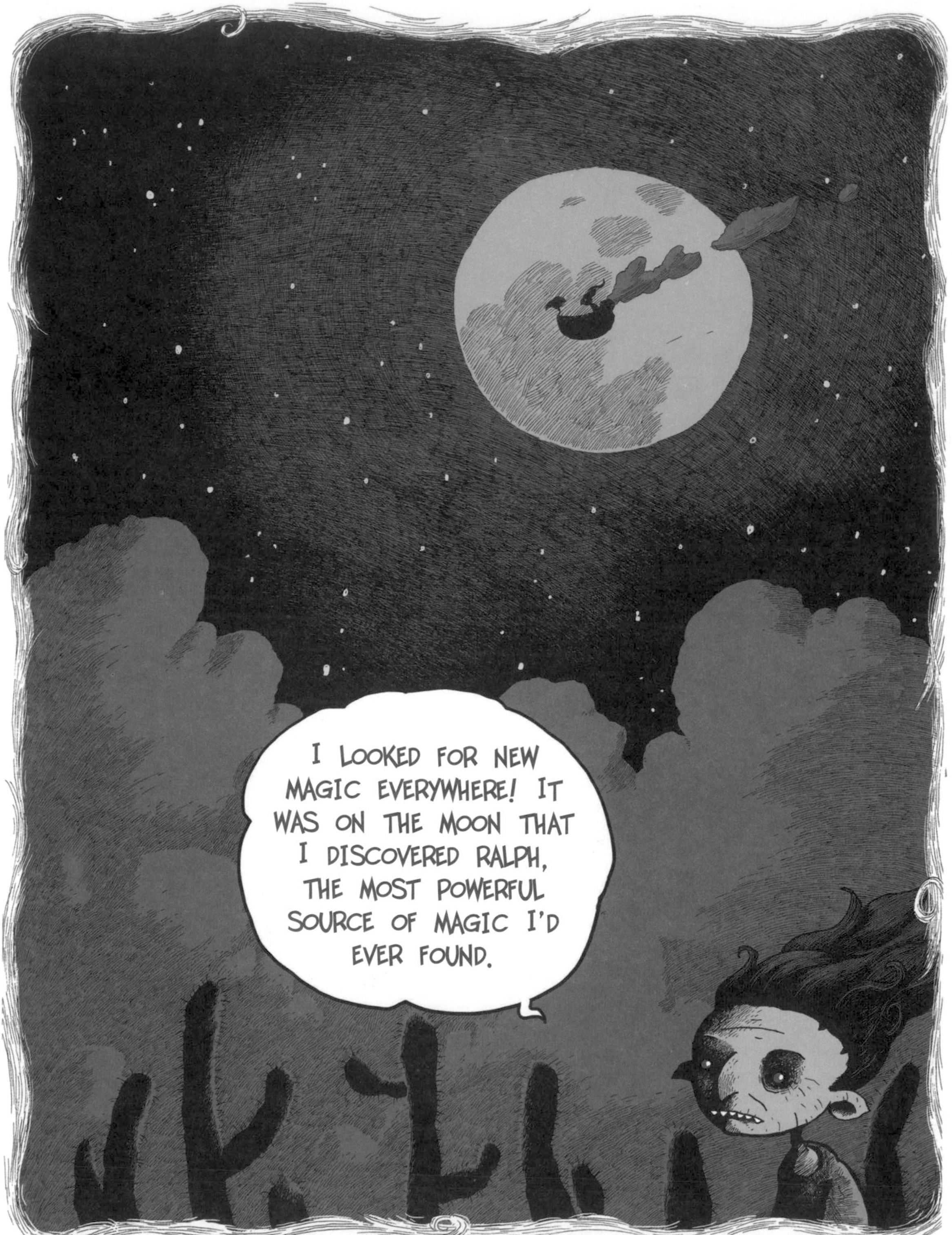
I LOOKED FOR NEW MAGIC EVERYWHERE! IT WAS ON THE MOON THAT I DISCOVERED RALPH, THE MOST POWERFUL SOURCE OF MAGIC I'D EVER FOUND.

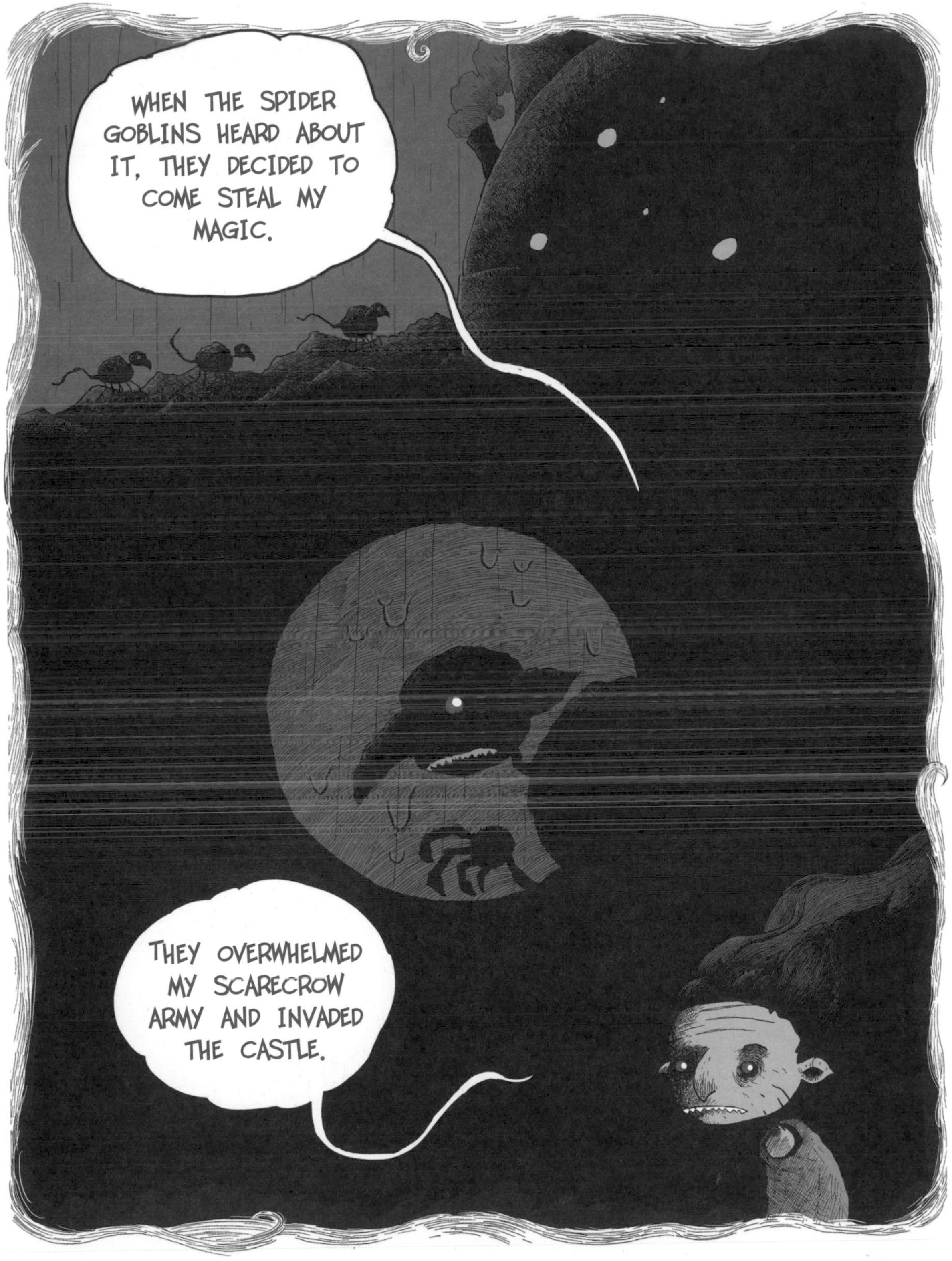
WHEN THE SPIDER GOBLINS HEARD ABOUT IT, THEY DECIDED TO COME STEAL MY MAGIC.
THEY OVERWHELMED MY SCARECROW ARMY AND INVADED THE CASTLE.

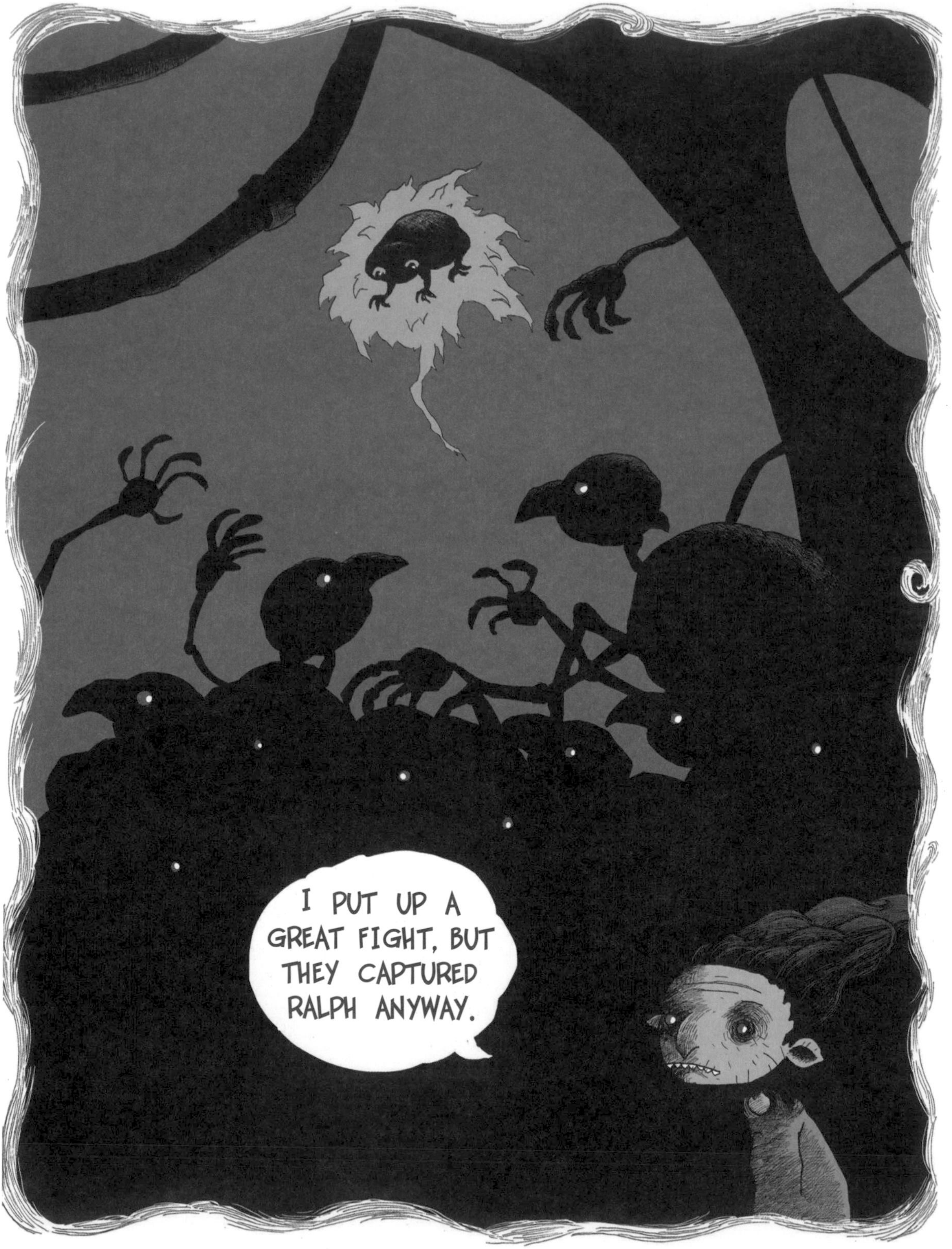
I PUT UP A GREAT FIGHT, BUT THEY CAPTURED RALPH ANYWAY.

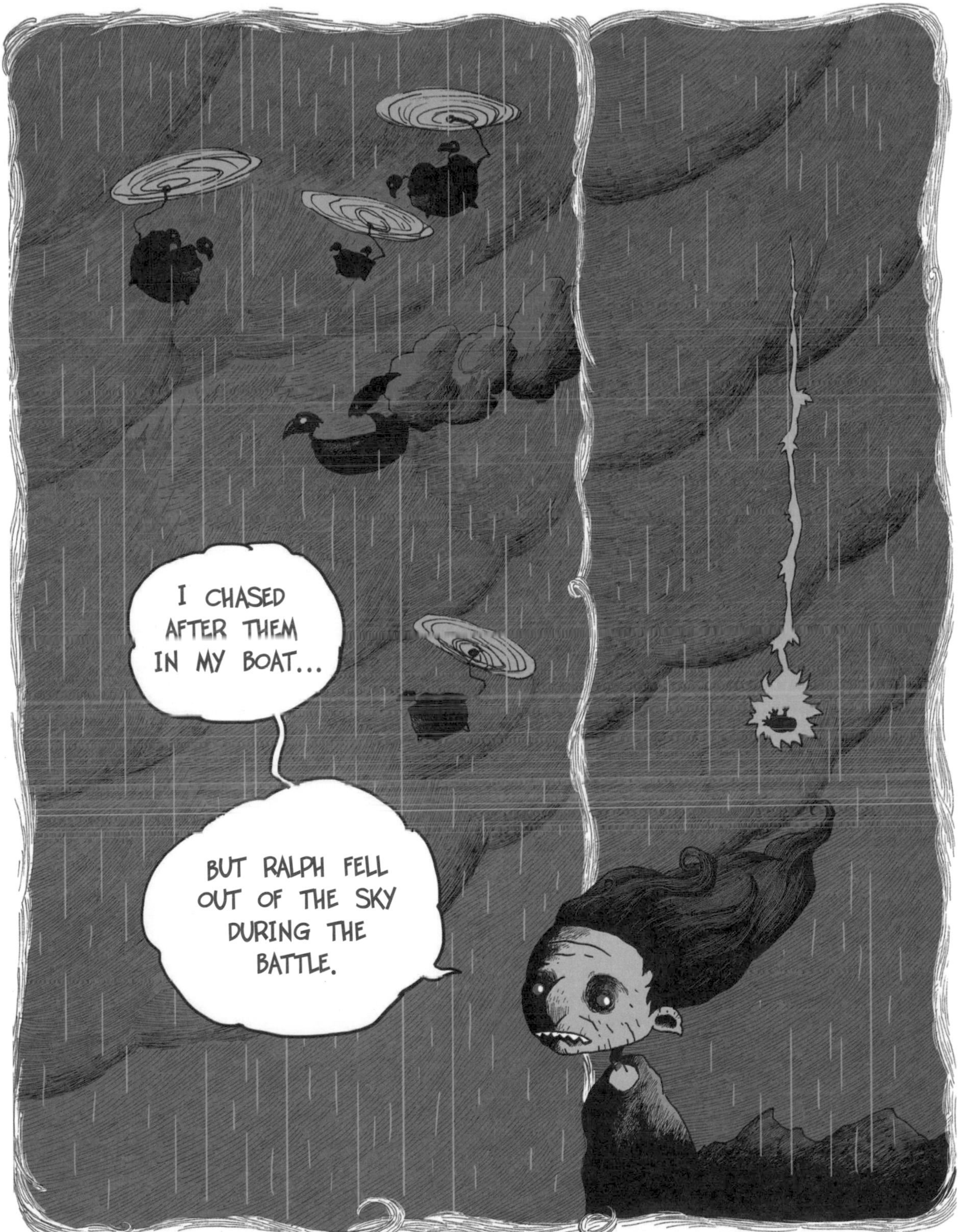
I CHASED AFTER THEM IN MY BOAT...
BUT RALPH FELL OUT OF THE SKY DURING THE BATTLE.

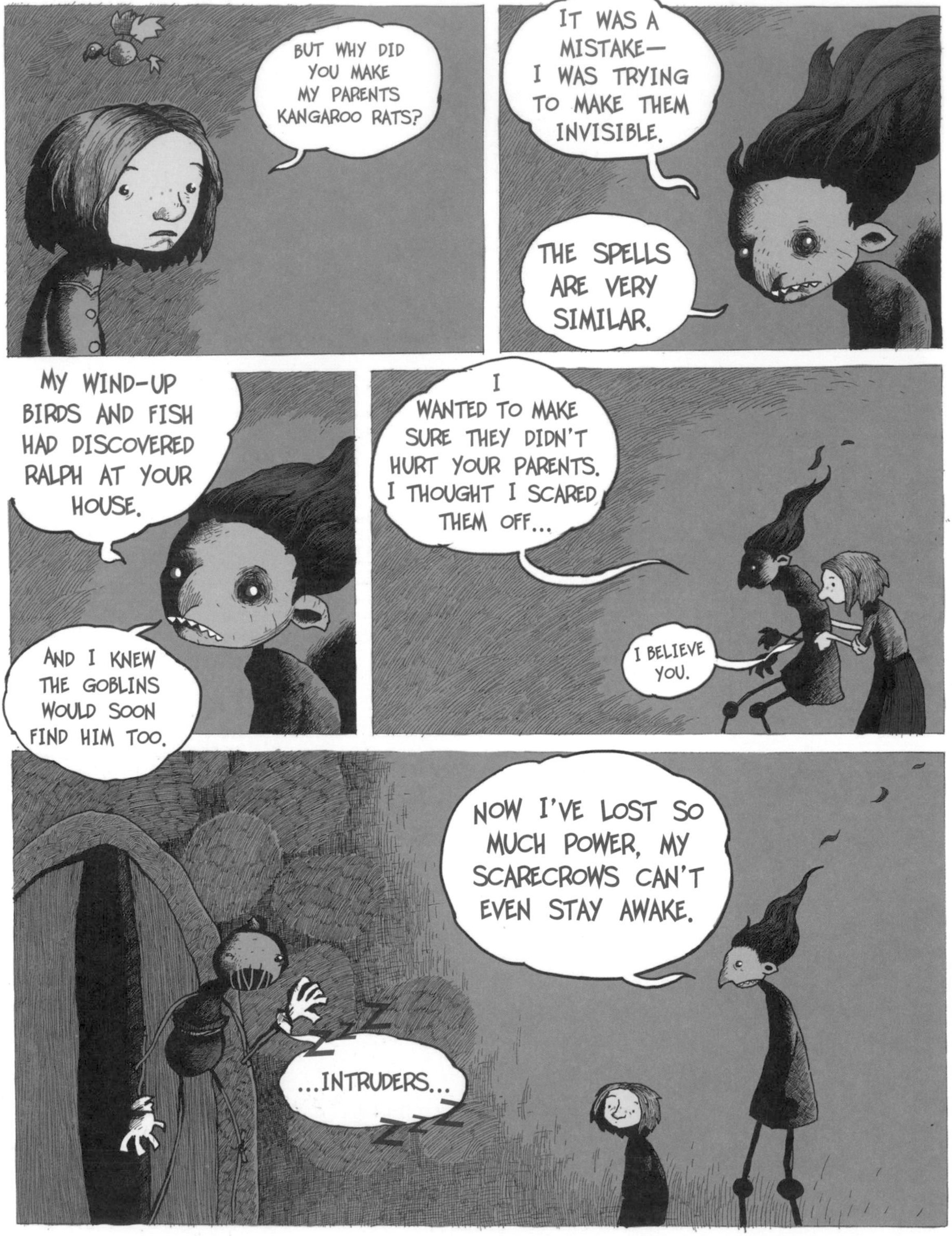
BUT WHY DID YOU MAKE MY PARENTS KANGAROO RATS?
IT WAS A MISTAKE— I WAS TRYING TO MAKE THEM INVISIBLE.
THE SPELLS ARE VERY SIMILAR.
MY WIND-UP BIRDS AND FISH HAD DISCOVERED RALPH AT YOUR HOUSE.
AND I KNEW THE GOBLINS WOULD SOON FIND HIM TOO.
I WANTED TO MAKE SURE THEY DIDN'T HURT YOUR PARENTS. I THOUGHT I SCARED THEM OFF...
I BELIEVE YOU.
NOW I'VE LOST SO MUCH POWER, MY SCARECROWS CAN'T EVEN STAY AWAKE.
ZZZ
...INTRUDERS...
ZZZ

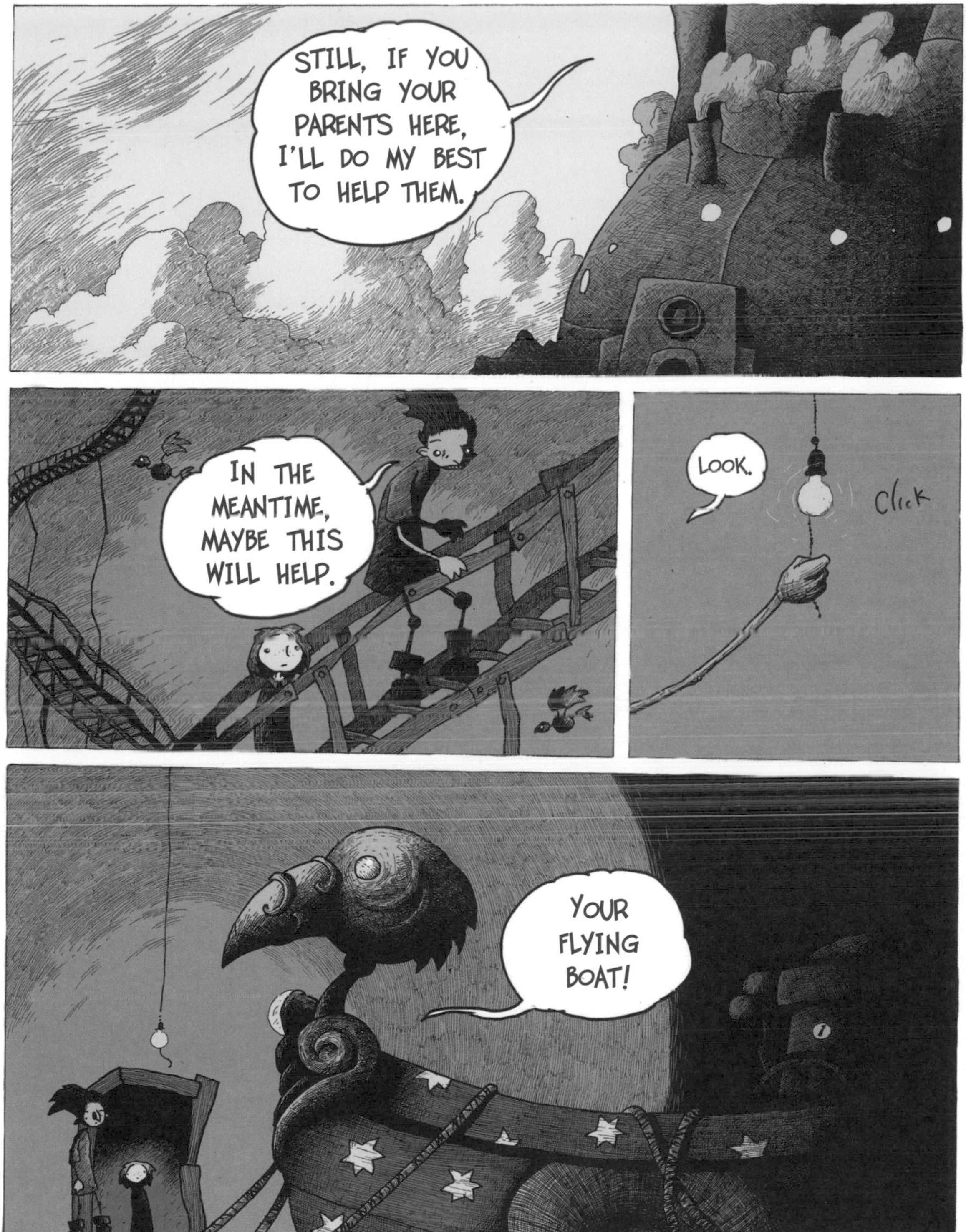
STILL, IF YOU BRING YOUR PARENTS HERE, I'LL DO MY BEST TO HELP THEM.
IN THE MEANTIME, MAYBE THIS WILL HELP.
LOOK.
Click
YOUR FLYING BOAT!

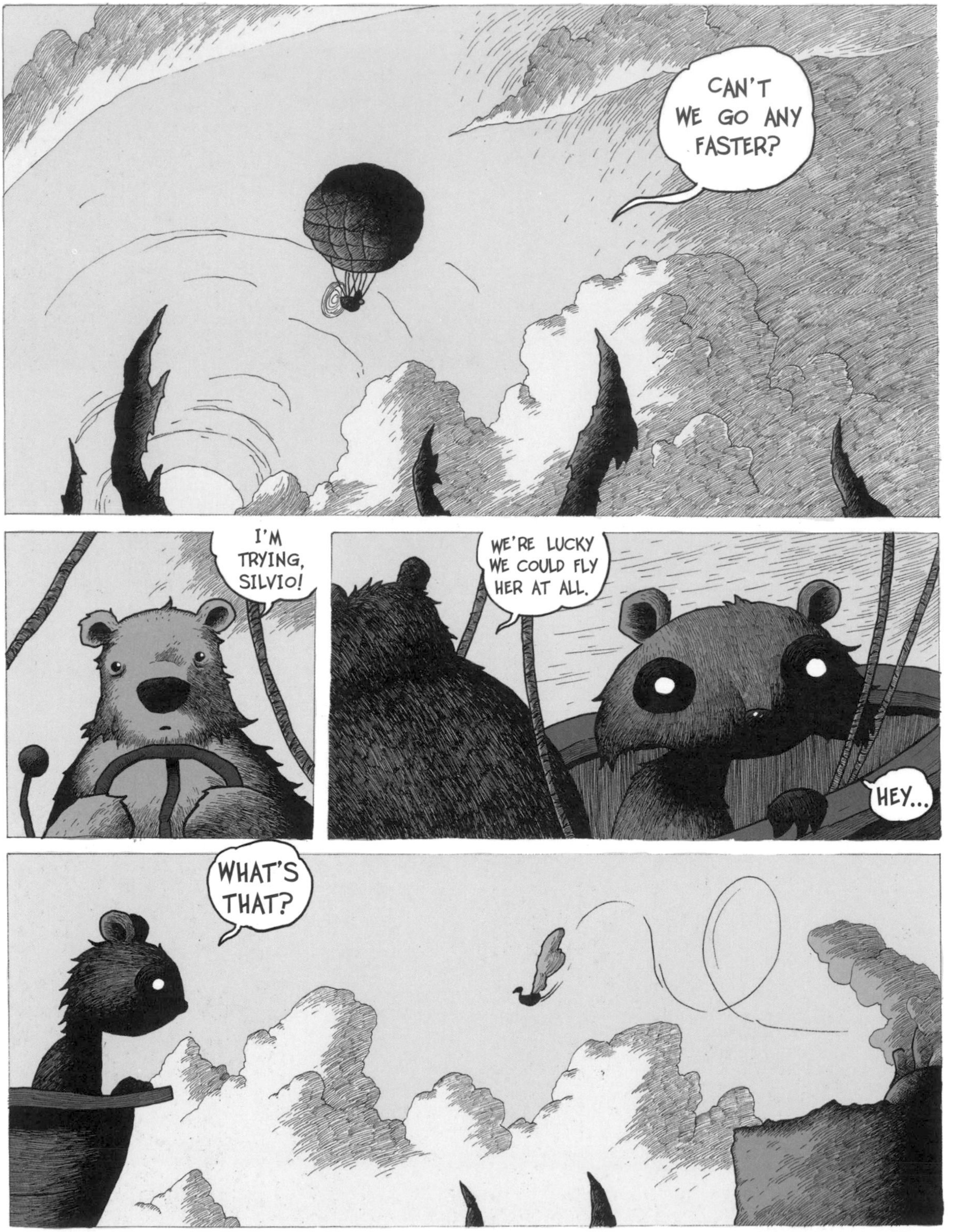
CAN'T WE GO ANY FASTER?
I'M TRYING, SILVIO!
WE'RE LUCKY WE COULD FLY HER AT ALL.
HEY...
WHAT'S THAT?

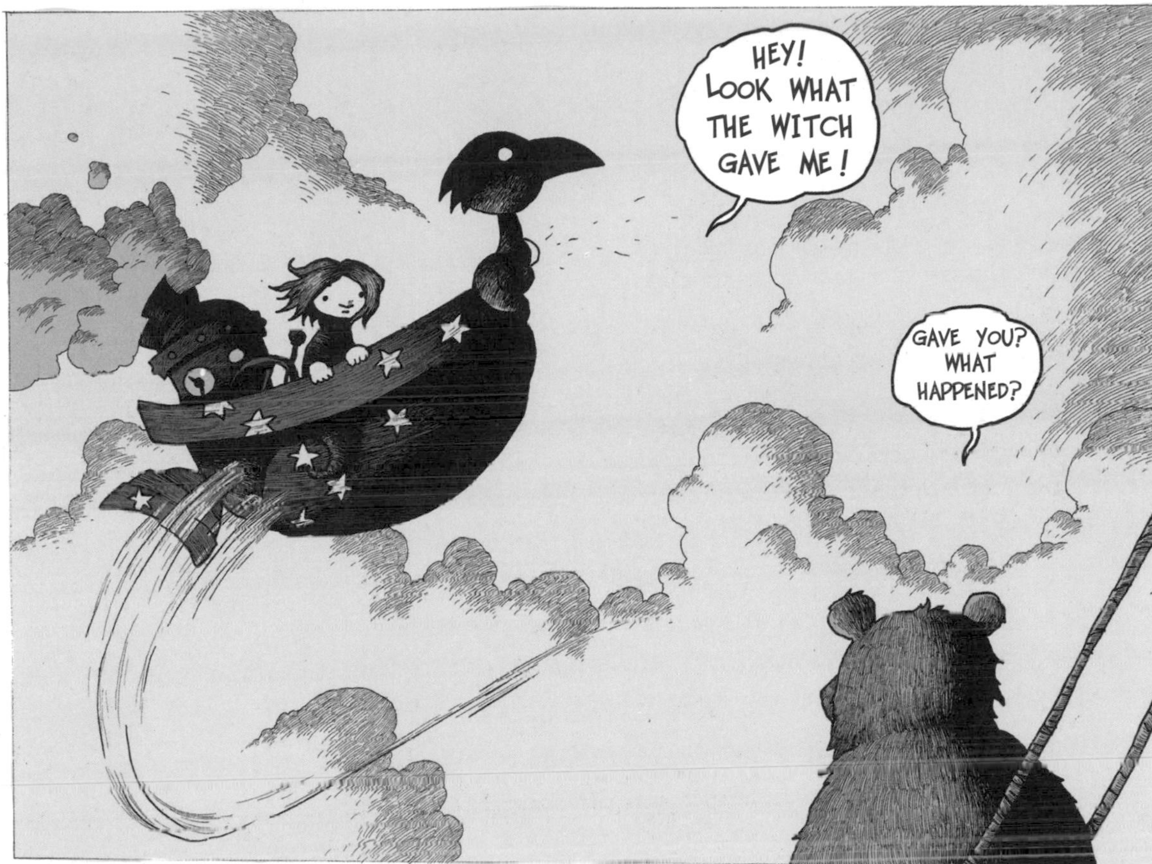
HEY! LOOK WHAT THE WITCH GAVE ME!
GAVE YOU? WHAT HAPPENED?

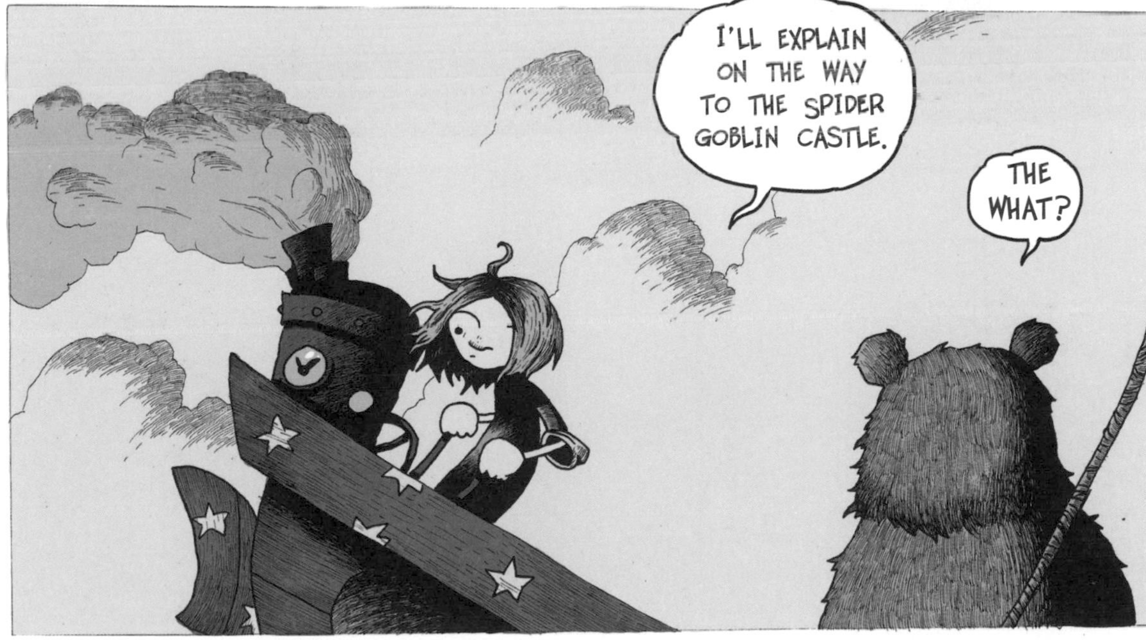
I'LL EXPLAIN ON THE WAY TO THE SPIDER GOBLIN CASTLE.
THE WHAT?

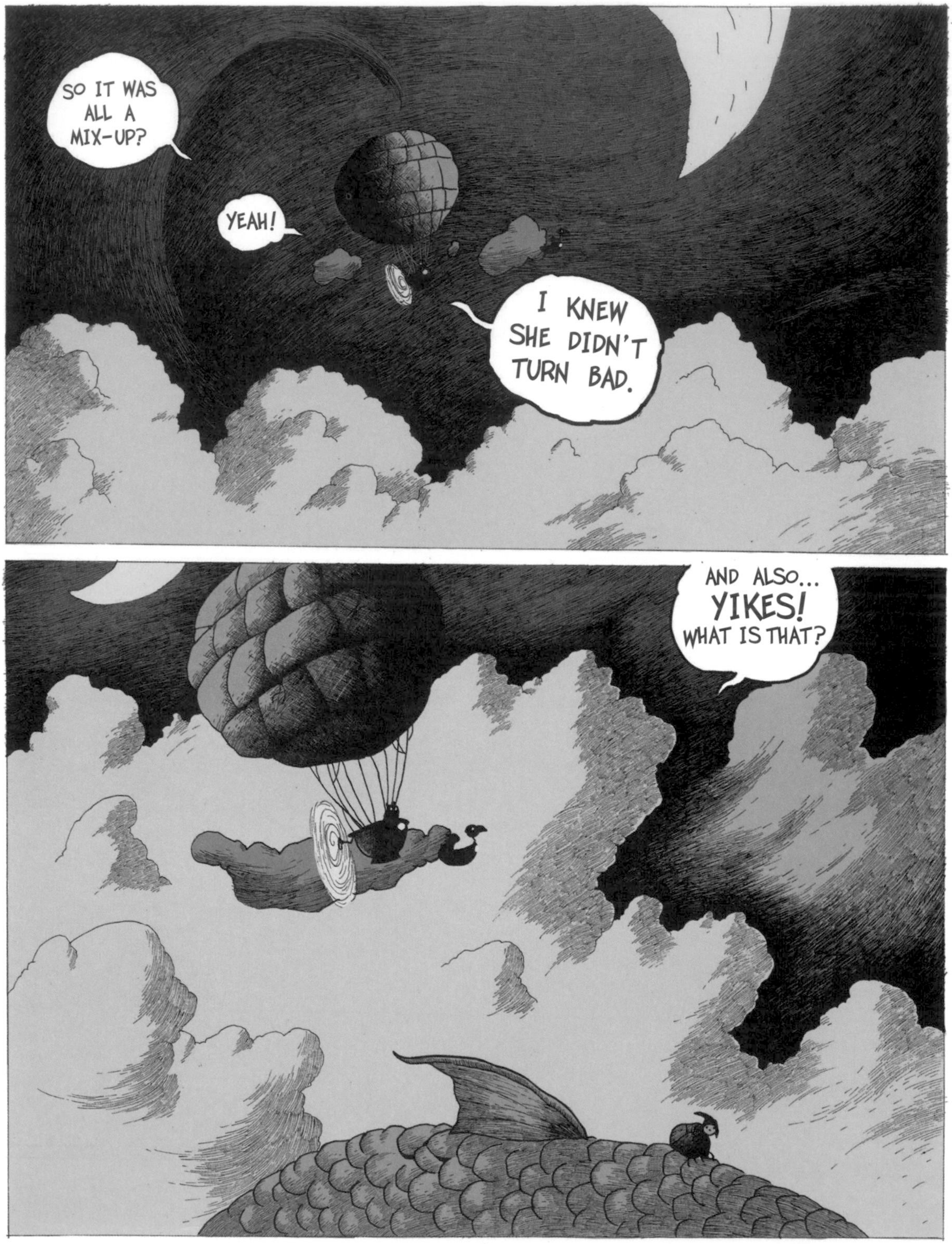
SO IT WAS ALL A MIX-UP?
YEAH!
I KNEW SHE DIDN'T TURN BAD.
AND ALSO... YIKES! WHAT IS THAT?

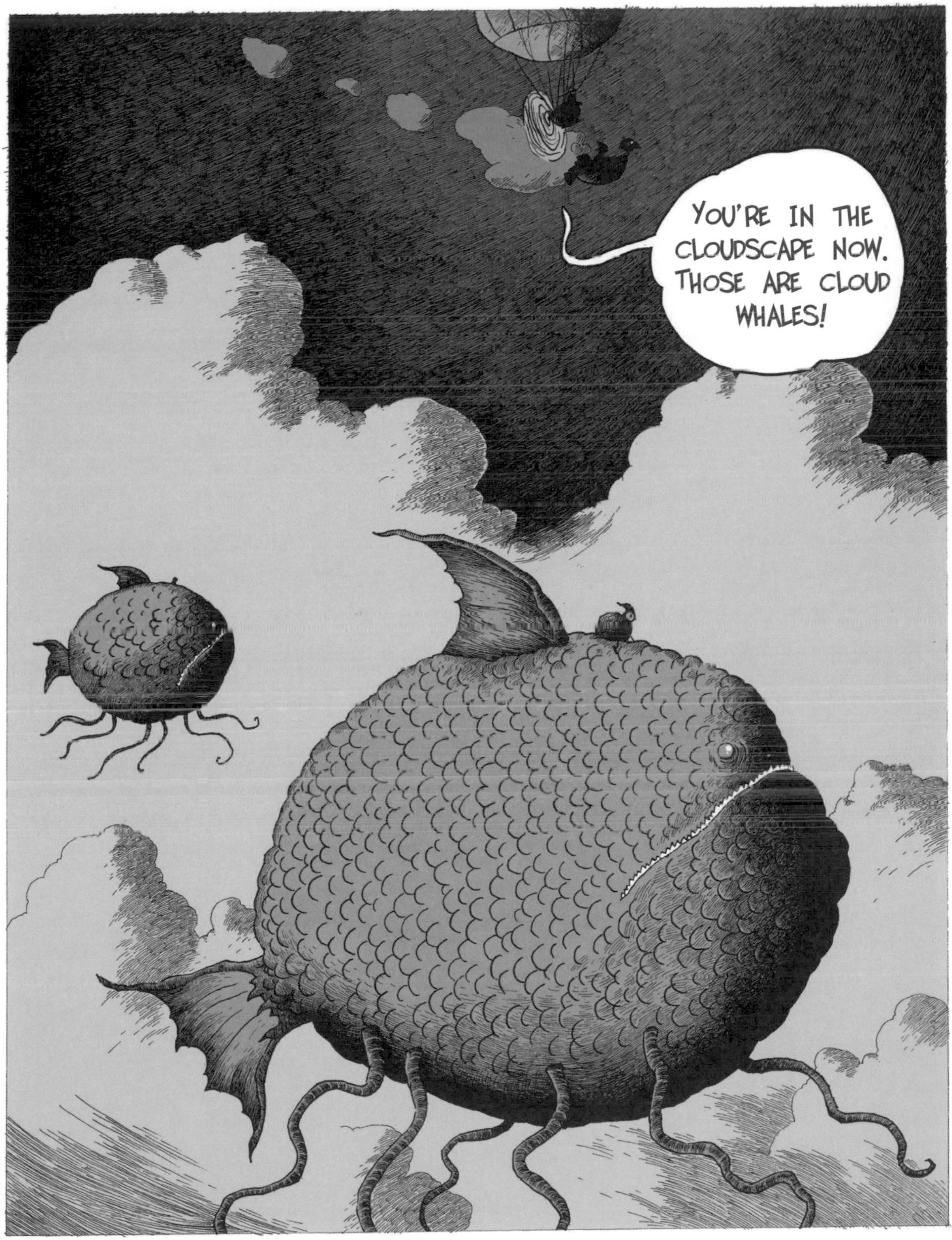
YOU'RE IN THE CLOUDSCAPE NOW. THOSE ARE CLOUD WHALES!

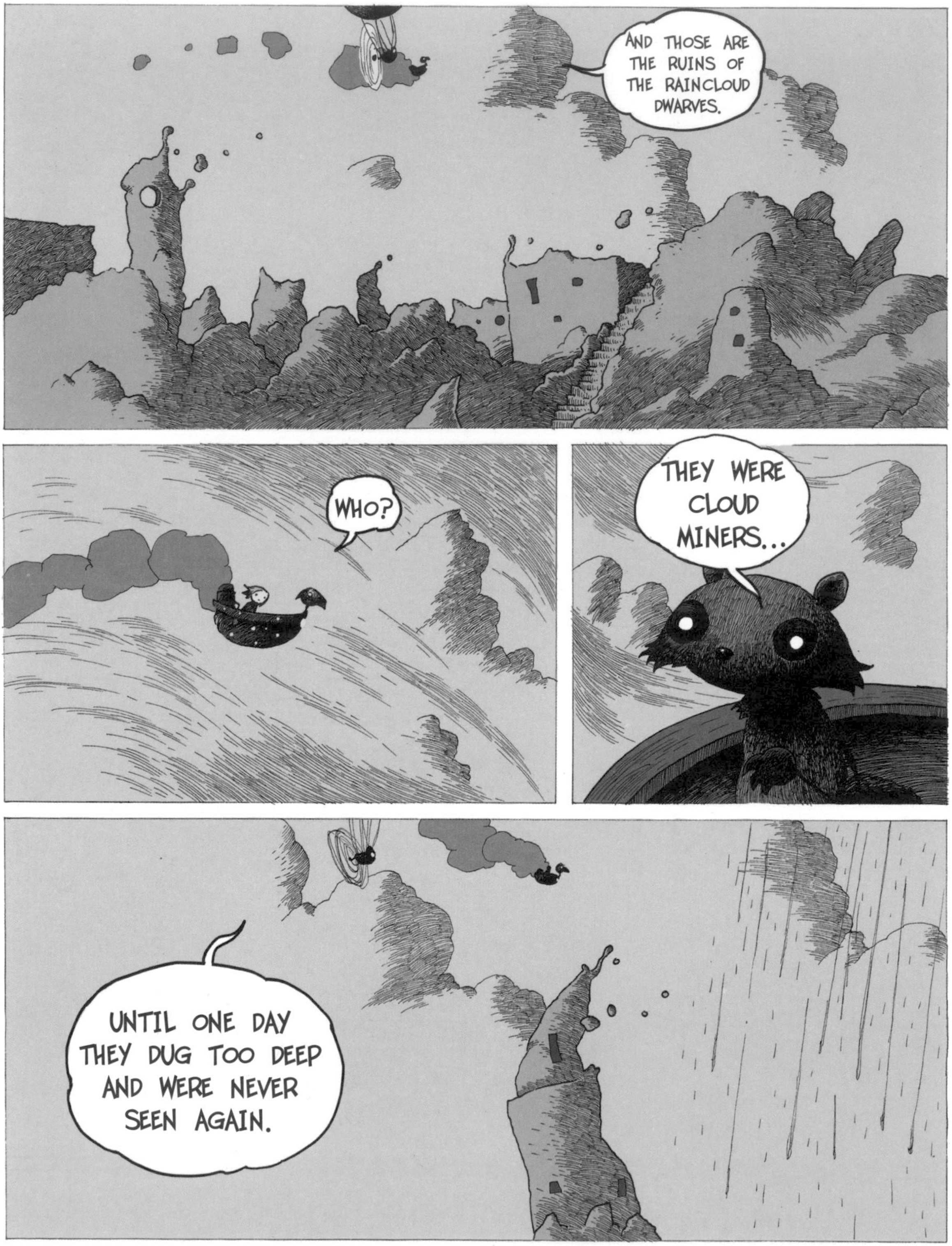
AND THOSE ARE THE RUINS OF THE RAINCLOUD DWARVES.
WHO?
THEY WERE CLOUD MINERS...
UNTIL ONE DAY THEY DUG TOO DEEP AND WERE NEVER SEEN AGAIN.

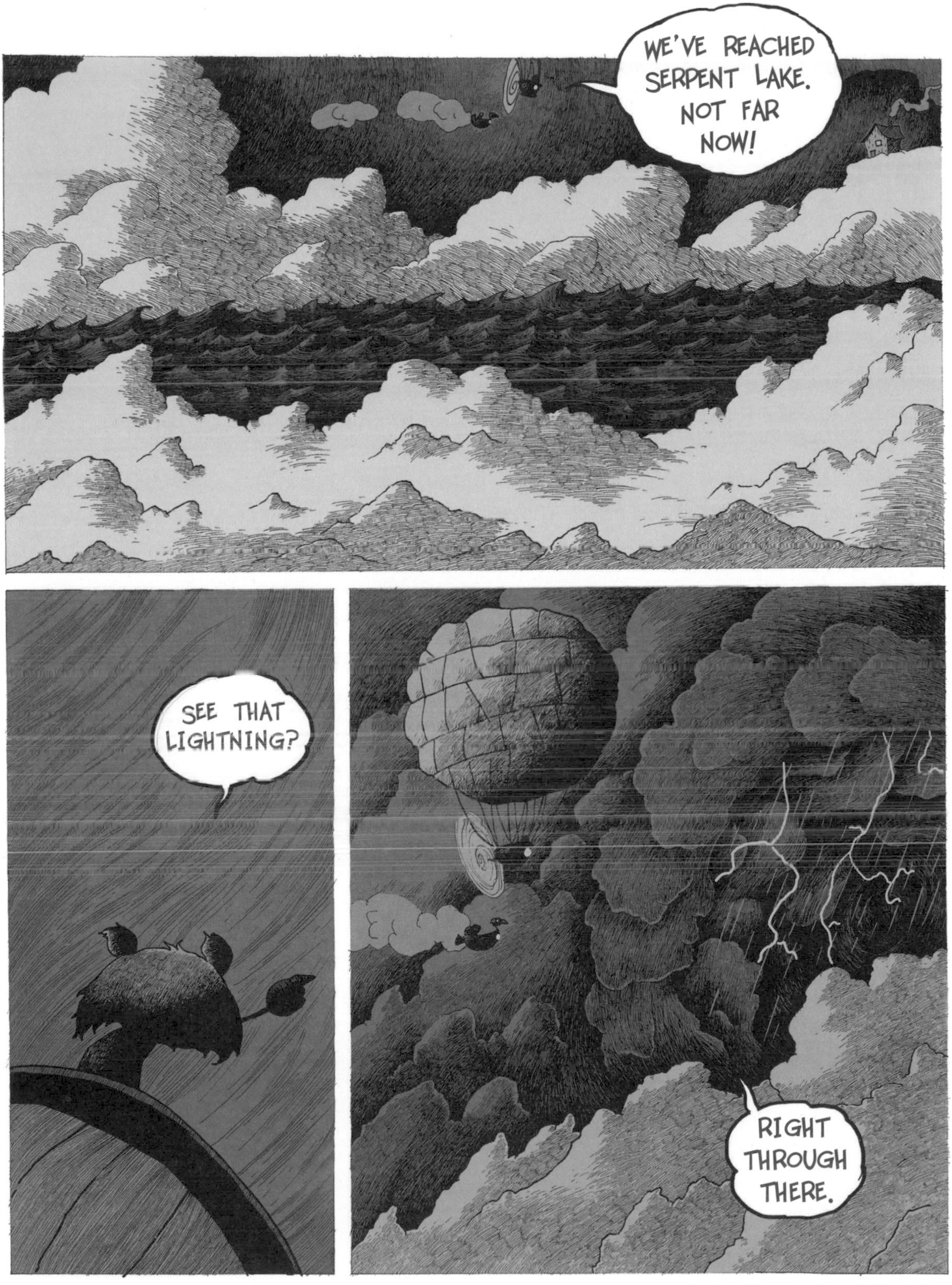
WE'VE REACHED SERPENT LAKE. NOT FAR NOW!
SEE THAT LIGHTNING?
RIGHT THROUGH THERE.

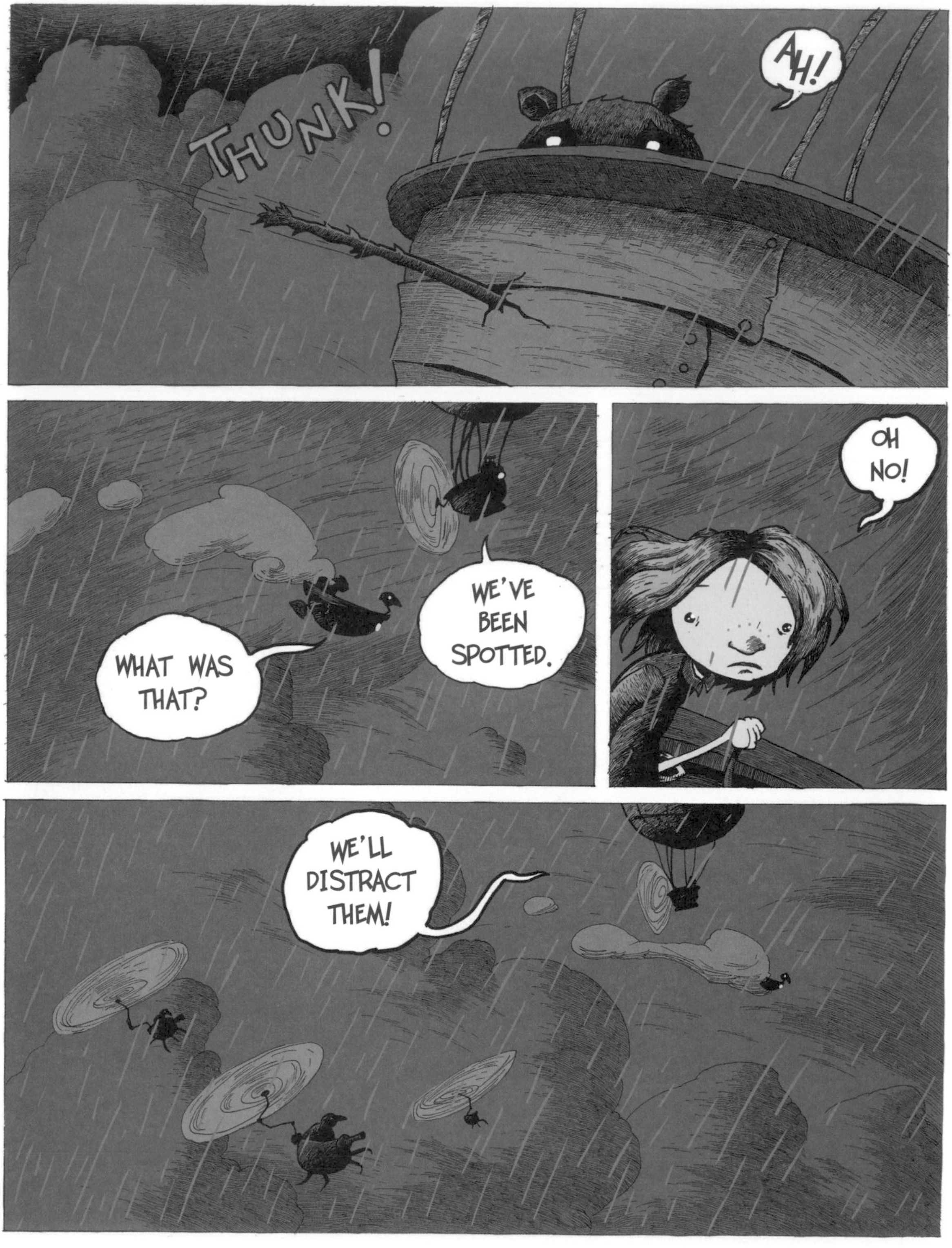
THUNK!
AH!
WHAT WAS THAT?
WE'VE BEEN SPOTTED.
OH NO!
WE'LL DISTRACT THEM!

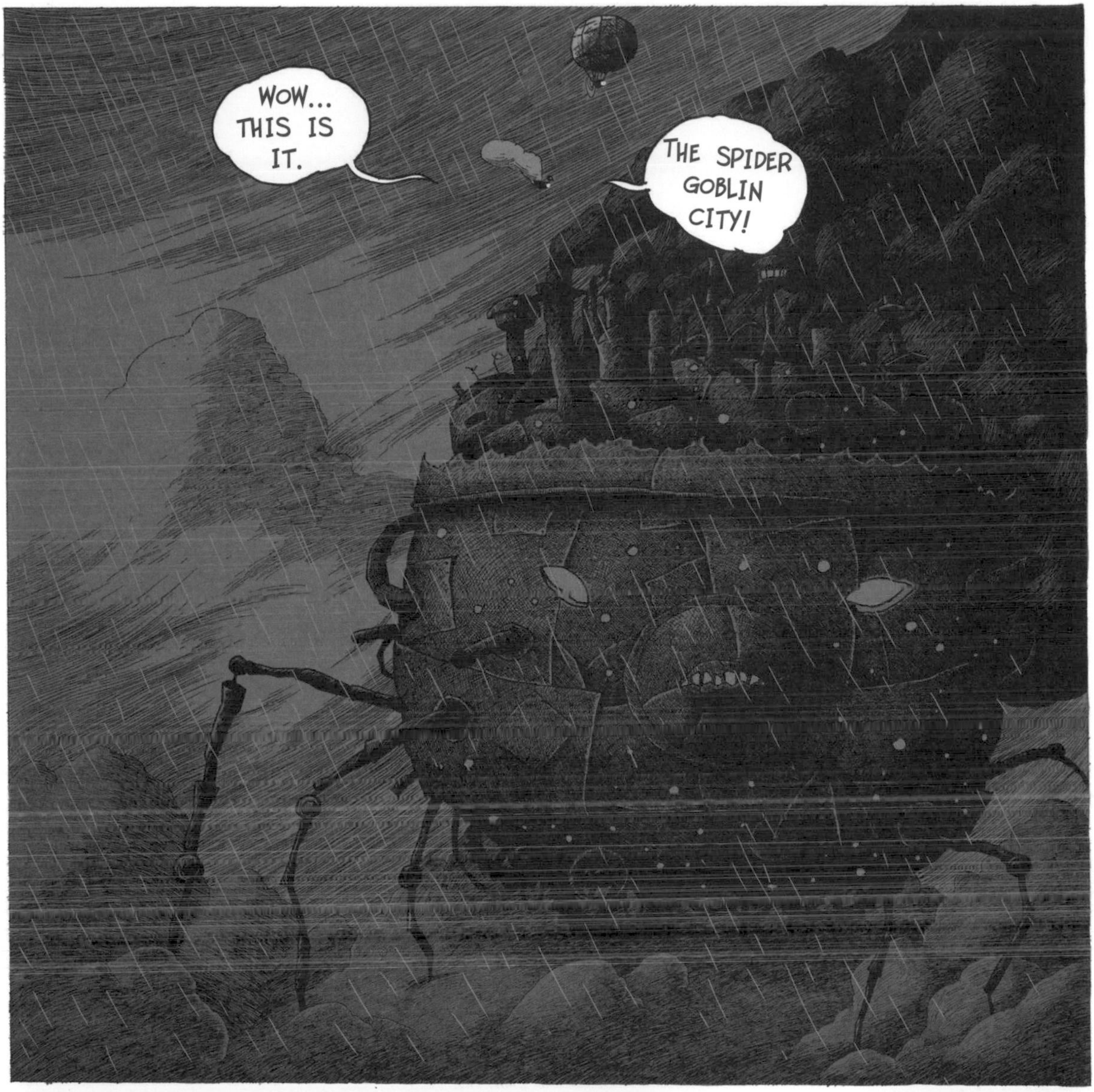
WOW... THIS IS IT.
THE SPIDER GOBLIN CITY!

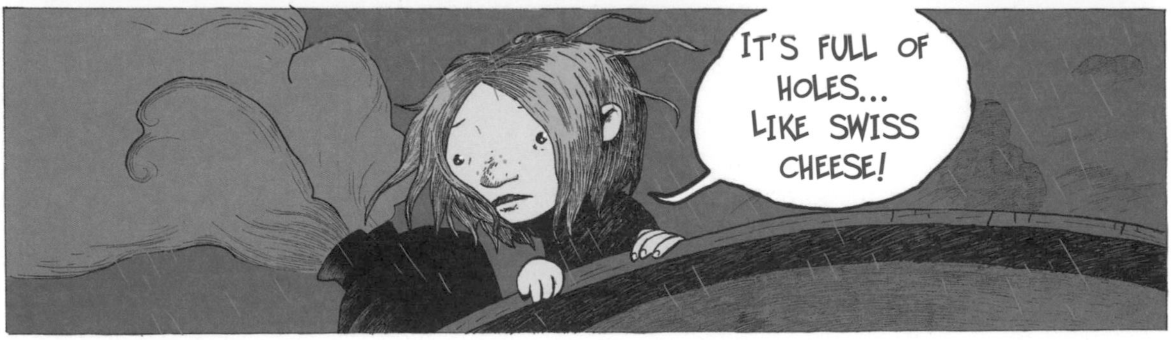
IT'S FULL OF HOLES... LIKE SWISS CHEESE!

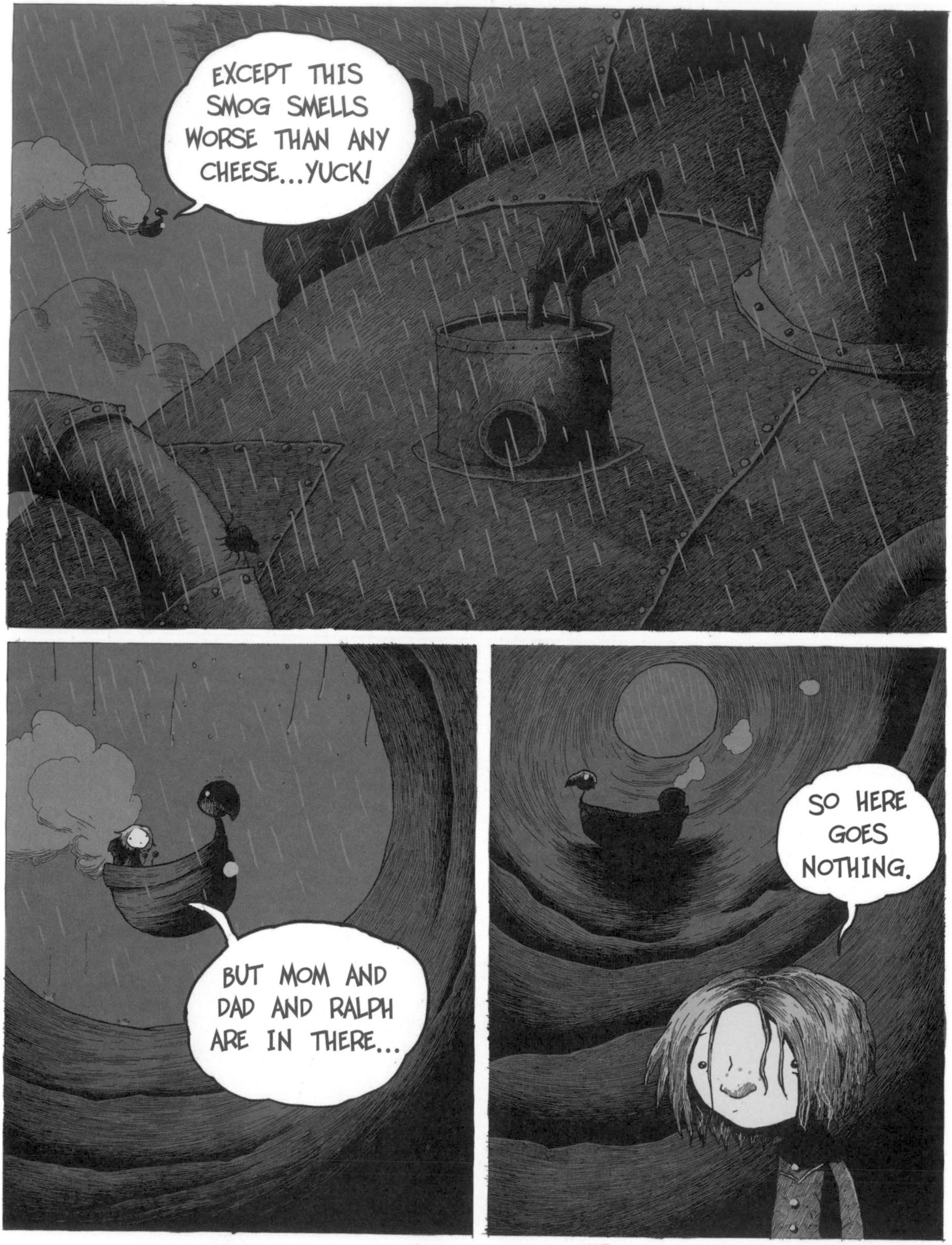
EXCEPT THIS SMOG SMELLS WORSE THAN ANY CHEESE...YUCK!
BUT MOM AND DAD AND RALPH ARE IN THERE...
SO HERE GOES NOTHING.

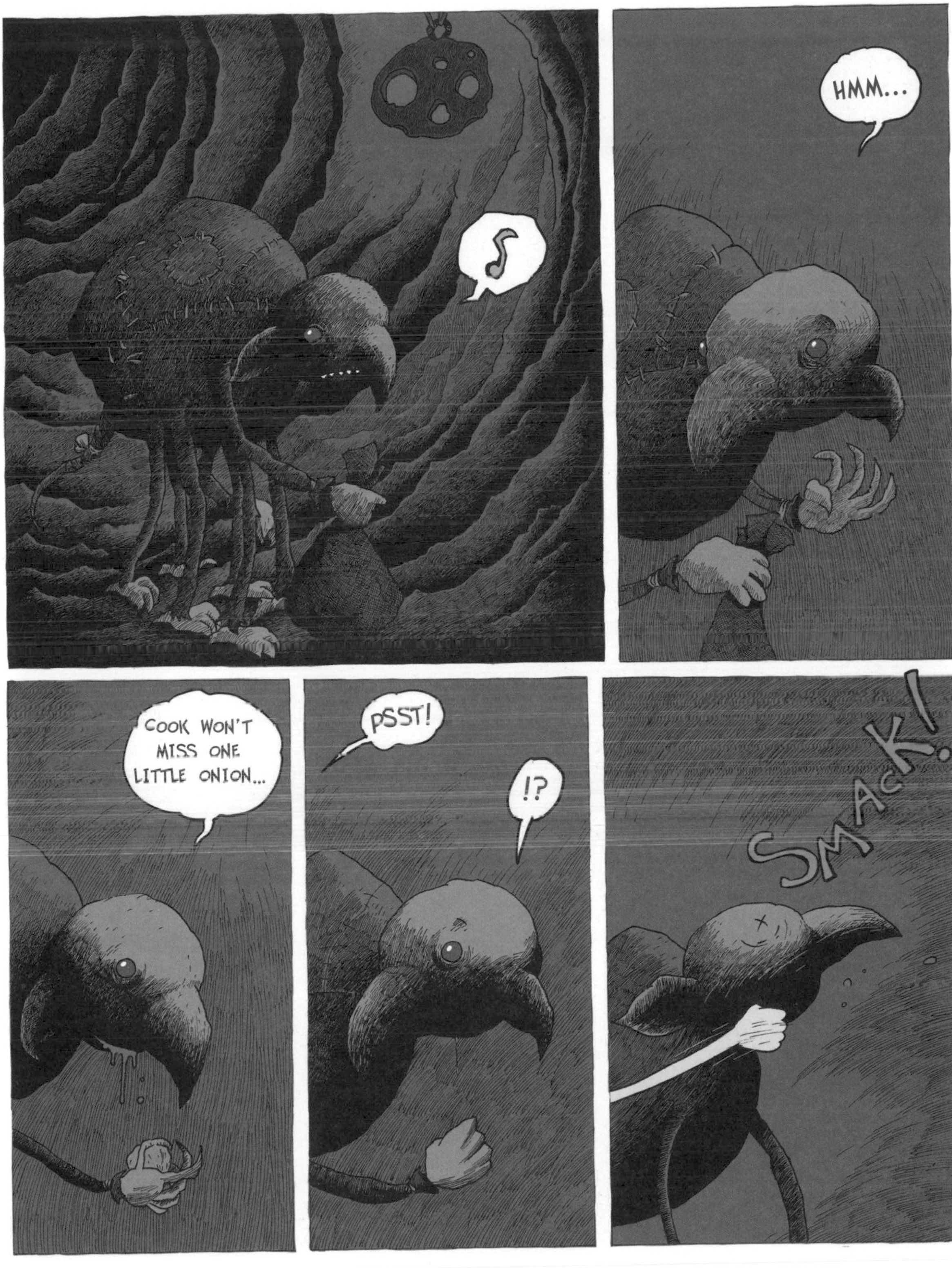

HMM...
COOK WON'T MISS ONE LITTLE ONION...
PSST!
!?
SMACK!

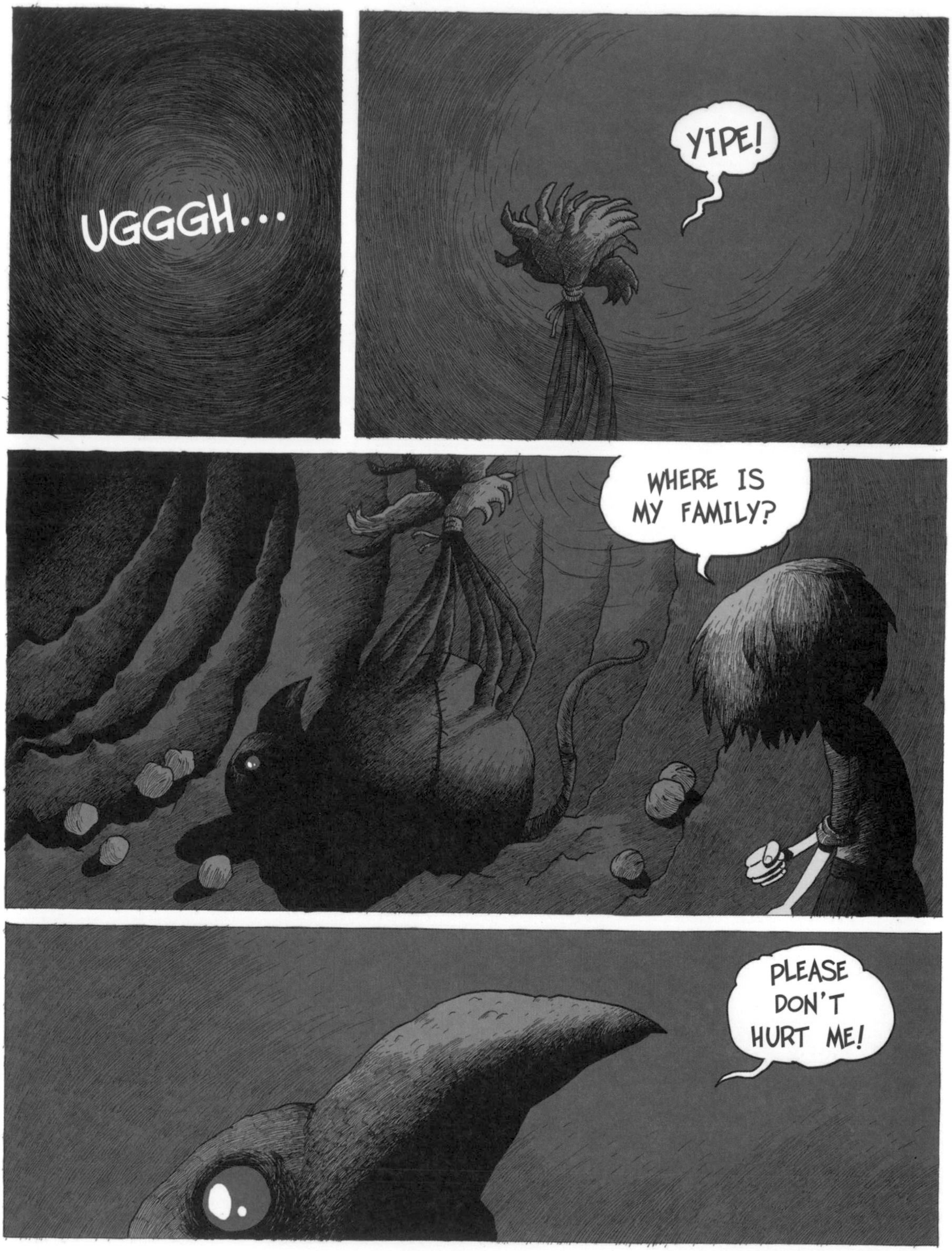
UGGGH...
YIPE!
WHERE IS MY FAMILY?
PLEASE DON'T HURT ME!

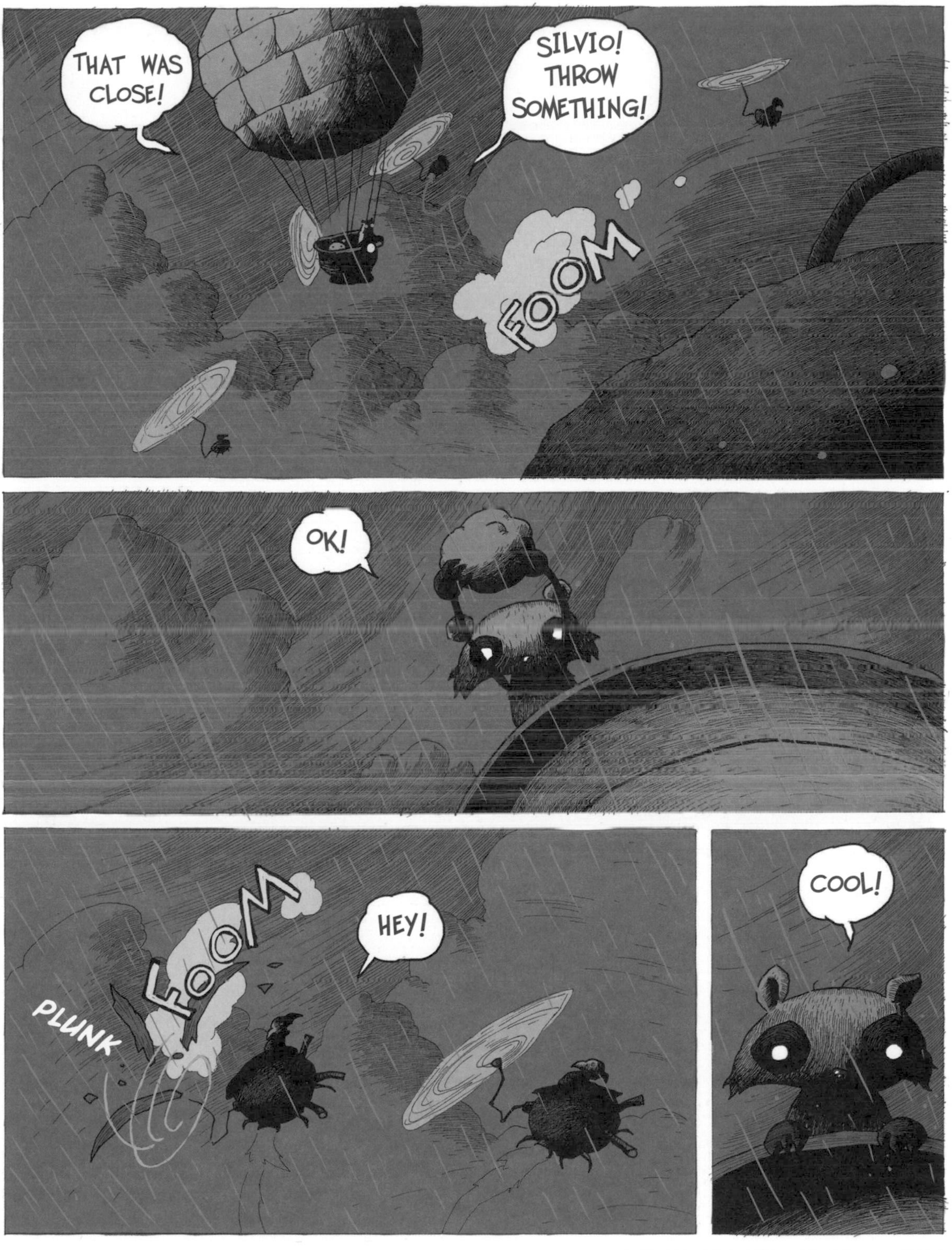
THAT WAS CLOSE!
SILVIO! THROW SOMETHING!
FOOM
OK!
FOOM
PLUNK
HEY!
COOL!

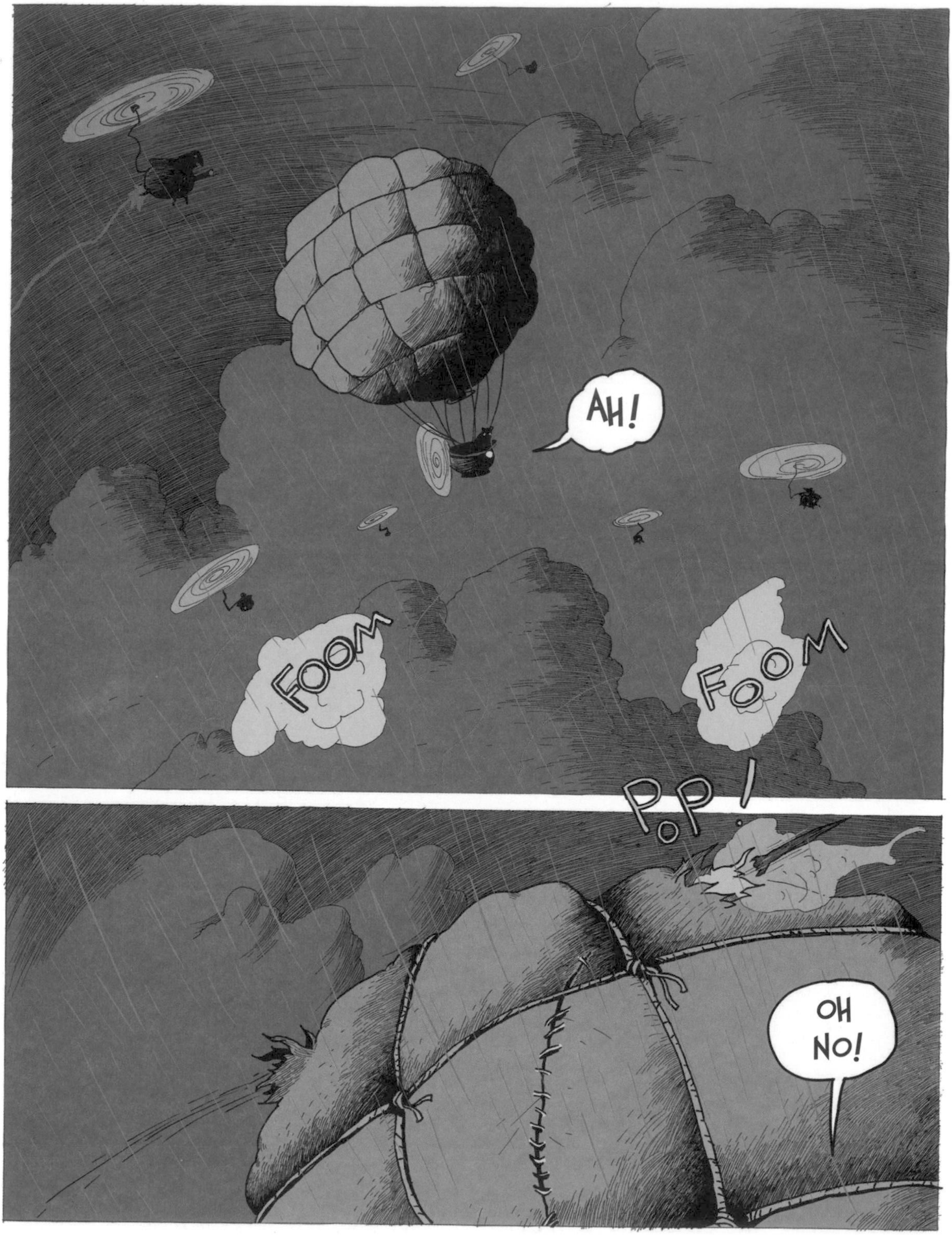
AH!
FOOM
FOOM
POP!
OH NO!

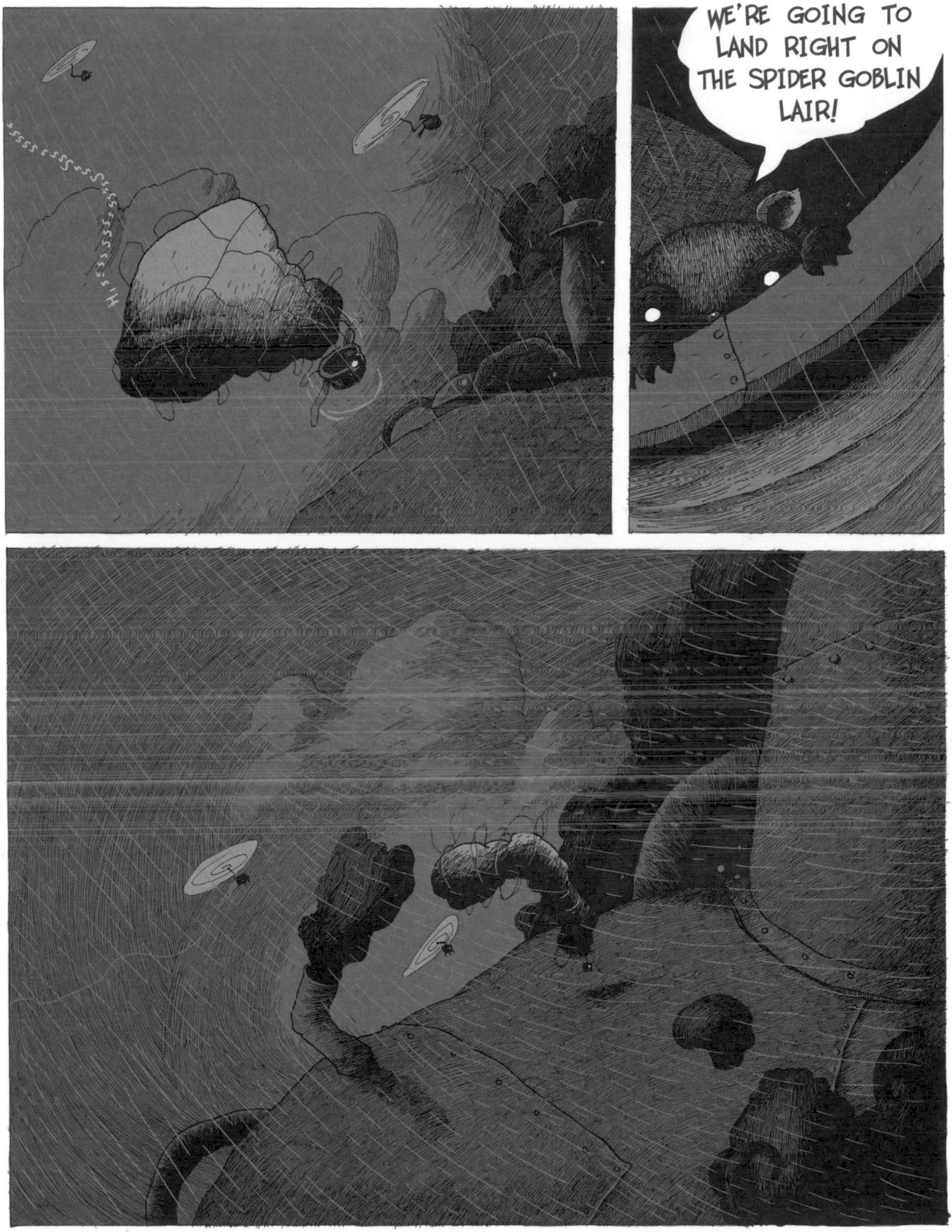
WE'RE GOING TO LAND RIGHT ON THE SPIDER GOBLIN LAIR!

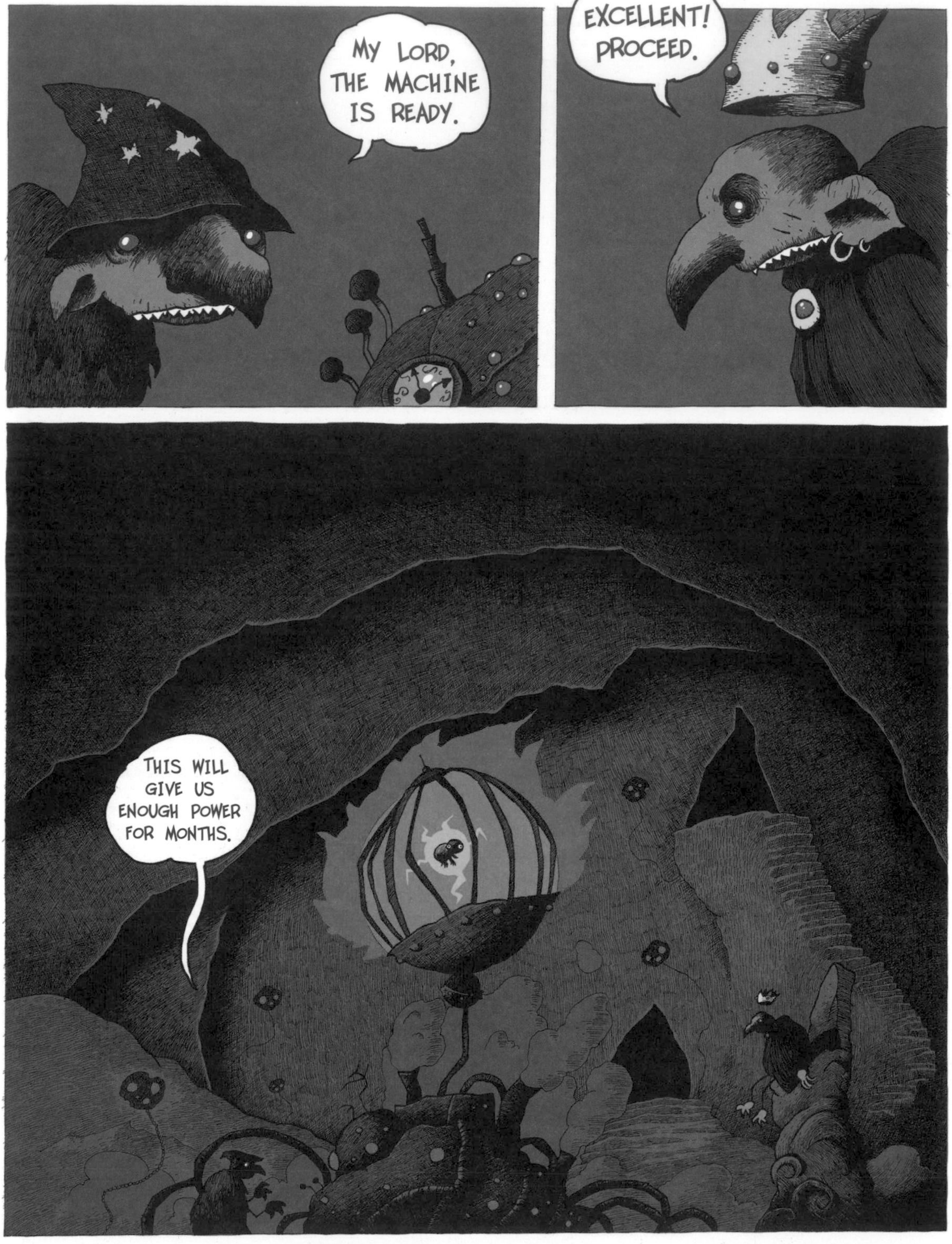
MY LORD, THE MACHINE IS READY.
EXCELLENT! PROCEED.
THIS WILL GIVE US ENOUGH POWER FOR MONTHS.

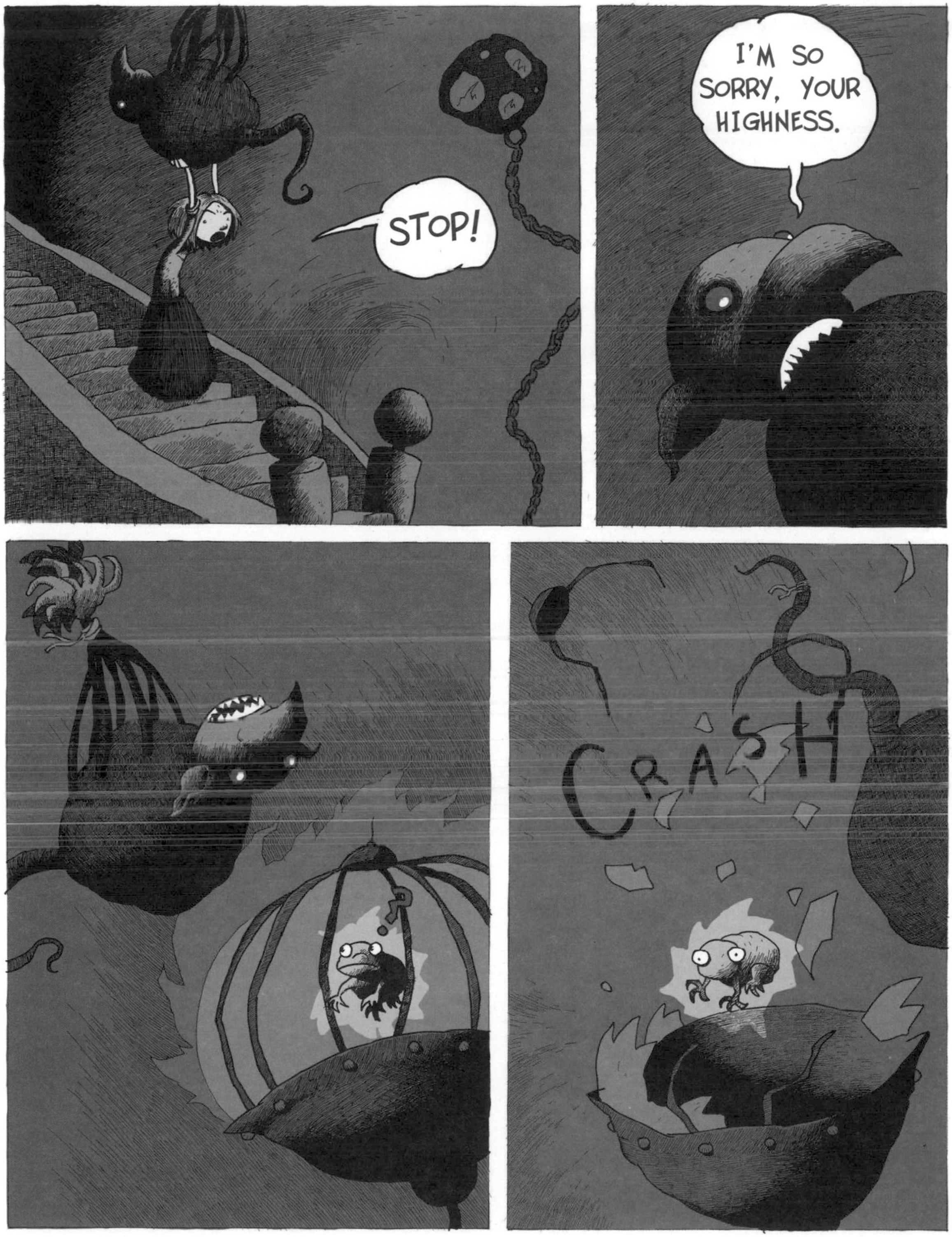
STOP!
I'M SO SORRY, YOUR HIGHNESS.
CRASH

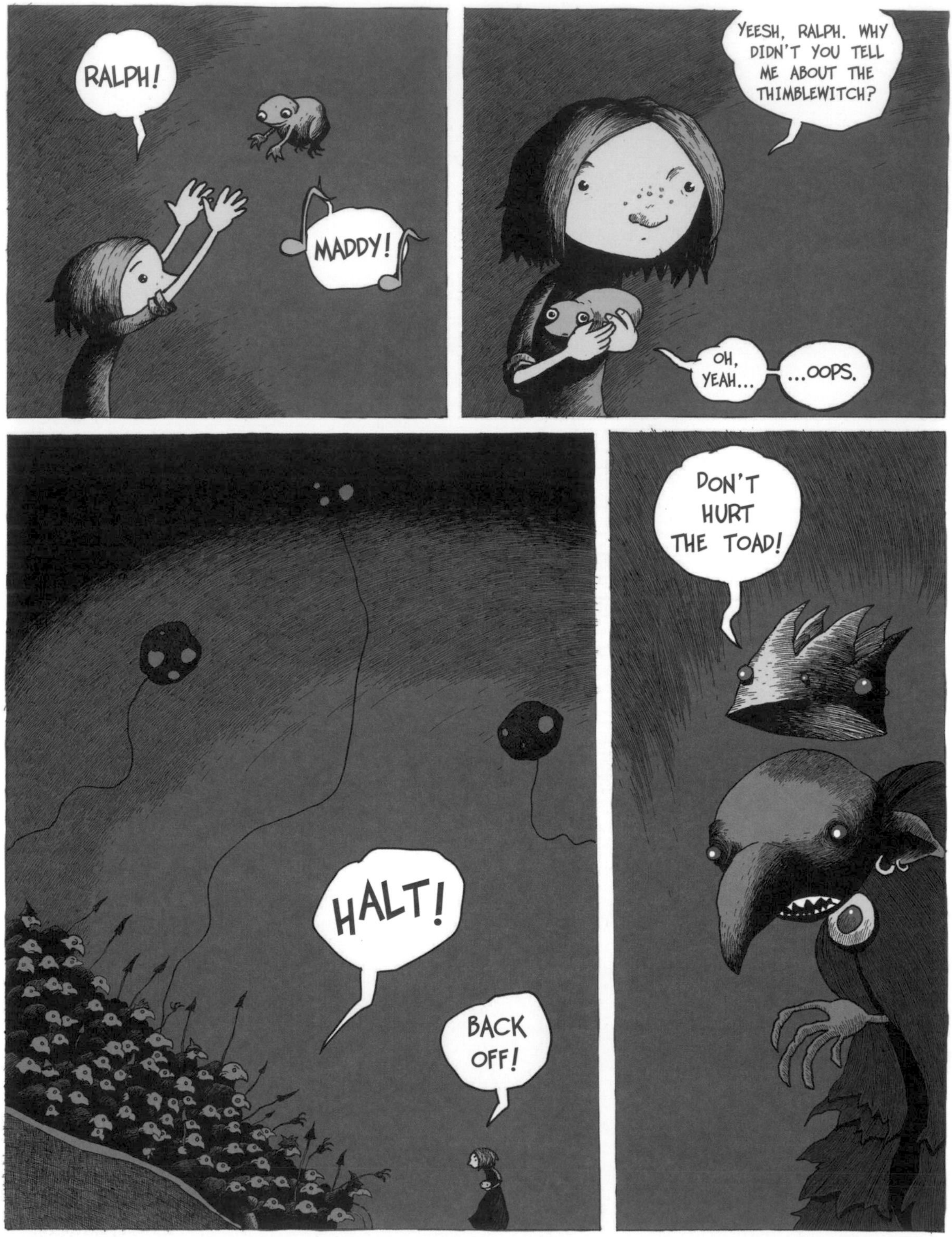
RALPH!
MADDY!
YEESH, RALPH. WHY DIDN'T YOU TELL ME ABOUT THE THIMBLEWITCH?
OH, YEAH...
...OOPS.
HALT!
BACK OFF!
DON'T HURT THE TOAD!

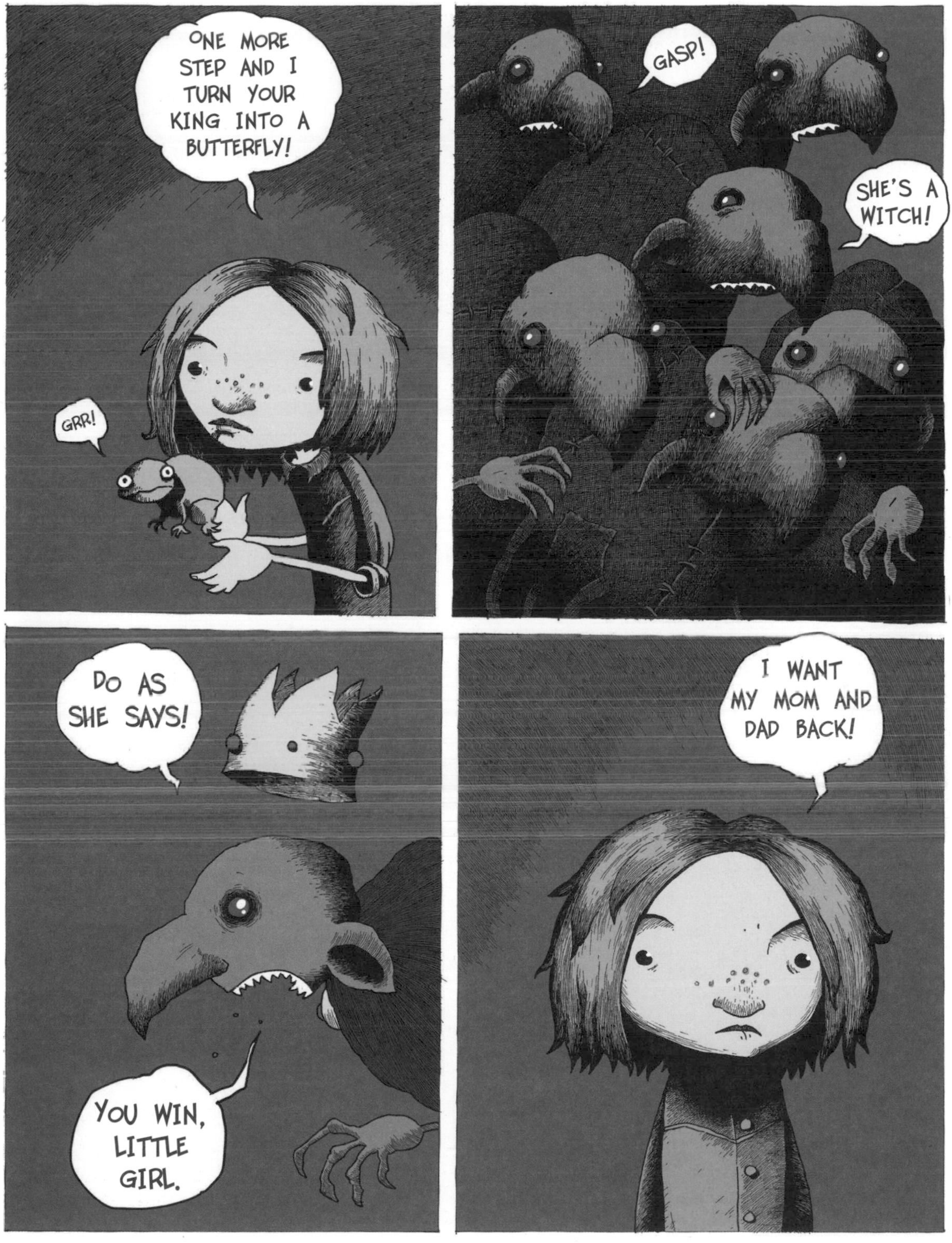
ONE MORE STEP AND I TURN YOUR KING INTO A BUTTERFLY!
GRR!
GASP!
SHE'S A WITCH!
DO AS SHE SAYS!
YOU WIN, LITTLE GIRL.
I WANT MY MOM AND DAD BACK!

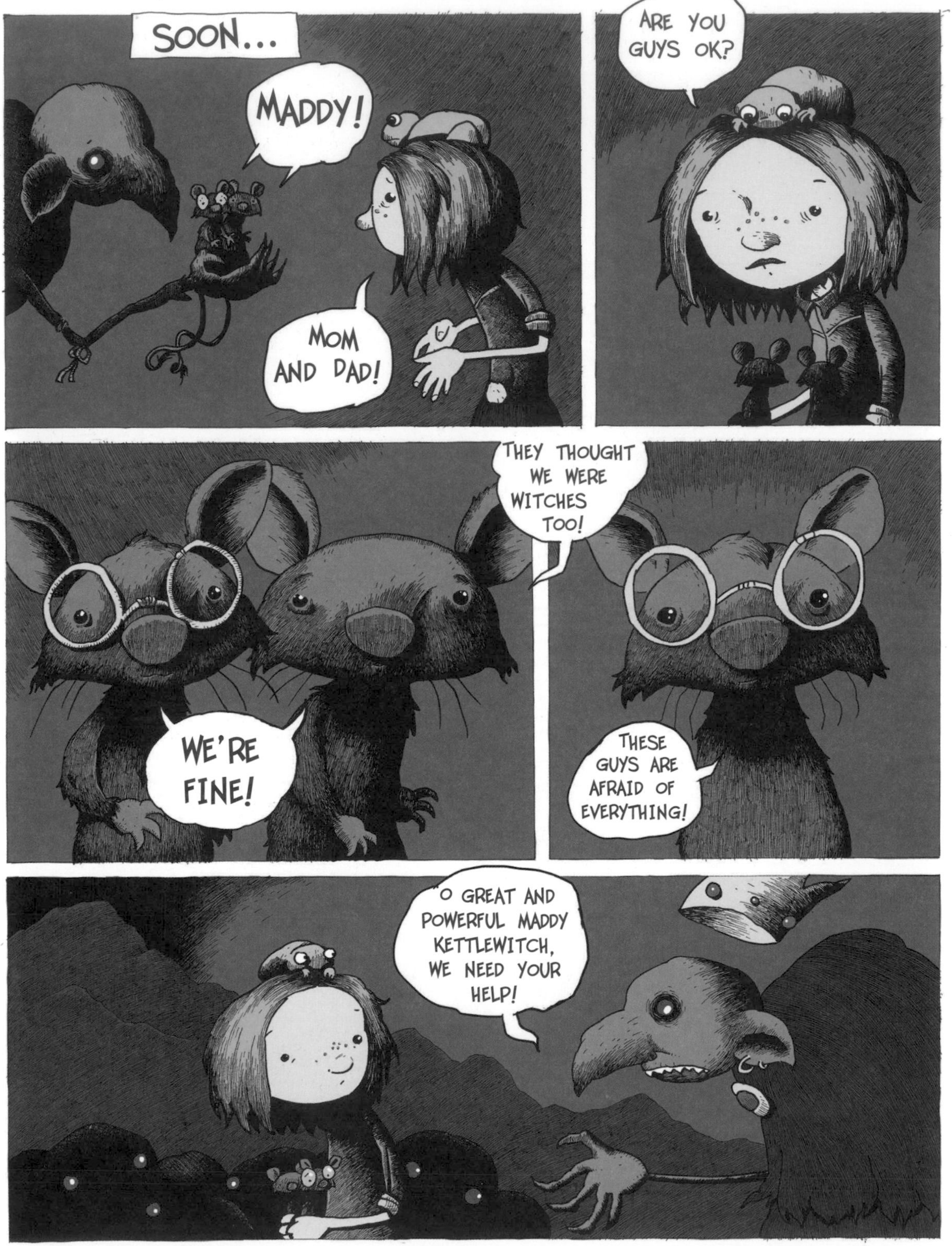
SOON...
MADDY!
MOM AND DAD!
ARE YOU GUYS OK?
WE'RE FINE!
THEY THOUGHT WE WERE WITCHES TOO!
THESE GUYS ARE AFRAID OF EVERYTHING!
O GREAT AND POWERFUL MADDY KETTLEWITCH, WE NEED YOUR HELP!

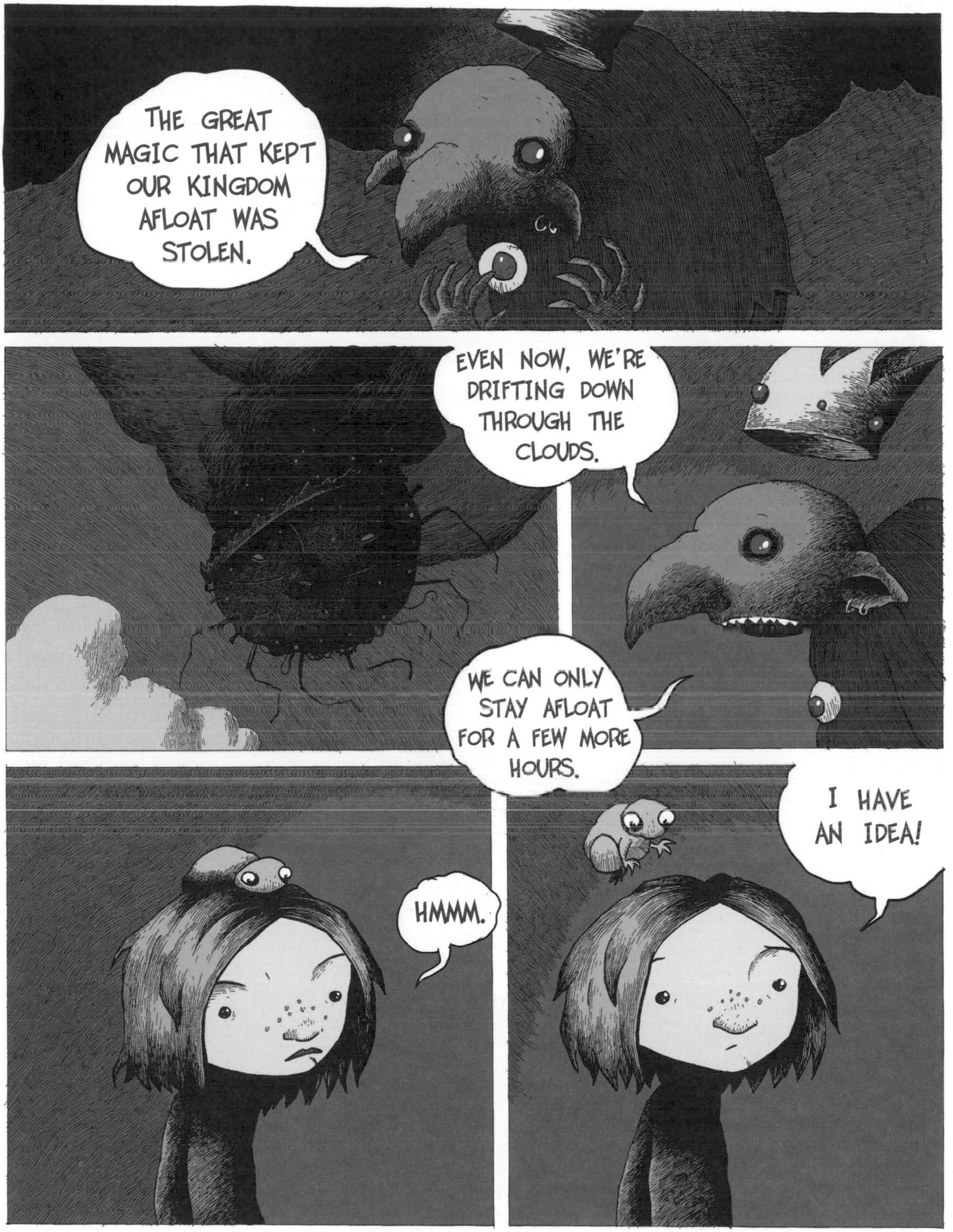
THE GREAT MAGIC THAT KEPT OUR KINGDOM AFLOAT WAS STOLEN.
EVEN NOW, WE'RE DRIFTING DOWN THROUGH THE CLOUDS.
WE CAN ONLY STAY AFLOAT FOR A FEW MORE HOURS.
HMMM.
I HAVE AN IDEA!

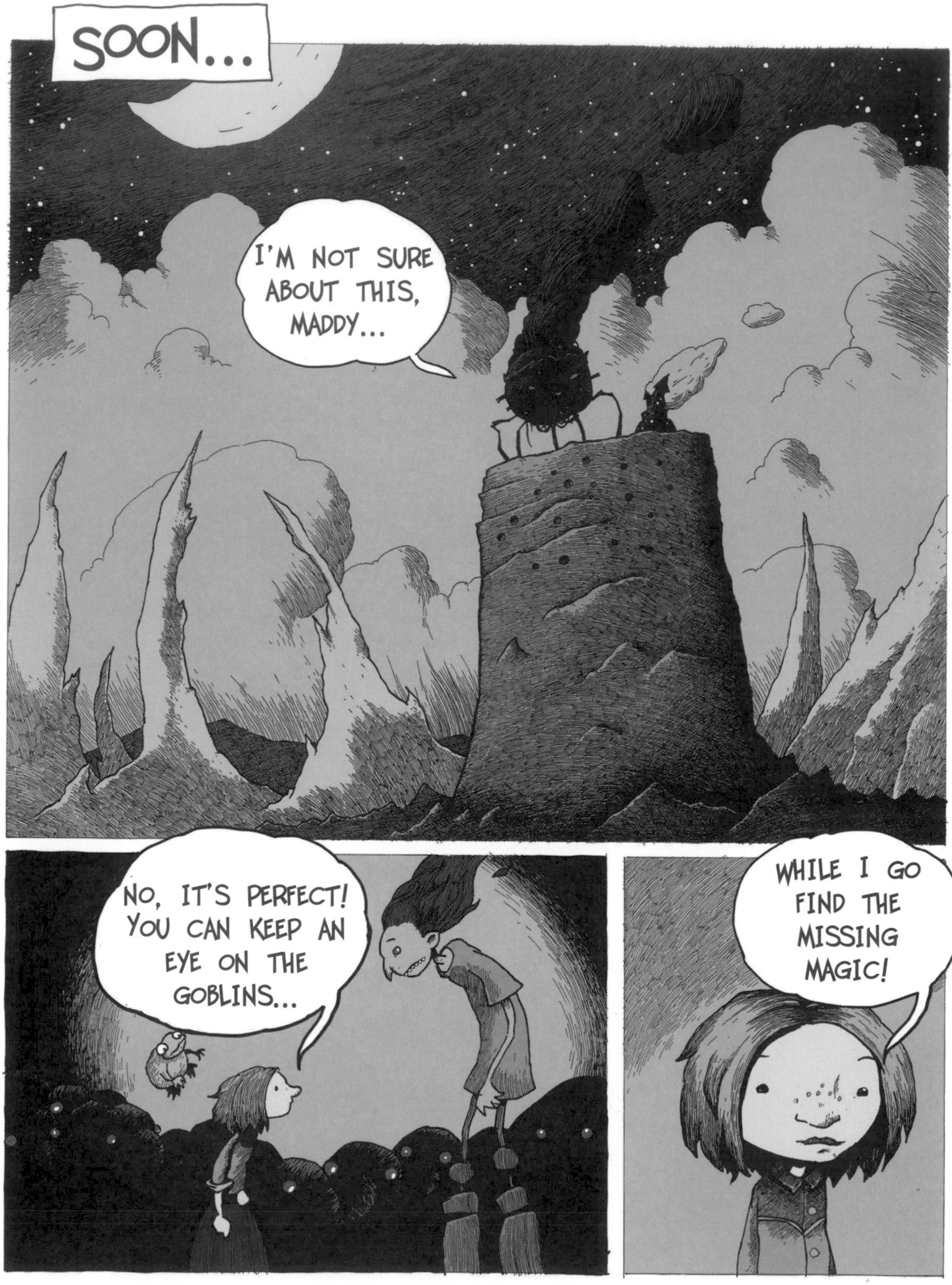
SOON...
I'M NOT SURE ABOUT THIS, MADDY...
NO, IT'S PERFECT! YOU CAN KEEP AN EYE ON THE GOBLINS...
WHILE I GO FIND THE MISSING MAGIC!

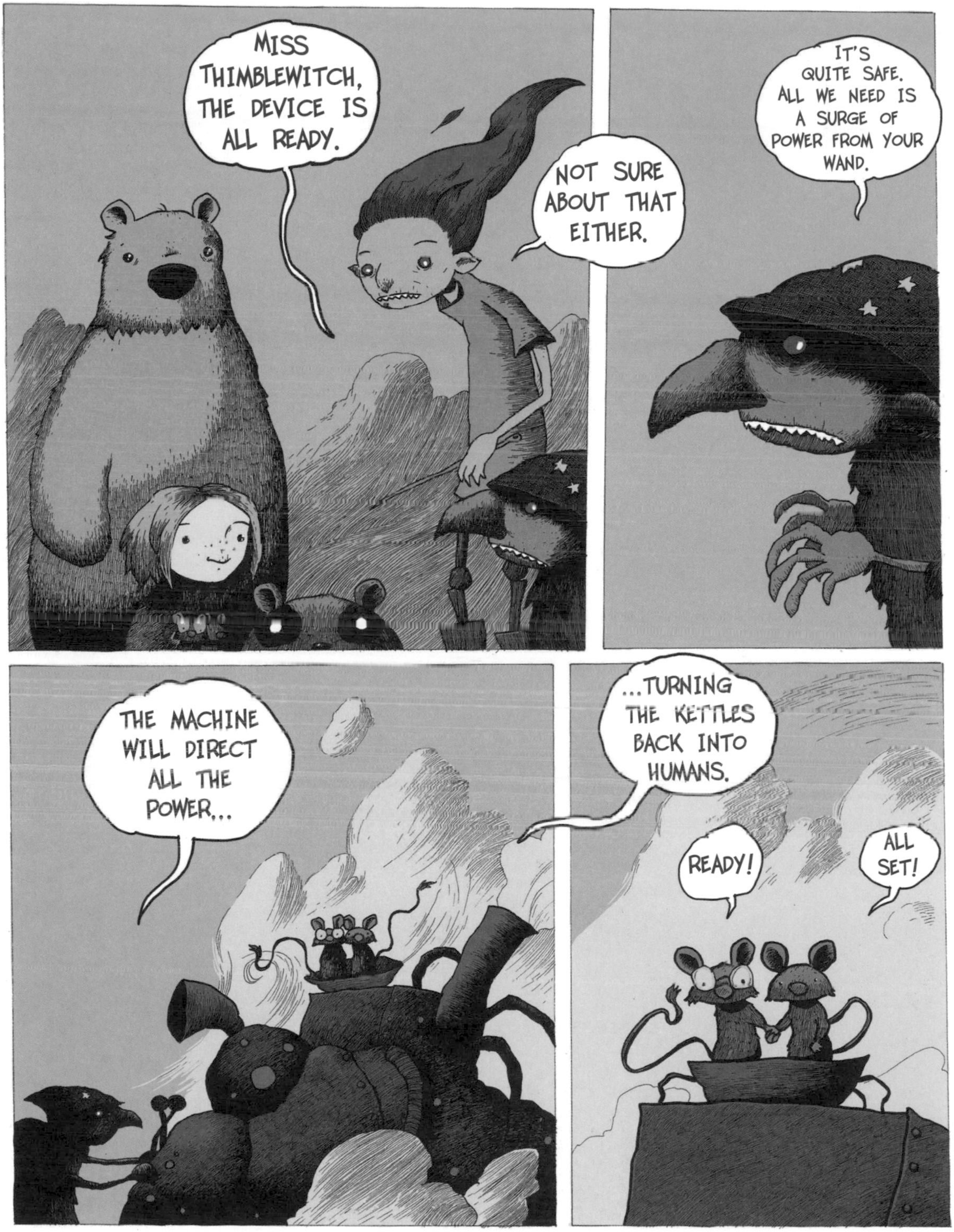
MISS THIMBLEWITCH, THE DEVICE IS ALL READY.
NOT SURE ABOUT THAT EITHER.
IT'S QUITE SAFE. ALL WE NEED IS A SURGE OF POWER FROM YOUR WAND.
THE MACHINE WILL DIRECT ALL THE POWER...
...TURNING THE KETTLES BACK INTO HUMANS.
READY!
ALL SET!

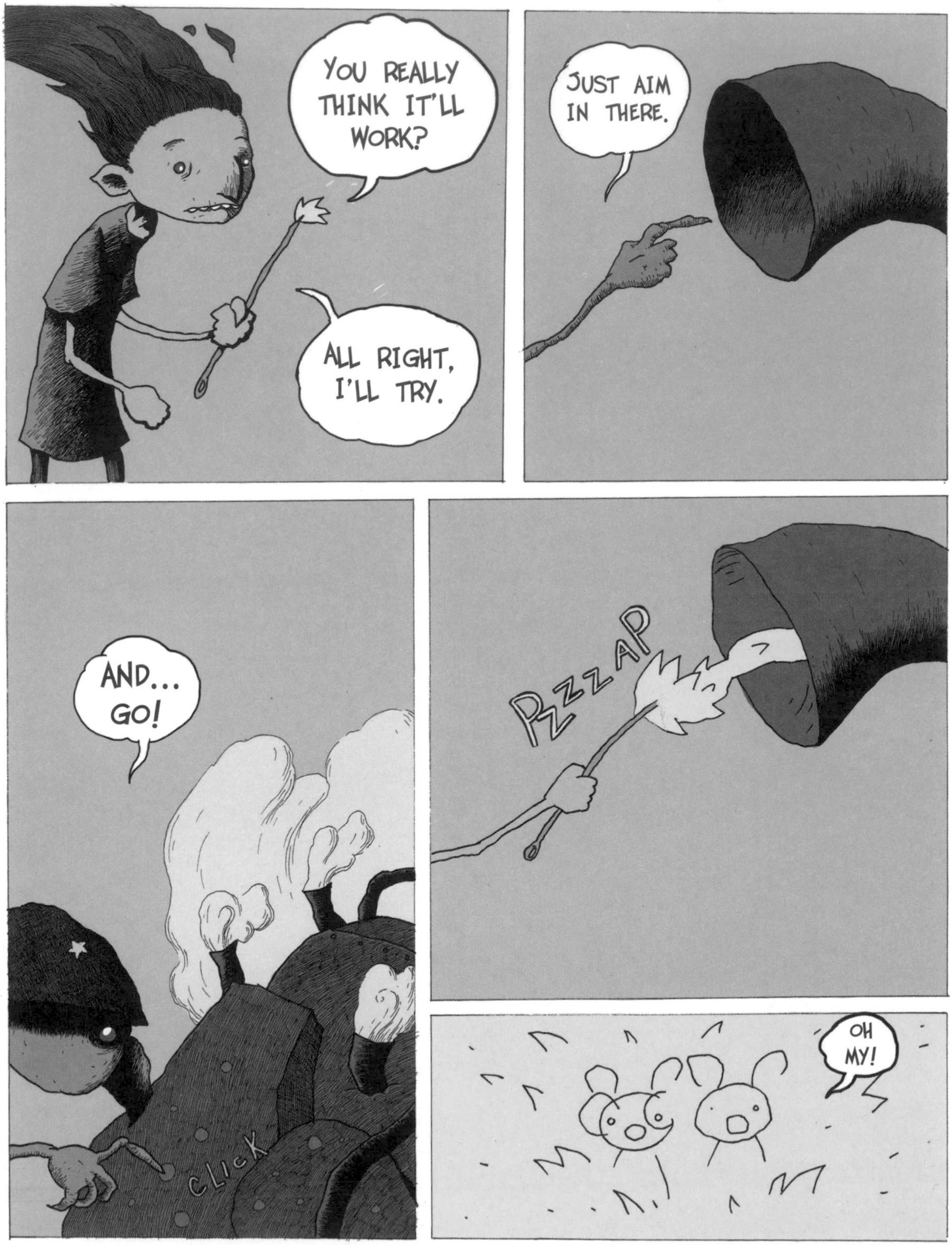
YOU REALLY THINK IT'LL WORK?
ALL RIGHT, I'LL TRY.
JUST AIM IN THERE.
AND... GO!
CLICK
PZZZAP
OH MY!

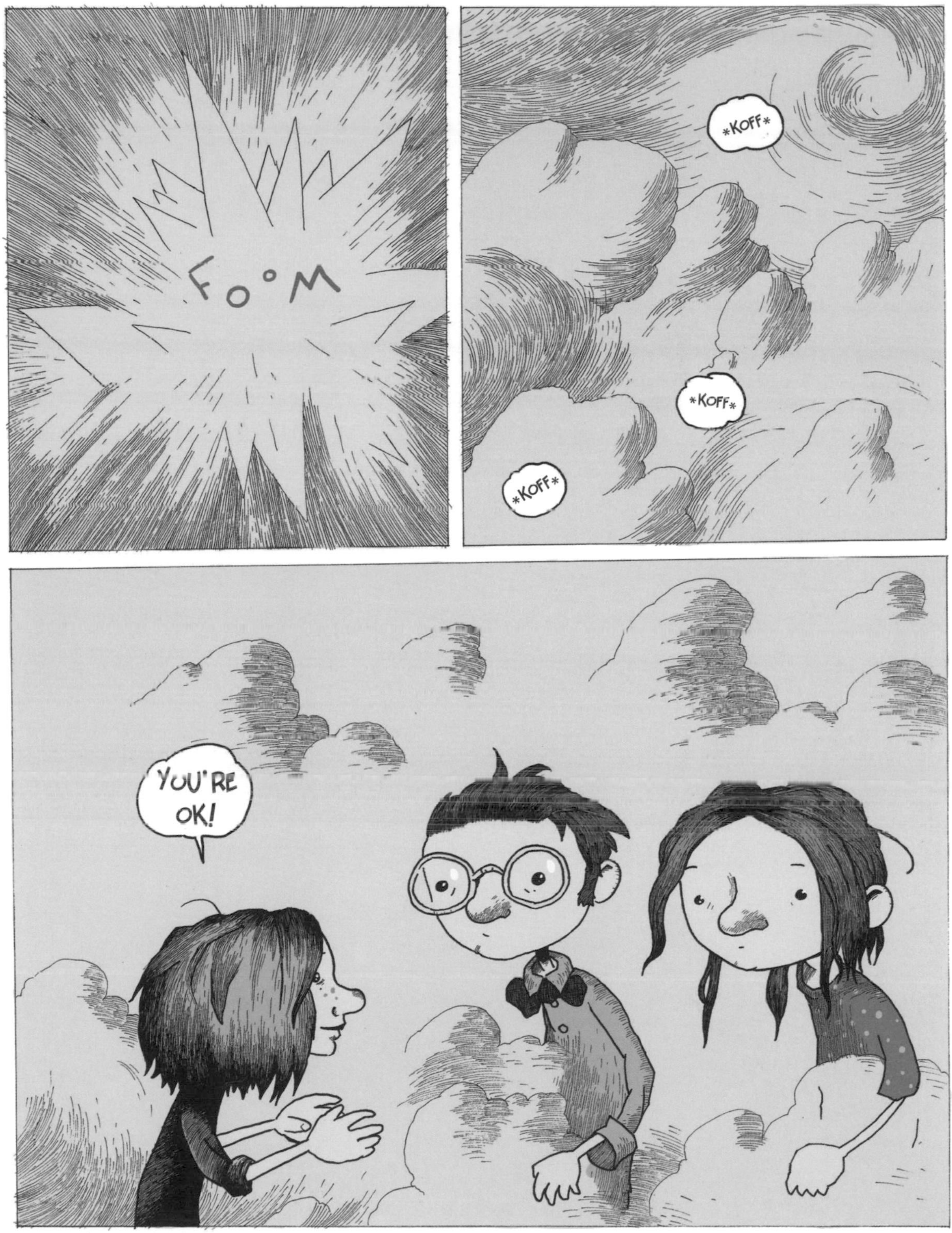
FOOM
KOFF
KOFF
KOFF
YOU'RE OK!

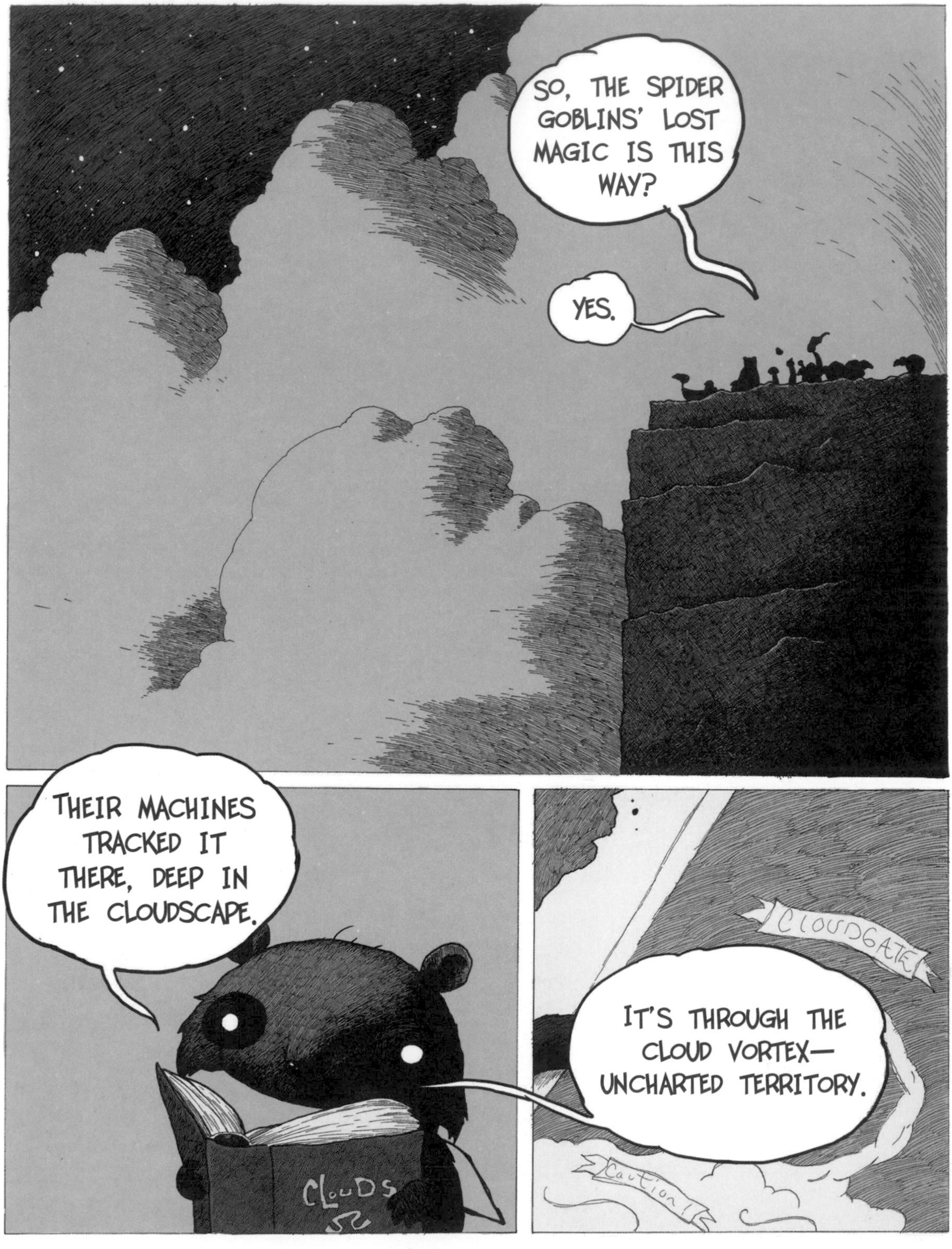
SO, THE SPIDER GOBLINS' LOST MAGIC IS THIS WAY?
YES.
THEIR MACHINES TRACKED IT THERE, DEEP IN THE CLOUDSCAPE.
CLOUDS
CLOUDGATE
IT'S THROUGH THE CLOUD VORTEX— UNCHARTED TERRITORY.
Caution!

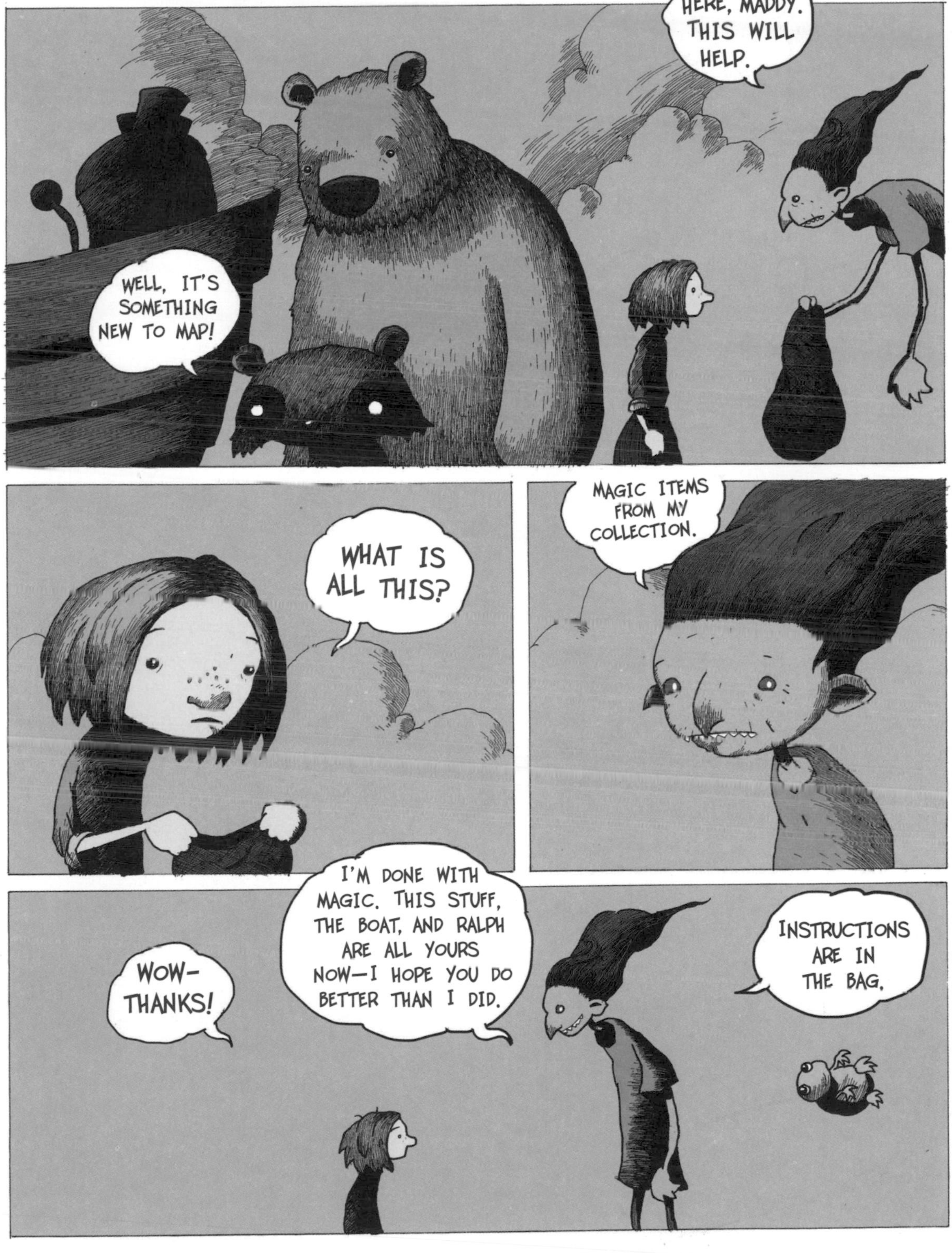
HERE, MADDY. THIS WILL HELP.
WELL, IT'S SOMETHING NEW TO MAP!
WHAT IS ALL THIS?
MAGIC ITEMS FROM MY COLLECTION.
WOW- THANKS!
I'M DONE WITH MAGIC. THIS STUFF, THE BOAT, AND RALPH ARE ALL YOURS NOW—I HOPE YOU DO BETTER THAN I DID.
INSTRUCTIONS ARE IN THE BAG.

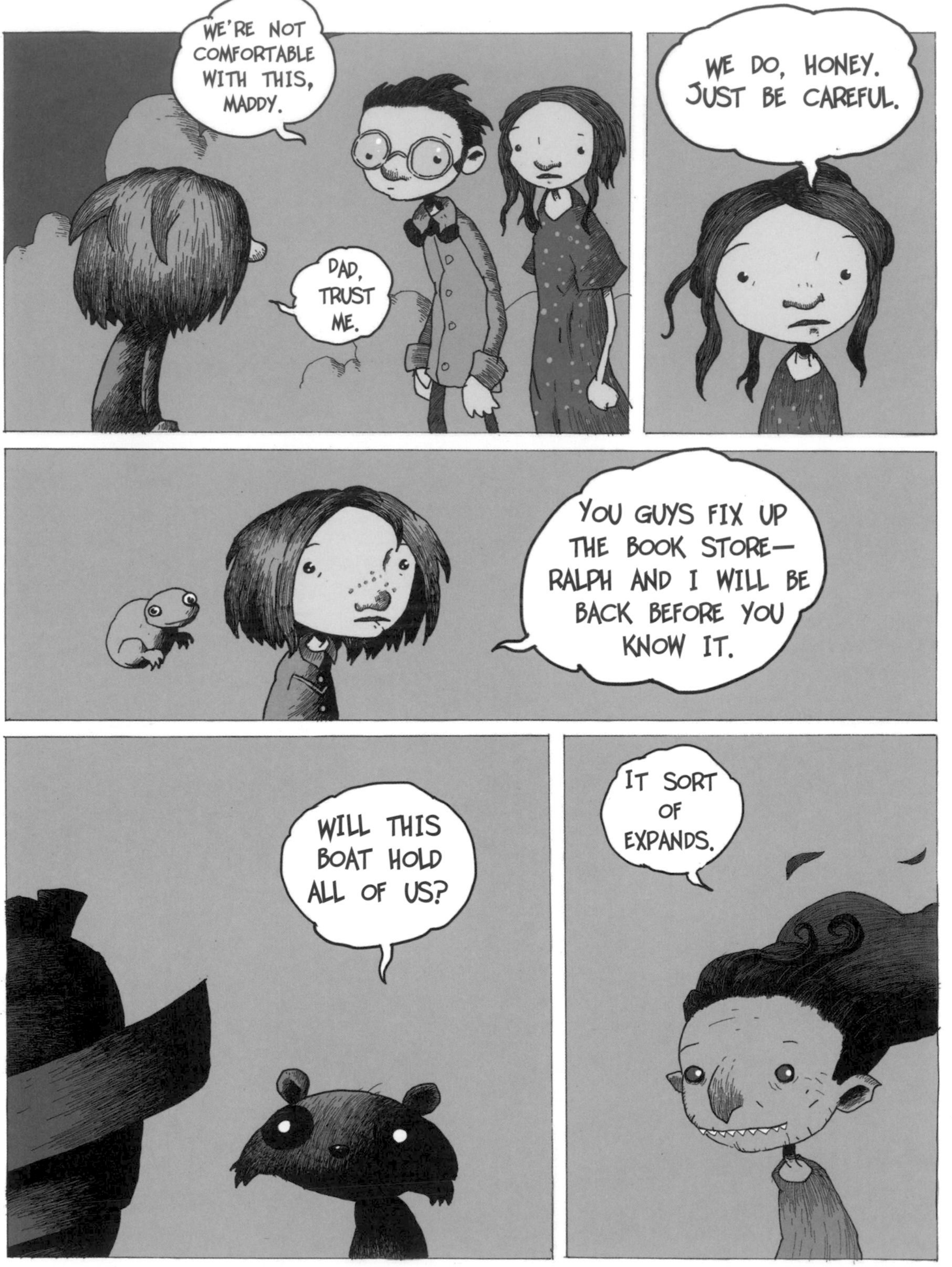
WE'RE NOT COMFORTABLE WITH THIS, MADDY.
DAD, TRUST ME.
WE DO, HONEY. JUST BE CAREFUL.
YOU GUYS FIX UP THE BOOK STORE— RALPH AND I WILL BE BACK BEFORE YOU KNOW IT.
WILL THIS BOAT HOLD ALL OF US?
IT SORT OF EXPANDS.

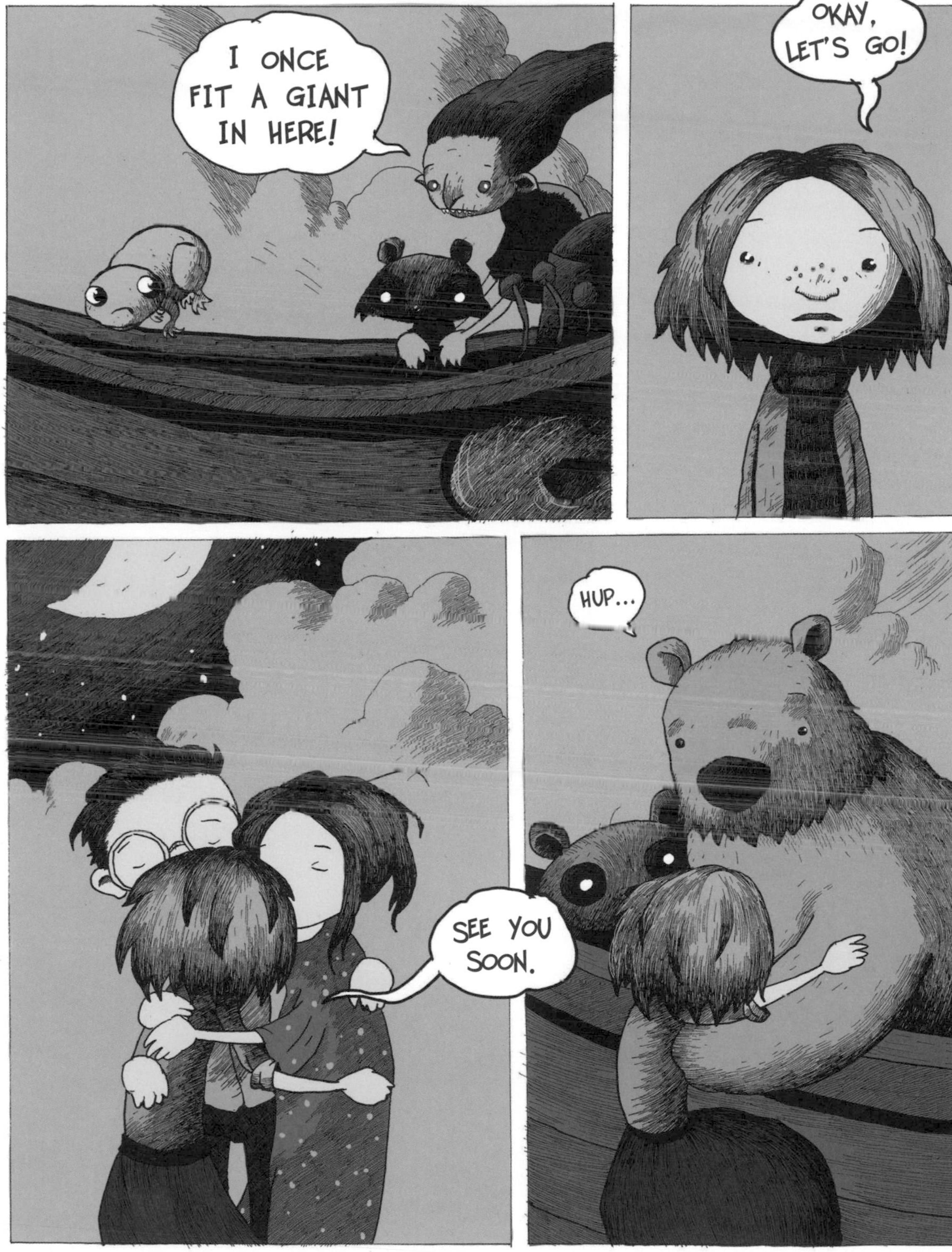
I ONCE FIT A GIANT IN HERE!
OKAY, LET'S GO!
SEE YOU SOON.
HUP...

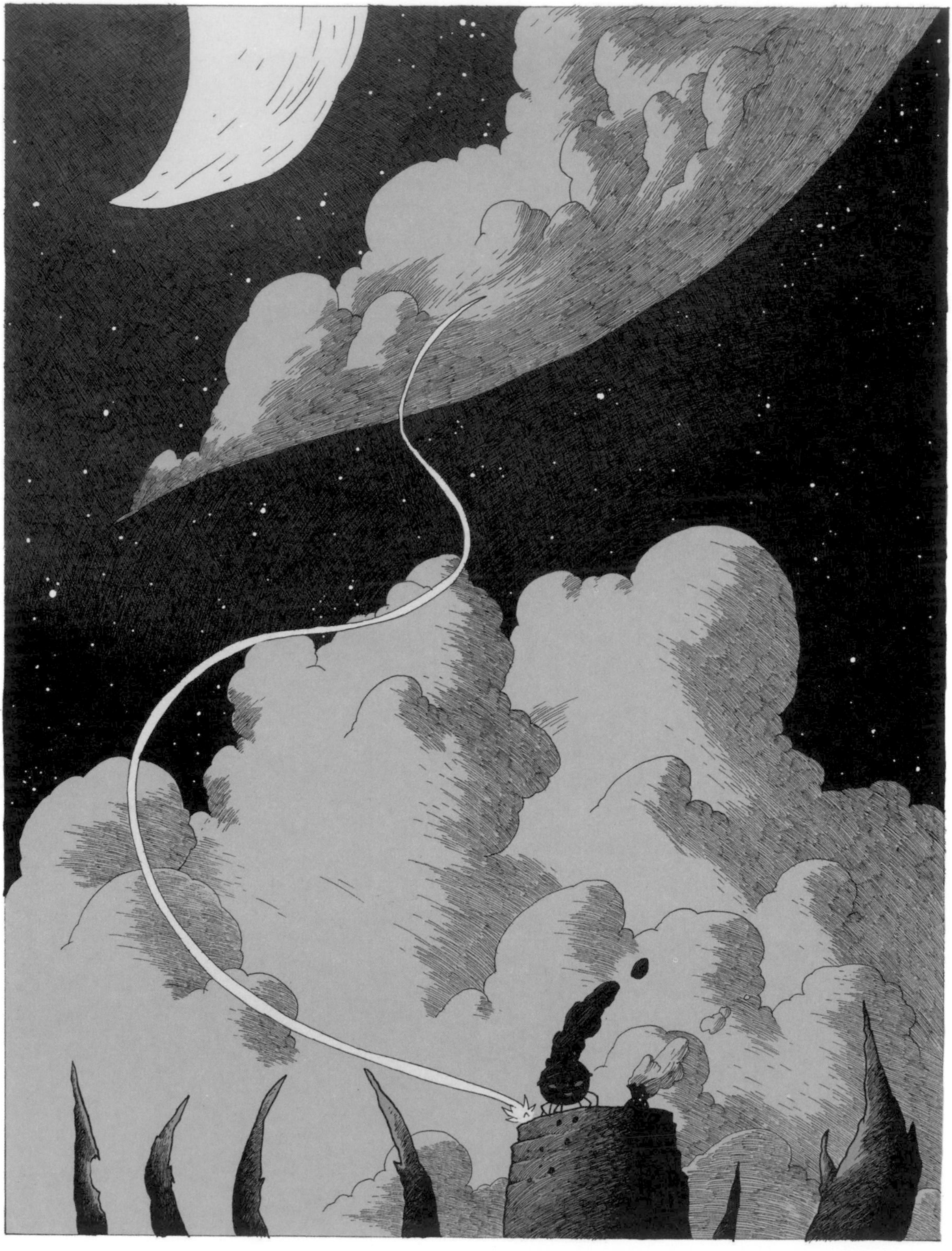

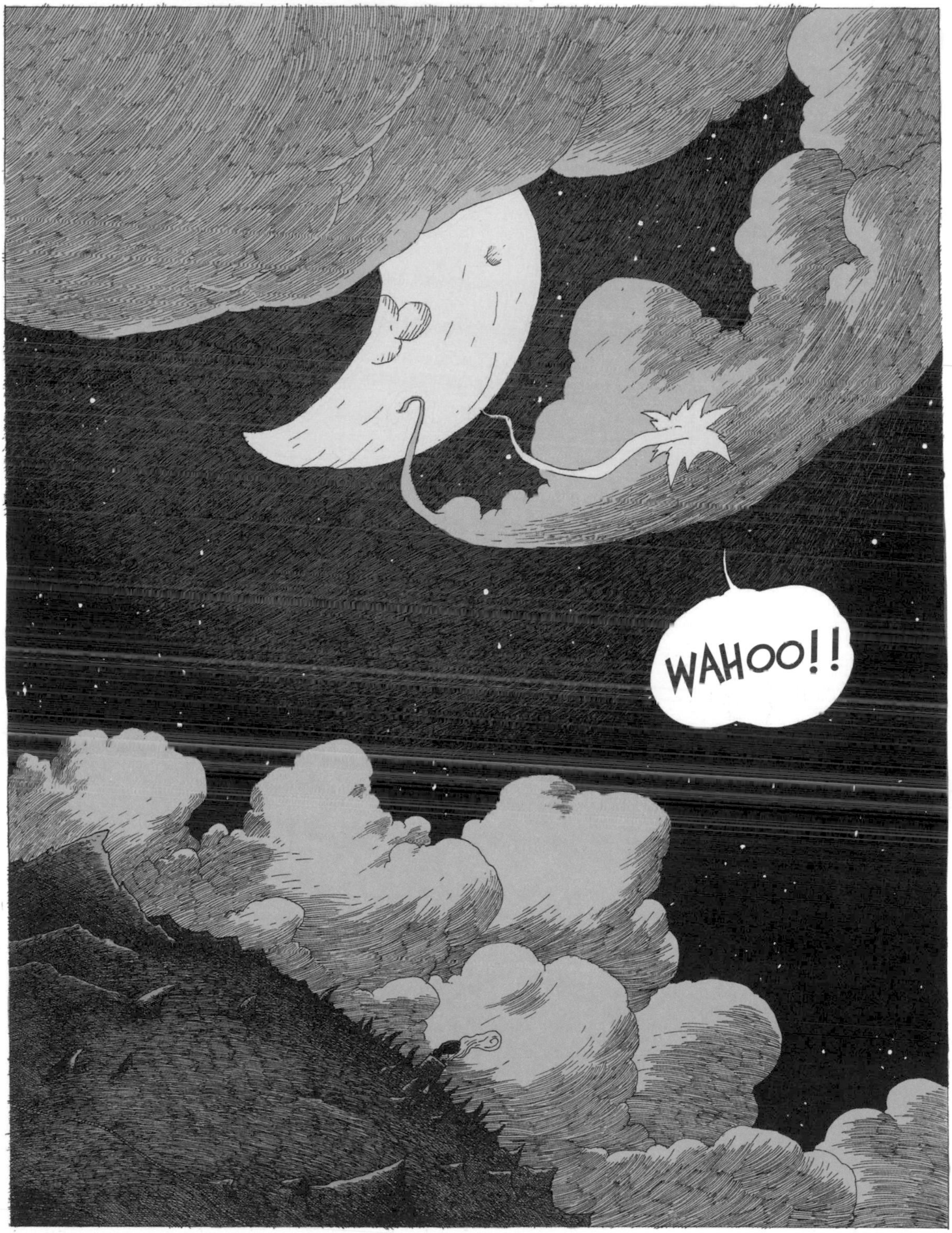
WAHOO!!

ERIC ORCHARD is an award-winning Canadian cartoonist and illustrator. His publishers and clients include First Second, Tor Books, and Scholastic Education. He lives in Toronto with his wife, two boys, and a parrot. *Maddy Kettle: The Adventure of the Thimblewitch* is his first graphic novel.

Find him online at www.ericorchard.com and twitter.com/inkybat.

ISBN 978-1-60309-072-8

Published by Top Shelf Productions, PO Box 1282, Marietta, GA 30061-1282, USA.
Publishers: Brett Warnock and Chris Staros. Top Shelf Productions® and the Top Shelf
logo are registered trademarks of Top Shelf Productions, Inc. All Rights Reserved.

Visit our online catalog at www.topshelfcomix.com.

Edited by Chris Staros and Leigh Walton.

Designed and lettered by Chris Ross with Eric Orchard.

First Printing, August, 2014. Printed in China.